CW00505033

The Ragged Slum Princess

a Victorian romance saga

HOPE DAWSON

Copyright © 2023, Hope Dawson
All rights reserved.

First published worldwide
on Amazon Kindle,
in February 2023.

This paperback edition first published
in Great Britain in 2023.

ISBN: 9798378636990

This novel is a work of fiction. The characters,
names, places, events and incidents in it are
entirely the work of the author's imagination or
used in a fictitious manner. Any resemblance or
similarity to actual persons, living or dead,
events or places is entirely coincidental.

No part of this work may be reproduced, stored
in a retrieval system, or transmitted, in any
form or by any means, without the prior
permission of the author and the publisher.

www.hopedawson.com

This story is part of

The Victorian Orphans Trilogy

Chapter One

As the sun set and the stars began to unfurl their twinkling blanket above the city of London, a warm breeze swirled through the East End, bringing with it the foul aroma of cheap ale, coarse tobacco and greasy food. Giggles, shouts and wild laughter echoed through the cobbled streets as merrymakers, looking to celebrate the end of a hard week's work, spilled out of pubs and onto the sidewalks.

While Mary wove her way through these throngs of people, she couldn't help but think of her father – God rest his soul – and his weak heart that had been crippled by more than just age. People claimed it had been a physical ailment that had taken him from this world prematurely, but Mary knew that his true undoing had been his drinking habit. He would often come home from the factory with empty pockets and a broken spirit. Unless Mary's mother could intercept him on his way to the pub, he would waste a whole week's worth of wages in a single evening.

"Blimey, Mary," her friend Fanny squawked. "Put a bit o' pep in yer step, will ye? If ye keep lookin' sour like that, yer sure to drive away all the men folk."

Fanny snorted with laughter as she playfully elbowed Mary in the ribs. The two of them were on their way to their favourite music hall, for their weekly night of music, dancing and having fun.

"Sorry," Mary smiled feebly. "I was thinking... about certain things."

"Yer always thinkin', luv," Fanny said, rolling her eyes in distaste. "Always got yer nose stuck in a book, too. Ya won't catch no bloke that way if ya don't take a gander at 'im."

"Are you telling me men don't appreciate a smart woman?"

"Maybe they do, but there's other things they like more."

"Like what?"

"Like these," Fanny replied, cupping her own breasts and jiggling them with her hands, making Mary blush.

"Or this," Fanny continued, slapping her backside.

Mary blushed even more, but her friend's cheekiness made her giggle as well. "I think you and I might be looking for different things in a man, Fanny."

She realised girls like them couldn't afford to believe in fairytales. But that didn't stop her from hoping that one day her very own knight in shining armour would come along.

"Do as ya like," Fanny shrugged. "But don't come cryin' to me when ya end up a lonely ol' maid in ten years' time."

Mary laughed, despite the fact that sometimes, in her darkest moments, ending up as a spinster was the very thing she dreaded. But surely, finding a husband who shared some of her interests wasn't too much to ask, was it?

Pushing those brooding thoughts aside, she quickly changed the subject and asked, "Who do you think will be performing tonight?"

"Who cares about that?!"

"I do."

Fanny shook her head. "Yer a right queer one, ain't ye? I ain't never met nobody who visits them dives just fer the tunes."

"Not *just* for the music," Mary countered, smiling a bit sheepishly. Because just like Fanny, she too visited the music halls in the hope of meeting the right man.

But unlike her friend, Mary didn't slip round the back each week with the first fella who took her fancy. She was after something less fleeting and far more meaningful than that. The thing she longed for most in a husband was love. Not just the physical kind, but the sort of love that set your heart on fire and nourished your soul. True love.

That was her dream anyway. But she knew her chances of achieving it were awfully slim. She only had to look at the families whose houses she cleaned as a chargirl. There was hardly any love in most of them.

The best a woman could hope for, or so it seemed, was to fall in love with her husband *after* they were married. And even those cases were rare, when friendship and mutual appreciation would grow into affection and devotion.

But that wasn't real love – not to Mary anyhow. She wanted a husband who would sweep her off her feet. Someone who'd come home straight after work, take her into his strong arms and make her feel appreciated. She would be his queen, regardless of how much or how little money they had. And in return, she would treat him like her king.

"Yer furrowin' yer brow again, Mary. I knows yer thinking."

"No, I wasn't."

"Go pull the other one," her friend snorted.

"I was daydreaming this time."

"Well, at least it brought a bit o' cheer to yer face," Fanny shrugged as they arrived at the music hall.

Waiting in the queue to buy their ticket, Mary studied the names of the performing acts on the bill, while Fanny threw flirtatious glances at several of the young men in the crowd.

And this pattern continued once they were inside. But that wasn't anything new to Mary. So it didn't surprise her much when she found herself alone by the end of the third act. Looking around, she just caught a glimpse of her giggling friend disappearing out the door with her latest conquest in tow.

Some people would have frowned upon Fanny's lewd behaviour – but those people didn't live and die in the slums. In Mary's world, girls and young women were expected to use their own judgement and fend for themselves. Chaperones and fine manners were for the rich.

"Good evening, Miss," a sonorous voice behind her said. "Great show so far, isn't it?"

She turned round, ready to deflect any unwanted advances. But the smiling eyes that greeted her had such a warm kindness to them that her usual reserves instantly softened a bit.

"Yes, the performers are lovely."

"Excuse me for asking, but haven't I seen you around before?"

"Since my friend and I come here regularly, yes, you might have, Mr–?"

"Lee. Henry Lee. And you are?"

"Mary King."

"Nice to meet you, Miss King." He glanced over his shoulder at the door through which

Fanny had disappeared, and then indicated the empty seat next to Mary. "May I keep you company for a while? I don't think your friend is coming back soon."

She nodded. "As long as you realise that, unlike my friend, I won't be lifting my skirts for you in the alley."

He blushed, but he recovered his wits quickly enough. "If that had been my intention, I would have struck up a conversation with your friend instead."

Mary smiled. His reply intrigued her. Other men would have laughed nervously while trying to put on an air of feigned innocence. She gestured at the empty seat and he sat down – happily, she noticed, but taking care not to appear too eager.

"Can I get you a drink, Miss King? A half-pint of ale perhaps? Or a tot of brandy?" He studied her, trying to guess her preference. "You don't seem like the gin drinking type to me."

"I'll have a shandy, please."

"Of course. I'll be right back."

While he went to fetch their drinks, she took the opportunity to scrutinise his appearance in more detail. He was broad in the shoulders, which told her he did some form of manual labour. But not as a factory worker, she thought. Because his handsome face and his strong hands had that weathered quality of someone who worked in the open air all day long.

Henry Lee was a pleasant man to look at, she concluded. Just as he returned with their drinks, their eyes met and he smiled at her. She gratefully accepted her drink and he sat down next to her.

"A toast," he said. "To an evening of music and beauty."

They clinked their glasses and took a sip, while she continued to peer at him. By now, she was curious to find out more about him.

"Do you come here often then, Mr Lee?"

"Yes, I love the music and the lively atmosphere."

"But surely, public houses have that too?"

"Pubs aren't quite my sort of place, to be honest. Too much drinking and brawling going on."

A good answer, she thought. But perhaps a little too easy, too obvious.

"And what is it you do for a living?"

"I'm a bricklayer," he replied before he jokingly flexed the biceps on his right arm for her. "You?"

"I work as a chargirl."

"So we're both gainfully employed. That's a good start, isn't it?" He smiled and gave her a playful wink.

"I'll say," she replied before taking a sip from her shandy. He was obviously flirting with her, but she had to admit to herself that she didn't mind. Not with him.

Before they could continue their conversation, the next singer was announced. While they listened to the lady's performance, Mary stole a few sideways glances at Henry. He genuinely seemed to be enjoying the music, which to her eyes made him look even more attractive.

And she only realised that her mind had been drifting – musing about things that might perhaps be – when the music stopped and everyone started clapping.

"That was beautiful, didn't you think?" he asked, turning towards her.

"Absolutely," she replied, hoping her embarrassment wasn't too apparent. "I have to say, Mr Lee, I'm fascinated."

"Fascinated?"

"Yes, by you: a bricklayer who loves the music hall."

"We're not all barbaric brutes," he quipped. "Would it surprise you to know that I can read and write? The nuns at the orphanage taught me."

"You were raised as an orphan?"

"Lost my parents when I was very young. I can't even remember their faces."

"I'm sorry to hear that."

He shrugged. "It was a long time ago and most of those nuns weren't too bad. So my childhood didn't exactly leave me scarred for life." He smiled, causing adorable little wrinkles to appear at the corners of his eyes.

"But being an orphan did leave me with one thing..."

"And what's that?"

"A deep desire to raise my own little family someday. And to do everything I can to make it a very happy family."

"That's sweet."

But did he actually mean it? Or was he merely saying it to make a good impression on her? Somehow he didn't strike her as the type who would lie to a girl in hopes of a quick fling. She had encountered men like that and they usually didn't go through this much trouble. Invariably, their tactics were coarse and easy to see through.

This man however, this Henry Lee the bricklayer, he seemed to be different. Her mind was telling her to slow down – *Don't go jumping to any conclusions just yet,* it cautioned her. But her fluttering heart was growing increasingly convinced that Henry was the real deal.

I need more time, she thought. *I want to get to know him better.*

The next stage act was a magician who, unfortunately, wasn't very good at his craft. But even a poor and boring performance had its benefits. Because it meant she and Henry could simply keep talking.

Leaning in closer, he whispered, "I hope you won't find my next question too forward..."

She inclined her head and waited with bated breath for whatever he was about to ask.

"But I'd rather not leave our next meeting to pure chance."

Neither do I, she nearly blurted out.

"So I'd be honoured if you would agree to see me again. Here perhaps? Same time next week?"

"Yes," she replied, "I would like that."

And I'll be counting the days until next Saturday comes round. A week could be such a long time.

"Or," he continued, throwing her the sweetest smile, "if you have some time to spare, we could go for a walk in the park tomorrow afternoon?"

Perfect!

Forcing herself to remain calm, she took a breath and said, "I think I would like that even more, Mr Lee."

Chapter Two

"O, my dearest sister! Look through yonder window and tell me if there is any sight yet of a brave and heroic knight approaching the castle." Abbie pointed at the kitchen window with one hand, while placing the back of her other hand on her forehead, to signify that she was in great emotional distress.

Her sister Jane rushed over to the window and peered outside. "Nope. Nothing to see out there." She giggled as she said it, because Jane never could keep a straight face when they were playing out their silly fantasies.

"Woe," Abbie lamented dramatically. "Will no one come and save us? Are we truly doomed to remain in this wretched tower for the rest of our lives?"

Jane covered her mouth with both her hands to stop herself from laughing. "Does a princess really talk like that?"

"Of course she does," Abbie said, permitting herself to drop out of character. "A princess is the daughter of a king and that makes her royalty."

She winked at Jane and wanted to resume their make-believe scene. But her younger sister wasn't through with asking questions yet.

"Why does the princess get locked up in a tower all the time? Is it because she's been very naughty?"

"No, usually it's because her father wants to marry her off to a villain or someone whom the princess dislikes very much. And when she refuses to marry this man, her father locks her up in a tower of the castle."

"For how long?"

"Until she changes her mind, I suppose. Or until a hero shows up to save her."

"But what if she doesn't like this hero either? Imagine a knight rescues her, but when he takes his helmet off, he turns out to be ugly. Then what?"

Behind them, their mother snorted with laughter.

Abbie frowned. Their play was as good as ruined now. Even though her sister did have a point. "I guess the princess would then refuse to be saved by the ugly knight."

"A princess can do that?"

"When you're a princess, you can do whatever you want."

"Except when the king locks you up in the tower?"

"Yes, except that." Abbie sighed and shook off the blanket that had served as the long trailing part of her pretend princess dress.

"Our father would never do anything like that to us," Jane stated confidently. "Not even if we were very naughty."

"No, he wouldn't. But then again, Papa isn't a king."

While Abbie folded up the blanket, Jane turned to their mother who was peeling potatoes. "Mummy, didn't your name used to be King before you married Daddy?"

"Yes, it was."

"Does that mean we're royalty?"

Mother laughed. "No, I'm afraid not. It's just a name, dear."

Jane moved to their mother's side and picked a piece of carrot from the pile of vegetables. "If Abbie and I were princesses, I wouldn't mind being locked up in a tower. Not as long as you were there too, Mummy. So you could bake biscuits and cake for us all the time."

"That's very sweet, my darling," Mother beamed as she placed a kiss on Jane's forehead. "Now, how about you girls lend me a hand preparing supper? Your father will be home in a short while."

Abbie and Jane were more than happy to help. Soon, the kitchen was filled with the mouth-watering aroma of the rich stew that stood bubbling over the fire. Abbie dipped a large wooden spoon into the pot for a quick taste.

Hmm, delicious.

They might not have been real princesses, she thought, but they had it better than most people in their street. They ate better, they wore nicer clothes – they even had a dozen or so books in the house. And despite the fact that Abbie was fifteen already, she and Jane still didn't have to join their mother when Mama went out charring for people. Papa said he wanted a different life for his daughters – one where they didn't have to slave and toil all day long.

Some of the neighbourhood children liked to tease them about it. Some did worse than teasing too. But Abbie tried not to let the taunts and the bullying get to her. For one thing, she herself barely understood how her parents managed. She simply assumed Mama and Papa were a bit smarter and more careful with their money.

"What's all that noise outside?" their mother asked, interrupting Abbie's thoughts. "You'd swear there was a parade or something."

Jane had already run to the front door to have a look. "It's Daddy," she shouted back. "And he's sitting on top of a carriage."

"He's what?!" Mother hurried to the front door as well, with Abbie following closely on her heels.

The scene on the street made their jaw drop. Father was indeed coming home on a large open wagon drawn by two horses led by a carter walking alongside them. People were staring and gaping, while a horde of excited children crowded around the slow-moving carriage.

"Hullooo, my darlings," Father shouted when he saw his wife and daughters standing in the door. He was sitting astride the covered load that had been secured with ropes on the flat-bedded wagon. Abbie couldn't see what it was, but it certainly looked big.

Father jumped off and ran the last few yards. Upon reaching their house, he fondly embraced his wife and kissed her.

"Henry Lee, what on earth have you done this time?" she asked with a curious smile. "What's on the wagon?"

"Something I bought for my precious wife and our dearest daughters," he replied with a twinkle in his eyes.

As the rattling carriage came to a halt in front of their home, he went over and pulled off the cover with a great flourish.

Mother gasped. "A piano?"

"It's just an upright of course," Father said with a hint of apology in his voice. "I would have preferred a proper grand piano, but I didn't think it would fit in the house."

He smiled at the gaping crowd in the street and added, "Guess that'll have to wait until we move to someplace bigger."

Then he gestured at the carter, who began to unload the piano with his helper.

"But Henry, why?" Mother asked.

"Because, my love, I know how you adore good music. And with this piano, you and the girls will be able to play music yourselves. So tell me, do you like it?"

He was beaming with pride, but Abbie could tell Mother was left a bit speechless. Father often bought them treats and surprises, small or big. A piano however – that was much more than a simple present.

"I love it, Henry. But darling, you know I can't play a single note. None of us can."

They stepped aside as the carter and his helper brought in the piano. "Where d'you want this, guv?"

"In the front room, please, my good man," Father replied. "Don't worry, Mary. We'll get a piano teacher. A really good one. For you and the girls."

"Another tutor, darling?" Mother asked, lowering her voice so none of the neighbours would hear. "Do you really think that's wise?

And how much did this piano cost? It looks expensive."

"That's just because it's brand new and shiny."

"Brand new?!"

"Of course. I wasn't going to buy some used piece of old wreckage, was I? Not for my queen and my two princesses."

He winked at Abbie and Jane.

"Henry, how much did you pay for it?"

"Over there by the wall, my good man," Father said to the carter, conveniently ignoring Mother's question.

"Henry..."

"Sorry, what's that, my love?"

"How much did you pay for this piano?"

"I won't lie to you, Mary: it wasn't cheap. But it's worth every single penny, I assure you."

Before Mother could press him to tell her the price, Father quickly thanked the carter and his helper and ushered the two men out the door – leaving his wife and daughters to stare at their new piano.

"It's very pretty," Jane said after a stunned silence.

"Of course it is," Father replied proudly as he returned to the front room. "And wait until you hear what it sounds like."

He opened the keyboard lid of the piano and merrily attempted to play a tune as if he was an accomplished pianist. But all he managed to produce was a random bunch of horribly off-key noises.

"Probably needs a tune up," he quipped.

Seeing the doubtful look on his wife's face, he went over to her and took her hands. "Don't worry about the money, Mary. You know I'd never do anything foolish."

He pulled her close and gave her a kiss.

She sighed and relented. Mama never could resist Papa's charms, Abbie chuckled inwardly.

"It's a very lovely instrument," Mother said.

"But not even half as lovely as you are, my dearest."

Mother shook her head and smiled. "Rascal."

Intrigued, Jane went over to the piano and pressed a few keys, more carefully than their father.

"I know I can be a bit of a clown sometimes, Mary," Father said while he gazed lovingly at his youngest daughter. "But just think, this piano is exactly the sort of thing our girls need if we want to give them a better future."

"I suppose if you put it that way," Mother replied, still somewhat uncertain.

"A bit of culture and education is their entry ticket into the middle classes, my love. We want our girls to have every chance of finding a decent husband, don't we?"

Abbie frowned and turned to the piano, where her sister was still cautiously trying out the sound of various keys. So being able to play this thing was supposed to improve her marriage prospects? She wasn't sure how she felt about that idea.

Chapter Three

Abbie's back and shoulders were painfully tense as she sat at the piano for her weekly lesson. With every false note she played, the discomfort only grew stronger. And unfortunately, she was making plenty of mistakes.

She could read the music sheet in front of her and she could hear the melody in her mind. But that wasn't how it sounded when she tried to play it. On paper, she saw the notes dancing gracefully across the staves. Her hands and her fingers however just didn't seem capable of putting that same sense of flow in the music.

"Miss Lee," her teacher Mrs Ashwin-Stokes sighed. "What have those poor piano keys ever done to you to deserve such harsh punishment?"

Abbie stopped playing. She knew what would come next. Mrs Ashwin-Stokes loved to ridicule Abbie for her lack of skill.

"Ma'am?"

"You're hitting the keys as if you're some sort of burly blacksmith hammering away at his anvil."

"I'm sorry, ma'am."

"Gentleness is what's called for. Your fingers should be caressing those keys, my dear. Not hammering them. After all, we're making music, not horseshoes." She gave a little sneering chuckle and glanced over her shoulder at Abbie's sister Jane, who tried to make herself even more invisible in the background.

"Here, I'll show you," the teacher continued as she sat down next to Abbie at the piano. With her eyes closed and her face turned up as if she were in a state of divine rapture, Mrs Ashwin-Stokes played a few bars.

When she was finished putting on her exaggerated display, she paused, let out a blissful sigh of delight and then looked at Abbie.

"That, Miss Lee, is how we play Chopin."

"Yes, ma'am."

"From the top, please," the teacher said haughtily while she stood up again. "And try not to make poor Mr Chopin turn over in his grave this time."

Abbie sighed in defeat. *Sorry, Mr Chopin,* she thought as she started playing once more.

It wasn't that she didn't like the music. Because she most certainly did. Its romantic dreaminess made it very easy to imagine herself wearing a beautiful gown and going to a grand ball where everyone stared at her in admiration... until she met the eyes of a dashing gentleman in a finely tailored suit.

"Miss Lee," the harsh voice of Mrs Ashwin-Stokes ruptured Abbie's reverie. "That's even worse than before. You're not putting in much effort, are you?"

"Sorry, ma'am."

"Remind me, how long have you been playing – or more accurately, hammering away at the keyboard?"

"A little over five years, I believe, ma'am."

With another disapproving sigh, Mrs Ashwin-Stokes said, "Your parents must love you very much if they insist on investing money in your musical education, when you so clearly haven't got an ounce of skill or talent."

Abbie bit her tongue. She ached to give this arrogant woman a piece of her mind. But instead, she forced a polite smile on her face and inclined her head.

Yes, her parents did love her dearly. And they wanted to give their two daughters the best possible education they could afford. She knew it meant the world to them.

Which was about the only reason she continued to endure the contempt and the humiliation that Mrs Ashwin-Stokes loved to meet out during these expensive weekly lessons.

The piano simply wasn't her instrument. Abbie had inherited her parents' taste for art and beauty, and she believed she had talent. She only had to close her eyes to picture herself on a stage before an entranced audience. Just not as a pianist.

They were struggling through another valiant attempt at a Nocturne, when a loud and urgent knock at the door made her jump.

Since Mother was out charring, Jane ran to the hallway and opened the door. Almost immediately her startled voice came back.

"Papa!"

Hearing the panic in her sister's voice, Abbie jumped up from her seat by the piano and went into the hallway as well. Outside, awkwardly fidgeting with his cap in his hands, stood a man whom she recognised as one of their father's fellow bricklayers.

"What's the matter?" she asked, sensing that something was terribly wrong. But as she reached the front door, her eyes gave her the answer to her question.

Father was lying in a wooden wheelbarrow, his grimacing face drained of any colour.

"Your pa took a nasty tumble, Miss," the man began to explain. "Fell off some scaffolding, he did."

"Oh, Papa," Abbie lamented as she rushed over to her father's side and ran a hand through his hair. He was drenched with cold sweat.

"Probably broke both his legs from the looks of it," the man continued. "Says his back hurts too."

"Has he been to the doctor's?"

"He didn't want to, Miss. So the foreman told me to take your pa home. Used the wheelbarrow, I did. Looks a bit crude, but it did the trick."

Abbie turned to her father. "Papa, you simply must see a doctor. I'll send Jane."

"No," he groaned.

"But Papa–"

"Those quacks are much too expensive and all they would do is give me a bottle of laudanum anyhow. Go fetch the bonesetter instead."

"If you say so," Abbie relented. "Jane, can you do that?"

"But I don't know–"

"Ask the neighbours. Someone will know and show you the way. Go."

Next, she turned to the man who had brought Father home. "Could you help me get Papa to the sofa in the front room, please, sir?"

"Of course, Miss."

When they entered the room, heaving and groaning, Mrs Ashwin-Stokes uttered a short yelp of shock and dismay.

"Heavens me! What's all this?"

"My father's had an accident at work, Mrs Ashwin-Stokes. I'm afraid we'll have to end our lesson prematurely this week."

At least some good would come out of this yet, Abbie smirked to herself without sensing the slightest trace of guilt.

"I see," the piano teacher said, looking at Abbie's father and wrinkling her nose as if the most foul and revolting creature had been dragged in from the street. "I suppose such are the dangers of manual labour."

With a short pretentious huff, she closed her music book and rose to her feet. "Still, I wish you a speedy recovery, Mr Lee."

"Most kind of you, Mrs Ashwin-Stokes," Abbie said, smiling politely. "Please allow me to show you to the door."

Her voice had sounded sweeter than summer honey, but secretly, she was itching to deliver a well-aimed kick to the posterior of this rude and pompous woman. Sending her flying onto the cobbled road outside would have been a very gratifying sight.

But Abbie wisely resisted the temptation to play out this particular fantasy of hers. Instead, she turned her mind and her attention to her poor father as soon as the piano teacher had left.

By the time Mother came home from work, the bonesetter had already been and done his job. As suspected, both of Father's legs were broken. He was sitting on the sofa now, looking rather miserable with his legs wrapped up in bandages to keep the wooden splints in place.

The moment Mother walked in, Abbie and Jane warned her what had happened. But her hands still flew to her gaping mouth when she saw her husband.

"Oh, my poor Henry!"

"It's not as bad as it looks, my love," he lied, trying to soothe his wife. "I'm as fit as a fiddle and these bones of mine will heal quickly enough. You'll see, I'll be back at work in no time. No time at all, I tell you."

"That's not quite what the bonesetter told us, Papa," Abbie said, contradicting her father and not liking it. "He said it would be six weeks, at least. And that you should rest and avoid putting any weight on your legs."

"Six weeks?" Mother exclaimed.

"Possibly more," Abbie replied. She stared at the floor, hating the fact that she was the bringer of bad news.

There was panic in Mother's eyes when she turned to her husband again. "How will we manage for so long? We need your wages to–"

"Bah," Father said, dismissing her concern with a wave of his hand. "Six weeks is nothing. It'll be over in a blink of an eye."

"Mama, if you're worried about the money," Abbie suggested, "I could go charring with you. I'm more than old enough to work, you know?"

"Yes, me too," Jane chimed in bravely. "It wouldn't be any trouble to us, I promise."

"Out of the question," Father replied. "I won't have my girls cleaning grates and emptying slop buckets at other people's homes."

"But Papa–"

He interrupted her with a gesture of his hand. "There's to be no argument about this." Then he smiled and added, "Please."

Abbie looked from her father's smiling face to her mother, who stood wringing her hands but didn't speak a word.

"I suppose you know best, Papa," she sighed. "But then at least let us cut back on some frivolous expenses, if only temporarily. For instance, I'm sure Jane and I could skip our piano lessons while you're laid up."

Out of the corner of her eye, she thought she saw her sister's face light up: Jane too seemed to like that idea.

But Father shook his head. "No, I don't see any reason to tinker with something as vital as your education, simply because I foolishly hurt a leg or two."

"You did more than hurt them, Papa. And I'm certain it wasn't foolishness on your part that caused it. But if we–"

"You're a sweet girl, Abbie," Father said. "And I know you mean well. But I'm telling you we'll be fine."

And that, she understood, was the end of the matter. Papa was right. They shouldn't worry about money. Hadn't he always managed their finances competently and effectively, like the responsible head of the family he was? Papa probably had savings, stashed away for a rainy day. And that was why he didn't seem at all concerned about his accident.

Yes, everything would be fine, she concluded. These few weeks wouldn't pose a problem. Papa was a clever and capable man.

Chapter Four

"Abbie dear," Father asked. "Will you play the piano for me, please? This miserable weather is hurting my poor bones and a bit of music will do me good."

He was sitting on the sofa, propped up with pillows for support. Close by, his crutches stood leaning against the wall.

"If you wish, Papa," she said. "But wouldn't you rather have Jane play something for you? She's much better than I am, you know."

He laughed. "I also happen to know she dislikes that piano even more than you do. Besides, she's busy in the kitchen baking oat biscuits."

"All right then," Abbie replied as she sat down in front of the piano with a dramatic sigh. "But don't say I didn't warn you. Let's pray I don't make your pain any worse."

"I'm certain it won't be that bad," he chuckled. "And since you're the one playing the music, it'll sound heavenly to my ears."

And with those words, he folded his hands and closed his eyes in peaceful anticipation of what was about to come.

Abbie thumbed nervously through the music books. In the end, she decided on a few of the easier pieces by Beethoven – feeling fairly confident she wouldn't make too much of a mess of those.

And as soon as the first notes drifted melodiously through the room, almost miraculously, her nerves began to fade.

That's because I'm playing for Papa, she knew. Even if she got every note wrong, he would tell her that he loved it... and probably mean it too.

How she felt sorry for him. More than two months had passed since he'd had his accident. And still he couldn't move about properly without some form of support.

He had tried going back to work of course. "I'm obliged to try," he had said. "As the main breadwinner, I mustn't fail in my duties towards my family."

But failed he had. His foreman had told him they didn't have much use for a bricklayer on crutches. And so Father had been sent straight home again, the weight of his bitter disappointment making him limp even more.

His slow recovery had Mother worried. Mama didn't voice her concerns out loud to the girls, but Abbie could tell. Mother was much more tense and less talkative than usual. And she worked longer hours, but it hardly made up for the loss of Father's income.

A loud and slow knocking at the door startled Abbie, putting an abrupt end to her music with a few jarring notes as her fingers hit the wrong keys.

"I'd better see who that is," she said, getting up. "Because Jane's probably up to her elbows in dough."

Keeping his eyes closed, Father nodded and smiled, "I'll wait here if you don't mind."

A second series of knocks sounded just as Abbie entered the hallway. Whoever it was, they clearly didn't have much patience, she tutted silently.

She opened the door and immediately her body froze in panic as she sucked in her breath. Before her stood a police constable, accompanied by an elderly gentleman and a young man, both of them well dressed.

"Good afternoon, Miss," the constable said politely, tipping two fingers to his helmet. "I'm Constable Perkins and this here is Mr Yates."

"How do you do, constable? Sir." She nodded a greeting to both of them and briefly threw a glance at the young man. The older gentleman must have been at least seventy, she judged. He had a slight stoop, but his piercing eyes were sharp. His wrinkled face had a lifeless grey quality to it and his mouth seemed to be permanently set in a disapproving scowl, as if he despised virtually everyone in life.

The young man who stood just behind his shoulder was about Abbie's age. He bore some resemblance to the older man, and she guessed they were related. His face was harder to read, but even so she couldn't detect any immediate trace of kindness in it.

"You are Miss Lee, I presume?" the constable asked. "Daughter of Mr Henry Lee, who lives at this address?"

"That's correct. How may I help you, constable?" She looked from the policeman to the elderly gentleman, who still hadn't spoken a word. All he did was stare at her with those intensely cunning eyes of his.

"Is your father in, Miss?" Constable Perkins asked. "Our business is with him."

"He's in the front room. But it's hard for him to get up. He's had an accident, you see, and–"

The policeman cleared his throat. "Could we perhaps come inside then, Miss? I believe it would be better if we explained our visit away from any prying eyes and ears on the street."

"Of course," Abbie replied nervously. Reluctantly, she showed the three men to the front room. Not knowing the purpose of their visit made her anxious. And Mr Yates' shrewd eyes only made those feelings worse. She tried to keep her hand from trembling when she opened the door to the room and announced the visitors.

"Papa, Police Constable Perkins and Mr Yates to see you."

Father sat up straight and tried to get to his feet, but the policeman gestured for him to remain seated.

"What's this about?" he asked, eyeing these surprise guests even more nervously than Abbie had done.

"Mr Lee," the constable began in a formal tone, "I regret to inform you that Mr Yates, here present, has obtained a court order against you. And that I have been instructed to escort you to debtor's prison–"

"Debtor's prison?!" Abbie gasped.

Constable Perkins frowned at her for interrupting him and then proceeded to finish his statement. "Where you shall remain until such time as your debt to Mr Yates has been repaid in full."

"This must be a mistake," Abbie protested. "Papa, tell them."

But her father sheepishly stared at the floor and shook his head. "It's no mistake, princess. We're deep in debt and I was afraid this day would come."

"What's going on?" Jane asked. She stood in the doorway, having come from the kitchen after hearing the consternation in her sister's voice.

"They're taking Papa to prison, Jane!"

"Our Papa? To prison? That's impossible."

When Mr Yates finally broke his stony silence, his voice was as harsh and as icy as the look in his eyes. "I've had quite enough of this family drama. Constable Perkins, please perform your duty. I have other, more important business to attend to. So I would rather not stand here and listen to this man's hysterical offspring."

But Abbie quickly manoeuvred herself in between the policeman and her father. "We refuse," she spoke out defiantly. "I don't believe a single word of this."

"What you believe is irrelevant, young lady," Mr Yates snapped. "The Court has ruled in my favour. Your father has been declared insolvent."

"Simply because an accident has prevented him from earning any wages for two months? That seems a bit harsh and rather unfair to me. How is Papa supposed to work in his current condition?"

Mockingly, Mr Yates grinned at her. "You poor, ignorant creature. Your dear Papa was up to his neck in debt long before he stupidly broke his legs. The accident was merely the final straw. My patience has run out and I have the Law on my side."

Helplessly and fearful, Abbie turned to Constable Perkins for support. But he could do nothing more than force a polite smile onto his face.

"I'm afraid Mr Yates is right, Miss. The Court has spoken and your father must go to prison for his debts. I have here a copy of the ruling." He handed her the piece of paper and added, "You'll see that the debt is indeed substantial."

Abbie's eyes darted over the court order, which seemed authentic enough. When she saw the amount her father owed, she reflexively drew in a sharp breath of air.

"But that's... That's a small fortune."

"Quite," Mr Yates agreed with a thin smile on his pale, bloodless lips.

"Papa..." She looked at her father, her incredulous eyes begging him to explain how this could have happened. But he remained silent and buried his face in his hands, too ashamed to meet her eyes.

Not getting any help from his side, she turned to Constable Perkins and Mr Yates instead. "How can we ever repay such a vast sum?" she asked, her voice trembling. "We are only modest people. Papa is a bricklayer and Mama is a charwoman."

Mr Yates sniffed scornfully. "Observe, Percy," he said to the young man by his shoulder. "Here comes the sad tale of woe and hardship. Followed, no doubt, by the usual crocodile tears and an impassioned plea for leniency."

"Which of course won't show them, Grandfather," young Percy smirked.

"Not in the slightest. The poor are all the same. Always trying to lie and worm their way out of their problems. Always blaming others for the misery they created themselves. And always playing obvious tricks on you by appealing to your feelings of charity."

"It's revolting," Percy said, raising one corner of his upper lip in disgust.

"They can't help themselves, lad. But you mustn't ever show them any mercy. It's for their own good."

Percy nodded and grinned, clearly appreciating his grandfather's so-called sage advice.

Abbie however gritted her teeth and angrily wiped away the hot tears that had sprung up in her eyes. How dared they talk about her family like that?

"We aren't poor," she snarled.

Mr Yates gave a mean little chuckle. "I can tell," he said, looking her up and down and then casting a few quick glances through the room. "The poor usually don't have a piano in their front room and neither do they wear pretty new clothes such as yours, Miss Lee."

A disdainful chill crept into his voice. "I suggest you start by selling those. If you live within your means and stop having fanciful ideas above your station, then perhaps there's hope your family might succeed in repaying your debt."

At this point Constable Perkins tactfully cleared his throat to interrupt the bickering. "Mr Lee is allowed to take a few personal belongings with him to prison. But given his incapacitated state, perhaps you could lend him a hand, Miss?"

Abbie looked at her father, who still sat silently with his head in his hands – ashamed and broken.

"Certainly, constable," she said. "I'll go and pack a change of clothes and some necessities."

She turned to her sister, who hadn't moved from her spot in the doorway, her face still frozen with shock and disbelief. "Jane, darling. You run and find Mama in the meantime. At this hour, she's probably charring at the Robinsons. Hurry!"

With her sister despatched, Abbie left her father with the three men and went upstairs to pack a carpet bag for him.

Clean shirts and undergarments, an extra pair of trousers, a fresh bar of soap. Oh, and I mustn't forget Papa's shaving things.

Rattling off the list of items in her head helped her to keep her anxious mind under control. It wouldn't do to panic. Papa needed her and she had to be practical about this. But there were so many questions that kept coming at her – like a terrifying horde of enemies hurling themselves at the barred gates of a castle.

Why had this happened? How had Papa amassed such an impossible mountain of debts? Why had he never mentioned it to them?

Or perhaps Mama did know, and the two of them had decided to keep it a secret from her and Jane.

And more importantly, how in heaven's name were they going to get out of this horrible mess? Would they need to hire a lawyer and fight the court's decision? But where would they find the money for that?

Abbie had just stuffed the last item in Papa's carpet bag – his favourite pipe – when she heard her mother's voice. Quickly she snapped the bag shut and carried it down the stairs.

Mama seemed to be sharing very similar doubts. Because when Abbie entered the front room with the bag in her hand, Mama asked Mr Yates the question that had been on her own mind as well.

"But how are we supposed to pay back the money my husband owes you when he's in prison?"

She was sitting next to Papa, their hands entangled as if they were clinging on to each other for dear life, while Jane stood behind them and had wrapped her arms around Papa's neck.

This sorrowful scene didn't mollify Mr Yates however. Abbie doubted anything could touch that man's heart.

Probably because it's surrounded by a thick layer of ice, she thought darkly.

"There are always ways and means to obtain money, Mrs Lee," he replied evenly. "As I suggested to your eldest daughter, begin by selling off all these niceties of yours." He gestured vaguely around the room, visibly offended by what he considered to be wasteful luxuries his debtors couldn't afford.

"Furthermore," he continued, "I understand that you are a charwoman?"

"Yes, that's correct, sir."

"Then you can repay part of your husband's debt by working for me. For free, obviously. I shall leave my card and I expect you to present yourself at my address tomorrow morning."

"But I'm charring for another family tomorrow morning," Mother protested dimly.

"Then change your schedule, woman," Mr Yates bit back forcefully. "And now, let's finally conclude our business of the day. Constable Perkins?"

One frosty look from the old man was enough to rouse the constable into action. "Time to go, Mr Lee," he said, moving towards Abbie's father.

Jane and Mama both started crying and tightened their grip on Papa. "No, please," they whimpered. "Have mercy."

"Don't make this any harder on yourselves, Mrs Lee," the policeman grumbled. "Your husband's going to prison whether you like it or not."

Mr Yates raised his chin somewhat and the effect was that he seemed to be looking down at this exchange with an air of indifferent superiority. His grandson Percy on the other hand made little attempt to hide his glee.

"Mama, please," Abbie spoke calmly. "Just let the constable perform his duty." They had lost this fight, so there was no use in resisting the inevitable. There would be more battles yet, she had no doubt.

Also, she didn't want to give Percy the enjoyment of witnessing further drama at their expense. She even forced back her tears, to deny him the pleasure of seeing her cry.

But after Father had been led away by the three men, on his crutches and with his carpet bag, the girls fell into their mother's arms. Where they wept until the evening came and the world turned dark.

Chapter Five

"No, I shan't have it," Mother said, wringing her hands uneasily and pacing the room. "I won't let you come with me, my darlings."

"Why not?" Abbie asked. She didn't want to cause Mama any more grief, but she deliberately struck an assertive and mildly defiant tone. They'd hardly had any sleep the night before, having been kept awake by their troubled minds, worrying about how Papa was faring in prison and how they would get him released.

Yet despite the sleep-deprived fogginess in her head, one thing was clear as crystal to Abbie: she would join Mama as a chargirl. And her sister Jane had declared the same intention.

"When you were born, your father and I swore that we would spare you this cruel life of manual labour," Mother said. "And I intend to keep that promise he and I made to each other."

"But everything's changed now," Abbie argued. She recognised the fear and doubt in Mama's face. And she knew she would win this argument, if she pressed her case long enough. In her view, they had no other choice. "It's the most sensible thing to do, Mama."

"Nonetheless–" Mother bit her lip. Her defences were beginning to crack and she was on the verge of giving in. The only obstacle was this silly promise, made many years ago when she and Papa had been young and full of grand, well-meaning ideals.

"The work will be much quicker this way," Abbie insisted. "If we share it among the three of us, we'll be done in no time. That means you'll be able to take on more customers. Which should help towards repaying Papa's debts."

Jane decided to chip in too. "Besides, we have to let go of our tutors anyway, and without Papa the house is going to feel awfully empty if it's just Abbie and me. So please take us with you, Mama."

"Precisely," Abbie said. "We can do lots of things: cleaning out fire grates, washing up dishes, dusting, mopping floors – all chores we've done many times for you here at home."

Mother let out a long and miserable sigh. "You're right. You brave and sweet angels of mine." Tears came to her eyes and she quickly dabbed at them with her sleeve. "You can come with me."

Abbie and Jane chirped happily and both embraced their mother.

"I shan't like it," Mother warned, pulling her girls close to her. "But I suppose we haven't got much choice."

"We'll make you proud, Mama," Jane said.

"I know you will, my darlings. You always do." She planted a firm kiss on each girl's head and took a deep breath to steel herself. "Let's be off then. We don't want to keep Mr Yates waiting. Especially not on our first day."

When they arrived at the address, Mother gave the girls a quick once-over, smoothed down her own apron and then she knocked. To Abbie's surprise, it was Percy who answered the door.

"Why, if it isn't the Lee family," he beamed smugly. "Sans Papa, obviously." He smiled at Abbie as if he had just made the drollest remark and was now expecting them to laugh and chuckle in the face of such delightful wit.

Pompous ass, she bristled inwardly.

"Good morning, Mr Percy," Mother greeted politely. "We've come to clean the house, as instructed. Is your grandfather in?"

"He most certainly is, Mrs Lee. Please, enter." He stepped aside and, with an exaggerated courtly flourish of his arm, he gestured for them to come in.

"First door on your left," he said as they crossed the doorstep into the dim and sparsely decorated hall.

They found Mr Yates finishing off the last of his breakfast in the dining room. A hasty glance around told Abbie that the house was in dire need of a thorough clean. Everything seemed to be covered in a thick layer of dust, old newspapers littered the floor, while stacks of dirty crockery encrusted with leftover food were threatening to make the sideboard collapse.

An odd, mouldy smell hung in the air as well, and Abbie wondered if it was emanating from the stained carpet, the peeling wallpaper or the grimy looking curtains.

She was beginning to suspect Mr Yates was the kind of moneylender who loved to make a good profit but hated the very thought of spending it.

"Mrs Lee," the old man said with a short and business-like nod of the head. Abbie and Jane however weren't deemed worthy of being acknowledged with more than a quick glimpse from him in their direction.

"Good morning, Mr Yates," Mother replied politely. "Where would you like us to start?"

"I hope you don't expect me to tell you how to do your job, Mrs Lee?" He stared at her with those cold, hard eyes of his boring into her. "You can start wherever you like. As long as this house is clean by the time you leave."

Mother pulled a pained face and looked around. She too had seen the state Mr Yates' home was in. "I'm not sure if we'll be able to manage it all in one day, sir."

"Then do the best you can and come back tomorrow." Carelessly throwing down his napkin, he stood up to leave the room. "I have an appointment in town, but Percy will remain here. To keep an eye on things and to ensure you don't steal anything while I'm away."

Mother gasped in shock. "Mr Yates, I assure you–"

"Never you mind, Mrs Lee," he interrupted arrogantly, pausing with one foot already in the hallway. "Going forward, I expect to see you on my doorstep every morning. There will be plenty of cleaning, cooking, washing, mending and whatnot for you to do."

Without any further ado, he slipped into his coat, put on his hat and went outside, leaving a stunned silence in his wake.

Under the grinning gaze of Percy Yates, Mother took a deep breath. "We'd better get cracking. I'll start dusting and sweeping. Jane, you can do the washing up in the kitchen. And Abbie, you clean out all the fire grates."

"There are fresh coals in the cellar," Percy said helpfully. "I'll just stay out of your way, shall I?"

"In the absence of your grandfather, you're the master of the house, sir," Mother replied. "You may do as you please."

"In that case," he laughed, "I shall be putting my feet up in the front room." He grabbed the morning newspaper from the table and saluted them with it as he left the room.

Abbie rolled her eyes the moment he was gone. She was about to comment on what she thought of this badly neglected house and its two residents, but Mama quickly gestured to keep her mouth shut.

"Chop chop," Mother told them. "We've plenty of work to do. And talking won't help us to get it finished any sooner."

Abbie helped Jane to carry all the dirty dishes and cutlery to the kitchen, and then she proceeded to clean the fire grates in the bedrooms. They clearly hadn't been emptied and cleaned in ages, with a thick layer of ashes spilling out onto the floor. Abbie wondered how anyone still managed to get a fire going in those grates. Or perhaps, she smirked, Mr Yates didn't often light a fire, in order to save on coal.

By the time she came to do the grates in the downstairs rooms, her flushed face was smeared with soot from wiping away the sweat with her dirty hands and sleeves.

"Ho ho," Percy exclaimed with a chuckle when she entered the front room. "It's a good thing I know it's you behind that blackened visage, Miss Lee. Or else I might have thought you were some savage from the African heartland."

She refused to reward his dimwitted attempt at humour with so much as a grin. "I've come to do the grates, sir," she said instead. "Would you prefer me to come back later?"

"No, don't take any notice of me, Miss Lee," he replied in that annoyingly cheerful tone of his. Even his smile seemed to mock her. "The fire grate is all yours. Lord knows it needs a good cleaning out."

Percy's head disappeared behind his newspaper again and Abbie went over to the fireplace, where she knelt down and began to scoop out the ashes into her bucket.

"Must be quite the change for you," Percy's amused voice sounded. "All this manual labour, I mean." He lowered a corner of the newspaper and studied her. "You strike me as the type of girl who's used to a more comfortable existence."

"Papa and Mama do their best to give us a good life," she replied, keeping her eyes firmly on what she was doing. "But my sister and I are no strangers to a bit of hard work."

"I'm sure your dear Papa has done the best he could," Percy stated earnestly. But then he burst out laughing and added, "Too bad he ran up such a massive debt in the process."

Abbie gritted her teeth and continued to clean out the fire grate. Deep inside however, his taunts were riling her up. And in her mind, she had a rather satisfying vision of stuffing a red hot piece of coal in his callous mouth.

"Don't you resent your father for these altered circumstances of yours?" Percy asked with morbid fascination.

"Why would I?"

"Because you, your sister and your mother will need to work your fingers to the bone for several years if you're to repay his debts. Doesn't that anger you?"

"No," she replied, straightening her back and looking him straight in the eye, her posture proud and defiant. "I'll do anything it takes to get my father out of prison."

A wickedly evil grin appeared on Percy's lips. "Most admirable. The man who wins your hand in marriage will be counting himself lucky with such a determined and devoted wife."

Blushing, she averted her eyes and turned her attention back to the fireplace. The grate was clean now and she hurriedly started stacking a fresh pile of coal in it. But even with her back to Percy, she could feel his gaze on her.

"What about you, sir?" she enquired politely. If she couldn't perform her duties without talking to him, then at least she could try to steer the conversation onto safer topics and away from herself. "You live with your grandfather? Or are you merely his guest?"

"No, I'm not a guest, I'm afraid. My mother died after giving birth to me, you see. And then my father drank himself to death shortly afterwards."

He said it in the most casual manner, as if he was informing her about something as trivial as the timetable of the local omnibus.

"I'm sorry to hear that, sir."

He shrugged his shoulders. "It happened a long time ago. The only reason I know their faces is because my grandfather used to have a picture of them. When my father died, the old man took me in and raised me."

"That's decent of him," Abbie said. She had finished laying the fresh coal in the fireplace and got up off her knees.

"Very decent. Especially since he already was a widower back then. Mind you though," he added, laughing, "I suspect he resented having to pay a nursemaid to look after a young child. He's the tight-fisted sort, as you may have noticed from the state of this house."

"We certainly have our work cut out for us," she agreed, brushing off her apron before gathering up all her things.

"Who's more to be pitied, I wonder?" Once again, the corner of his lips curled up in that mocking smile. "Me, the poor orphan? Or you, Papa's precious princess who's reduced to working as a chargirl to pay off her father's debts?"

Refusing to take his bait, Abbie kept her mouth shut and headed for the open door. "I'm done here, sir. I'll see if my sister needs any help in the kitchen and then we'll all be back tomorrow."

"Lovely. See you tomorrow, Miss Lee. In fact–" He paused, barely suppressing his mirth. "I'll see you every day from now on, for the next two or three years."

Biting her tongue, she closed the door behind her. But the sound of his laughter in the room echoed through her head until she reached the kitchen.

"You look upset," Jane said, washing up the last of the pots and pans. "What happened?"

"I don't know what's going to be worse," Abbie said after she had let out a long and angry breath. "Cleaning this grubby house, or putting up with Percy Yates."

Her gut told her it would be the latter.

Chapter Six

A bitter wind blew its ice-cold breath over the muddy streets, causing Abbie to pull her shawl even more tightly round her shivering shoulders. With deep regret she thought of all the warm and pretty clothes they used to have, before they were forced to sell most of their wardrobe, together with the rest of their belongings.

But those were merely material things, she told herself. One day, when Papa's debts were repaid, they would be able to buy new and nicer clothes again.

One day...

Abbie was on her way to visit her father in prison for the first time. Mama had already been to see him, but when she'd come back home afterwards, she had locked herself in the bedroom and cried for hours. Even a week later, Mama still didn't want to talk about it. The only bit of information Abbie and Jane had succeeded in prying out of her was that Papa seemed to be coping reasonably well in prison.

So Abbie had decided to go and see for herself. She missed Papa awfully and she was eager to meet him, talk to him and simply spend some precious time with him.

But part of her was also feeling apprehensive about the visit. She still hadn't managed to wrap her mind around the sad truth that – somehow – her father had accumulated so much debt that he was sent to prison. She was dying to understand how it had happened, but she didn't know if she would have the nerve to outright ask him. Because the last thing she wanted was for Papa to become angry with her during her visit.

Arriving at the prison, she paused before entering and gazed up at the tall building. It didn't look much out of place in the neighbourhood. Only the barred windows and the high, spearheaded iron fences betrayed the fact that this place was holding people captive.

People like her Papa.

Taking a deep breath, she pressed on and walked up to the gate. After giving the prison porter her name and the reason for her visit, she was let in and shown to a small office, where she had to sign the visitors book. From there she was taken to a spacious room with tables and chairs, where she was told to wait. Only two of the tables were occupied by what she assumed were inmates and their visitors, speaking in hushed tones. She sat down at the table furthest away from the others, so she and Papa would enjoy more privacy.

When her father finally arrived, still limping on his crutches, she had to fight the urge to jump up from her seat and throw her arms around him in a tight hug. Instead, she sat up straight, fought back her tears and put on a brave smile for him.

"Hello, Abbie my princess," he said, equally pleased to see her. "So nice of you to come." With some effort and a painful groan, he sat down.

Mama had been right, she thought. Given the circumstances, he was looking fairly well. Tired perhaps, as she couldn't help but notice the dark circles underneath his eyes. Other than that, he seemed to be in fine health and good spirit.

"Wild horses couldn't have kept me away from you, Papa. How are you?"

"Not too bad, my love. This place isn't like most prisons. I've yet to meet any real criminals, since everyone's here for the same reason."

"Debt?"

"Yes, we're all in the same boat. Doesn't mean there's much camaraderie though. Some of the men can be a bit irritable and unfriendly at times."

A worried frown appeared on Abbie's face, as she imagined her father having to deal with loud and uncouth inmates. But he patted her hand and soothed, "Nothing I can't handle, princess."

"I've brought you something," she said, placing a small parcel wrapped in brown paper in front of him.

"A gift? For me?" He smiled, untied the piece of string and opened the parcel. "Tobacco," he said, looking at her appreciatively. "Thank you, my dearest. This stuff is as good as currency in here."

"Why's that?"

"They make you pay for anything beyond the mere basics. Meals are usually poor fodder like gruel, dry bread with a few crumbs of cheese and the weakest tea you've ever tasted."

She grinned awkwardly as she thought of the meagre pauper's meals she, Mama and Jane ate at home these days. Good food and Sunday roasts were a thing of the past.

"There's a lot of bartering going on," her father said. He slipped the tobacco in the inside pocket of his vest and softly patted the little bulge it made. "So I'll keep this very safe. Do you think you could bring any more next time you visit?"

"I'll try, Papa. But we really have to watch every penny, and things aren't easy at home."

She felt bad for saying it and she would have loved to make his stay in prison more comfortable. But the more frugally they lived, the sooner they could repay his debt.

"Of course, of course," he replied hastily, turning away and blushing with shame. Then he cleared his throat and forced himself to look at her again. "How are you all doing? Your mother didn't say much when she visited. I'm afraid she cried more than she talked."

"We do our best," she shrugged. "Jane and I go out charring with Mama every day. So no more private tutoring obviously. And we've had to sell the piano, along with a cartload of furniture and other things."

"We'll get it all back, princess." There was fire and conviction in his voice. Or was it desperation, she wondered?

"I promise," he continued. "As soon as I walk out of here a free man, I'll work twice as hard. And then we'll buy even nicer things."

She tried to smile, but she didn't share his enthusiasm. "The trouble is, Papa," she started saying, weighing her words so she wouldn't hurt his feelings. "Everything we've sold so far only covered a small part of your debts. Mama, Jane and I will have to work for two or three years to pay it all back."

Again, he dropped his gaze, too ashamed to face her. "I'm sorry, my love. It's my fault you have to go through this awful ordeal. Please forgive me."

"I don't care about the work, Papa. Truly, I don't. But it also means you'll be stuck in here for a few more years. How will you manage?"

He looked up, smiled at her and stroked a loose lock of her hair that was dangling down the side of her face. "My sweet princess. I don't deserve a daughter as caring and devoted as you."

"You mustn't say that, Papa. I love you. No matter what."

Something about this bittersweet moment between them gave her the courage to ask the question that had been on her mind for so long.

"Papa," she began, hesitantly at first, "I hope you won't find it rude of me to ask, but..." Her confidence faltered. Fortunately though, he finished the question for her.

"How did I end up having so much debt?"

"Yes. You don't have to tell me if you don't want to. I realise it's none of my business."

"Seeing as you're working to pay off my debts, I'd say it is your business. And you have every right to know, my dearest."

Letting out a miserable sigh, he folded his hands and placed them in front of him on the worn and rough surface of the wooden table.

"The truth of the matter is I've been borrowing money for years. Just a little at first. You know, to pay for unexpected bills or to tide us over until I got my next wages. Never had any trouble paying it back."

He smiled at her, as if he was sharing memories of happier times. Which, she mused, in a way he was.

"But then," he continued, "I became bolder." The smile vanished from his face and he gazed down at his hands. "Or perhaps foolish is a better word for it."

He fell silent for a moment, and Abbie thought she saw an emptiness in his sad and hollow eyes. But she held back her desire to speak, allowing him to tell his story in his own time.

"I started borrowing money for larger expenses – things we didn't necessarily need. But I knew they would bring a smile to our faces and give the three of you joy."

He looked up at her, his eyes pleading and urgent. "I so wanted our little family to be happy, Abbie."

"I know, Papa," she replied softly, placing a hand over his folded hands. They felt cold to the touch and they were trembling slightly.

"But that's when things got out of control," he said. "Whenever I couldn't repay a loan, I simply took out a new one to pay back the older debt. That worked splendidly for a while, but of course it meant my debts were growing, slowly and steadily. I thought I'd be able to stay on top of it all, until..."

He sighed, the memory too painful to him.

"Until you broke your legs and couldn't go to work?"

He nodded. "Mr Yates isn't a kind man. These moneylenders seldom are, but he's certainly one of the hardest."

"Then why did you borrow from him?"

"I was running out of options, Abbie. Some of these men didn't want to lend me any more money, because they were concerned I wouldn't be able to pay them back. I guess you could say they were smarter than me."

Abbie thought of Mr Yates with his stiff and arrogant appearance, a heart colder than ice, and a mind as rigid as his old back. Smart wasn't a word she would have used to describe him. Cunning felt much more appropriate.

"I did it because I wanted us to have a good life, Abbie," Father said, fixing his sad and sorrowful eyes on her. "I wanted to provide for my wife and my two girls. I wanted to make you proud of me."

"But we are proud of you, Papa. We–"

"No," he interrupted. "There's nothing to be proud of in me. There's only shame. I've failed you all miserably." He pulled back his hands, dropped his shoulders in utter defeat and slumped in his seat. "Please forgive me."

Before she could reply, he pushed himself up and took his crutches, while silent tears ran down his agonised face. She rose to her feet as well and wanted to tell him that it was all right and that he should stay with her a little while longer. But as he began to limp away from her, she understood his pride had been badly hurt and that he needed to grieve in peace.

"I'll be back soon," she called after him. "And I'll bring more of your favourite tobacco." A few people stared at her and then resumed their own conversations. Her father merely nodded and resumed his lonely departure from the room.

Abbie sighed and made her way out of the prison. No matter how foolish, reckless or irresponsible Papa had been, she couldn't bring herself to hate him for it. Or even to blame him for the harshness of their current situation.

He was her father and she loved him. And everything he'd done – no matter how misguided it might seem to anyone else – he had done it for the good of his family.

When she emerged onto the street, the gathering darkness of the evening was beginning to show itself, adding to her already gloomy feelings. But despite all this, she could sense a strong determination in herself as well.

They would overcome these problems. They would pay back all the money Papa owed and they would be a happy family once more. She would work very hard for that.

Even if it meant dealing with the likes of Mr Yates and Percy.

Chapter Seven

On wash day, the kitchen in Mr Yates' house was filled with a distinctly unpleasant and rancid odour, emanating from the tub in which the dirty linen had been soaking overnight in lye soap. But this foetid smell was the least of Abbie and Jane's bothers.

Because now the girls had to scrub everything clean on the washboard, bleach and boil the white pieces and then put it all through the wringer mangle. An arduous grind that was hard on their aching backs and perhaps even harder on their hands, due to the harsh chemicals they had to use.

The fact they were washing the men's undergarments didn't make their task any more agreeable either.

They laboured in silence for a while, until Jane stood up straight to stretch her back. She sighed and asked, "Do we have to keep doing this, Abbie?"

"Of course we do, silly. These clothes aren't going to wash themselves, you know. But we're nearly done, so don't despair."

"No, I didn't mean the washing. Although I do dislike this part of our work." She lifted a pair of soggy cotton drawers from the tub and shivered in disgust. "I meant how much longer do we have to be chargirls?" she asked as she began to scrub the drawers on the washboard.

"For quite some time still, I'm afraid," Abbie replied. "We've only just begun repaying Papa's debts."

"What would happen if we stopped working?"

"Then we wouldn't be able to pay off the debt and Papa would have to stay in prison forever. We can't have that, can we?"

Jane shook her head and fell silent. When Abbie looked at her, she could tell her sister was brooding.

Small wonder. Only a month ago, their days were mainly filled with music, reading, studying and some light household duties. Now, they were a pair of common skivvies cleaning out chamber pots and doing a whole range of other menial tasks.

She tried to think of something encouraging to say, but Jane spoke first.

"And what if we just stopped working for Mr Yates?" she asked, lowering her voice. "I don't like him. He frightens me. And Percy's even worse."

"I know, sweetheart." Abbie's heart bled for her younger sister. "And believe me, I would much rather stay as far away from those two as possible. But we don't have any other choice."

"If you say so," Jane sighed. "Promise me one thing though."

"And what's that?"

"Promise me we won't be chargirls for the rest of our lives?"

"I'll gladly give you my word on that one. When this is over, we won't be washing other people's dirty laundry ever again." She tossed the last of the drawers into the large kettle to be boiled and bleached.

And that's when an idea struck her. Something that was sure to lift her sister's spirits.

"Do you remember the games we used to play when we were little? The ones where we pretended to be princesses?"

A faint smile appeared on Jane's face as those particular childhood memories came back to her. "Yes. What about them?"

"Why don't we do that now?"

"You must be joking. We're too old for that sort of thing."

"My dearest sister," Abbie chuckled. "You make it sound as if we're a pair of old spinsters. One is never too old to play a princess."

She grabbed a tea towel and draped it over her hair like an improvised veil headdress. "Behold, I am Princess Abigail."

Jane tried not to laugh, but she couldn't prevent a little snort from escaping her. Abbie's fantasies were simply impossible to resist.

"Here we are," Abbie lamented. "Two unhappy princesses, trapped in the smelly old manor of the greedy Baron Yates and his wicked grandson Percy."

Her sister burst out laughing. "That's precisely who they are! And this place certainly is old and smelly."

Encouraged by Jane's reaction, Abbie continued her role of the princess in distress. "Woe is us," she exclaimed with great dramatic conviction. "Are we fated to be enslaved in misery forever? Or shall Fortune smile upon us and send us a brave and handsome prince?"

"Make that two handsome princes, please," Jane said with a cheeky grin. Soon, the two of them were in stitches, coming up with silly lines and spinning an absurd fairy tale, while they bleached and pressed the washing.

Time passed quickly this way, and they almost forgot about their worries and the endless drudgery that threatened to dominate their lives for years to come.

Until the door suddenly opened a crack and Percy's head appeared in the doorway. Abbie and Jane's heart skipped a beat and their laughter instantly died.

"So much jolly merrymaking in here," he smirked. "Mind if I join you? I was feeling a bit bored and I could hear you laughing all the way to the sitting room."

Not waiting for a reply, he fully opened the door and strolled into the kitchen, oozing with cocky self-confidence.

"Apologies if we distracted you, sir," Abbie said. "We'll work more quietly." She tried not to blush and wondered how much he had overheard. What if he had been eavesdropping by the door? And for how long?

"Nonsense," he said, taking visible delight in their embarrassment. "I wouldn't want to deny you a little joy and pleasure. How very dull life would be without a bit of fun."

He paused and smiled as he watched them pulling wet clothes through the mangle – standing a pace too close for comfort. Abbie and Jane avoided meeting his gaze and doubled down on their task with considerably more attention and focus than it actually required.

He's toying with us, she thought. But she decided it was best to let him enjoy his game, hoping he would eventually tire of it.

"Ingenious contraption this, isn't it?" he marvelled, pointing at the mangle the girls were operating. "So simple and yet so effective."

"It gets the job done, sir," Abbie replied, humouring him while her muscles strained to turn the handle.

"I say, Miss Jane," he spoke with a particularly sardonic grin on his face, "I do believe that's a pair of my drawers you have in your hands there. I bet you've never touched a man's undergarments before."

Jane winced at his scandalously unseemly remark, while Abbie turned red with barely suppressed rage. She could have slapped him in the face for making such a vulgar comment to her younger sister.

But in the unfair world they lived in, that sort of angry reaction from her – even though it was merited – would have been deemed a far greater transgression than his foul-mouthed words.

Where's Mama when you need her?

She knew their mother was somewhere upstairs, cleaning the bedrooms. If only she'd been in the kitchen. Not even Percy would have dared to be this bold with Jane and Abbie's mother around.

Feeling ever so protective, Abbie wanted to get her sister out of the kitchen and away from Percy's cynical smut as quickly as possible.

"Jane, darling," she said. "Why don't you take this first pile of clean laundry outside to dry?"

Her sister hesitated briefly, flashing a wary look at Percy, as if she was nervous about letting Abbie alone with him.

"Don't worry," Abbie reassured her. "I'll bring out the rest as soon as I'm done."

Grateful for the opportunity to slip away, Jane grabbed the damp laundry and left, casting one final glance over her shoulder on her way out.

With some luck, she'll run into Mama and tell her, Abbie prayed. In the meantime, she wanted to get the last bit of washing through the mangle as quickly as possible. The sooner she too could get away from Percy, the better. Her arms and shoulders would be painfully sore the next day, but she decided that was only a small price to pay.

"Just me and you then," Percy grinned as he kept staring at her while she toiled and slaved at the mangle.

Why had he come to the kitchen, she wondered? Even if he had heard her and Jane laughing, it wasn't proper for him to be here. But at the same time, as the hired help she wasn't in any position to tell him that. So why was he here? If he wanted tea or coffee, or a midday snack, he could have called out for it.

But it probably wasn't refreshments he was after, she guessed. She had heard the stories of what some employers got up to with their maids.

"Anything I can do for you, sir?" she asked as beads of sweat sprung up on her forehead.

"Oh, I'm sure there's plenty you could do for me, Miss Lee." Despite the smile on his face, there was an undertone to his voice that would have turned her entire body rigid with fear – if it hadn't been for the work she so desperately wanted to finish.

"Actually, I'm worried about you, Miss Lee," he said.

"Why is that, sir?" she enquired as politely as she could manage.

"You might think I'm jesting, but it's true. Watching you grind away at that machine, I cannot help but fear for your marriage prospects."

Abbie stopped turning the handle and stared at him, blinking in disbelief. What was he driving at this time?

"My... marriage prospects, sir?"

"Yes, you're jeopardising them. An educated young woman such as yourself labouring as a maid-of-all-work? Why, you're severely damaging your ability to attract suitable marriage candidates."

Having recovered her wits, she rushed to pull the last garments through the wringer. Their conversation was becoming much too bizarre and personal for her liking.

"Thank you for your concern about my future and my welfare, sir," she replied primly. She didn't, of course, for a minute believe he was being sincere. No, Percy Yates was up to some sort of trick. And she wasn't sure she cared to find out which one.

"Some men might not want to have anything to do with you," he said, "if they saw you engaged in this kind of work." He paused briefly and then added, with his typical grin, "Their loss, obviously."

Abbie picked up the damp pile of pressed laundry, eager to escape. "Duly noted, sir. Although I'm confident it'll all be fine in the end."

She headed for the door, but he took a sideways step to block her path, forcing her to stop and face him.

"I can make sure things will work out fine, Miss Lee," he said.

Fine for her, she thought? Or for him?

"No need, sir. I don't require saving at the moment."

She moved to be on her way, but he placed a hand on her arm and squeezed – a soft, yet determined touch that caused her to hold her breath.

"Are you running away from me, Miss Lee?" he whispered. "Do I make you nervous?"

Her mind was at a loss for words. All she could do was stare at his hand that was restraining her.

"You're not afraid of me, are you?" he asked, clearly enjoying the many signs that she was indeed afraid.

"Mister Percy?" Mama's voice sounded behind him. "Can we be of assistance to you, sir?"

Without any hint of shame or surprise, he let go of Abbie's arm and spun round, conjuring up a dazzling and perfectly innocent smile.

"No, I was merely asking your fine daughters how they were coping in their new role, Mrs Lee."

"Most kind of you, sir," Mama replied, her formal tone betraying her doubts about his true purpose.

"I need to take this laundry outside," Abbie said as she slipped swiftly past Percy. "Jane's outside and she's probably waiting for me."

She gladly left her mother to deal with Percy and went to join her sister in the small courtyard at the back of the house. But when the last of the washing had been hung out to dry, her legs were still shaking from fright.

Chapter Eight

Supper at the Lee residence had become a sad and silent affair. The poor quality and the meagre amount of food on the table was, in and of itself, enough to make Abbie want to weep. Especially since they had been used to eating far better than this.

But none of them made any comments about it. Mainly because they were always too tired to talk much after a long day of hard work. And also because there was no use in complaining. This was their lot in life now. The less they spoke of these things, the easier it was to accept them.

That's why they kept their heads down and ate in silence – the kind of silence that weighed heavily and made you forget you were hungry.

Abbie fixed her eyes on the chipped plate in front of her while she ate. But even then it was hard to ignore the bare walls around them. The same walls that had previously been adorned with small paintings, picture frames and all sorts of plain but charming knick-knacks.

All gone now, their absence painfully betrayed by the square and rectangular marks they had left behind on the walls. The house felt empty. There was no more joy in the air and Abbie found herself doubting if she still thought of this place as their home.

She stared at the fourth chair by the table. The one where Papa used to sit. No, she concluded, it didn't feel like home any longer. Not in the true sense of the word anyway.

She snapped out of her dark and brooding thoughts when there was a knock at the front door. The sound seemed to echo through the empty house, creating an ominous effect.

More bad news, Abbie fretted instantly?

The three women looked at each other, briefly frozen in the moment. But then the eerie spell was broken by another knock.

"Could just be one of the neighbours," Jane suggested.

"Go and have a look, Abbie dear," Mama said listlessly, before returning her attention to her food.

As Abbie got up and went to the hallway, her stomach grew tighter with every step. And by the time she opened the front door, it wouldn't have startled her if she had been greeted by the Grim Reaper himself.

Instead, the man standing on their doorstep was Constable Perkins – who, despite not being half as scary as Death, was looking quite gloomy.

"Constable Perkins," Abbie said cheerlessly.

"Good evening, Miss Lee. Might I come inside, please? I have news. About your father."

"Not very good news, judging by that look on your face?"

He shook his head and gazed at his black boots. "I'm afraid not, Miss."

With a resigned sigh, she stepped aside and gestured for him to enter. "My mother and sister are in the kitchen," she said as they walked the short distance to the back of the house.

"Mama, Jane, it's Constable Perkins. He says he has news about Papa."

Mother's hands flew up to cover her gaping mouth and Jane clutched the edge of the table. They too understood that whatever the police officer had come to tell them, it wouldn't be good.

"Evening, all," the constable said with a short nod of the head. "I wish there was a way I could soften the terrible blow you are about to receive, but alas, there isn't. Mrs Lee, it is with great sadness that I must inform you of your husband's death."

Mother broke down in tears, her shoulders shaking as she sobbed and wailed in misery. Abbie and Jane rushed to her side and wrapped their arms around her, engaging in a threefold embrace.

"What happened?" Abbie asked.

"Apparently, an inebriated fellow inmate got into a heated argument with your father. The dispute revolved around tobacco, I was told." He awkwardly fingered the edge of the police helmet in his hands.

"The situation got out of hand," he continued. "A fight broke out and by the time the guards regained control, Mr Lee was found dead on the floor."

Mother let out another salvo of sobbing cries as she buried her face in her handkerchief. Abbie and Jane held her tight, both for their Mama's sake as well as their own.

Killed in a common brawl. Why did Papa's life have to end like this? Beaten to death over some tobacco. If Mr Yates hadn't gone to court over the unpaid debt, Papa would never have been sent to prison. If that man had given Papa a little bit more time to recover from the accident...

Then Papa would still have been alive!

He would have been here with them and everything would have been as pleasantly wonderful as always. Instead, their lives had been ruined. And all because Mr Yates was so eager to get his money back.

Perhaps Jane was thinking along similar lines. Because she looked at Abbie and asked, "Does this mean we don't have to pay off the rest of the debt any more?"

"I don't know. Constable Perkins?"

The policeman stopped fidgeting, grateful for the short pause in the displays of feminine emotion he had been forced to witness. "To my knowledge, upon the death of a debtor, the debt is inherited by his heirs."

"What does that mean?" Jane asked, her hopes fading quickly.

Abbie sighed. "It means we'll be working for Mr Yates for quite a while still."

"One of you will have to go down to the prison," Constable Perkins said. "To claim Mr Lee's remains and to make arrangements for the funeral with an undertaker."

"I'll see to that," Mama answered, wiping away her tears. She took a deep breath and straightened her shoulders. "Thank you, constable, for bringing us the news in person. Apologies that you had to watch us cry."

"Think nothing of it, Mrs Lee."

"Shouldn't someone inform Mr Yates as well?" Abbie asked. She reckoned he wouldn't be half pleased. Even though for him, ultimately, Father's death didn't change much: he would still be getting his money back, one way or the other.

"Would you mind doing that, Abbie dear?" Mother said. "I can't bear the thought of having to face that man just now."

"I'll go with Mama," Jane said. "I don't particularly want to see Papa's dead body, but I want to see Mr Yates and Percy even less."

An hour later, Abbie arrived at Mr Yates' house. On her way over, she'd had time to think about how to break the news to the old man. Short and to the point was probably best, she had decided. Mr Yates hated anything melodramatic.

As she had expected, it was Percy who opened the door. "Miss Lee," he beamed. "What a delightful surprise."

"My apologies for calling on you at this late hour, sir. But I have rather important news that my family and I believe your grandfather should hear."

"Sounds intriguing. Have you won a small fortune at the races, so you can now repay your father's debts in full?" he quipped.

"Hardly, sir."

She hoped the dryness of her tone made him understand she didn't appreciate his attempt at being funny. Whether he cared was another matter.

"We were just having supper," he said. "But please, do come in. If it's important, as you say it is, I'm sure my grandfather won't mind the interruption."

"Very gracious of you, sir."

She entered the house and followed Percy to the dining room. The two men were having the soup Mama had made earlier that day, with some bread and a bit of hard cheese. Mr Yates could easily afford to eat better than that, Abbie knew. But he loved his money too much to spend it on good food.

"Miss Lee," he greeted her with an annoyed scowl. "I'm assuming you have a good reason to disturb us at this time of day?"

"I do indeed, Mr Yates. I have come to tell you that my father has died in prison."

She watched his face for any reaction. But there was none. Not even the slightest trace or hint of emotion. And certainly not sympathy. But she suspected his cunning mind was already trying hard to come up with a way to turn this setback into his advantage.

"Unfortunate," he said.

That's one way of putting it, she grumbled silently.

"But–" He sighed and threw down his napkin on the table. "I believe I have a solution. One that will benefit your family as well as myself."

Abbie was sure it would benefit him just that little bit more. "Sir?"

"I want the three of you to move into this house, as our live-in maids. You'll have free food and lodgings, so obviously I will need to halve your wages."

"Halve?!"

"Yes, I'm being generous. And don't forget, this way you won't have to pay rent any longer, so that's more money that can go towards your late father's debt. You're still free to continue your work for other households of course."

"A very elegant solution, Grandfather," Percy smiled smugly. "Wonderfully beneficial to all parties involved, I should think."

Yes, you *would think that, wouldn't you?* Abbie wanted to sneer at him. The idea of living under the same roof as Percy Yates filled her with revulsion.

And dread.

"Thank you, Mr Yates. I'll convey your proposal to my mother."

"Please do, Miss Lee."

"One practical question however, if I may. Where would we sleep?" She already knew there weren't any servants' quarters in Mr Yates' house.

"You have two options, Miss Lee. Either you sleep on the kitchen floor. Or you can use the small loft room. Once you clean up the cobwebs and chase out the rats, you should be quite comfortable up there underneath the rafters."

"Thank you, sir," she replied with a curt nod. *Generous indeed,* her mind added sarcastically. It sounded more like slavery to her.

But when she presented his plan at home, Mother decided –reluctantly– that it was the best thing for them to do.

"I don't exactly fancy the idea either," Mama admitted. "But like Mr Yates said, it'll allow us to make more savings if we give up our own home." Anxiously wringing her hands, she looked round the half-empty room. "Besides, this old place has too many memories about your Papa attached to it anyway."

The next day, they notified their landlord that they were leaving. And after they had sold most of what few belongings they had left, they arrived at Mr Yates' doorstep – each of them carrying two bags containing some clothes and a few bare necessities.

When Percy opened the door for them, his triumphant grin reached from ear to ear. "Welcome to your new home," he said.

His conceited tone made Abbie's skin crawl.

Chapter Nine

"Your turn to serve supper this evening, Abbie," Jane said. "And for your sake, I hope Mr Yates is in a better mood than he was yesterday. I couldn't do anything right, it seemed."

"Thanks for the warning," Abbie replied as she picked up the kettle of steaming hot soup. "But if he gets too rude, I just might be tempted to pour the contents of this onto his lap. Purely by accident, of course." She grinned and winked at her sister, before leaving the kitchen.

When she entered the dining room, Mr Yates and Percy were already seated at the table, discussing business. Mr Yates ignored her, as was his habit, and simply continued his monologue to his grandson. But Percy looked up and stared at her unashamedly.

Abbie served Mr Yates first, being very careful not to spill the slightest drop onto the crisp tablecloth. Not so much to please Mr Yates, but because she hated cleaning out the stains.

Next, she moved over to Percy's side. He didn't take his eyes off her for a moment while she ladled out his soup. His gaze unnerved her terribly, but she made sure her hands didn't tremble.

"Smells delicious, Miss Lee," he said after making a show of inhaling the aroma. "Was it you or your mother who made this?"

"My sister and I did, sir."

"Then you're both very talented young women."

"Quit the chit-chat, Percy," Mr Yates snapped. "You don't speak to the staff. You tell them what to do, that's all."

"Yes, Grandfather."

"You," Mr Yates said to Abbie with a dismissive wave of his hand. "Leave. We'll call you when we need you."

"Yes, sir," she replied, bobbing a quick curtsy and then heading for the door.

"See?" she heard Mr Yates say as she left the room. "That's how you handle these people, Percy."

Having closed the door, she silently pulled a face at the two men inside. She disliked both of them. But even so, she greatly preferred Mr Yates' rudeness over his grandson's creepy stares.

Just as she returned to the kitchen, their mother came in from her last charring job of the day – soaking wet from the rain.

"Mama," Abbie exclaimed, full of concern. "You look like you're drenched to the skin."

"I am, sweetie. Got caught in a downpour that lasted the whole way here."

"You should've taken the omnibus, Mama," Jane said. "Or a hansom cab."

Abbie grabbed a kitchen towel and started dabbing at their mother's wet clothes with it.

"Walking's cheaper, Janie dear," Mother replied to her youngest. "And Abbie darling, it's no use. These clothes are soaked."

"Then go and change in some dry ones, Mama. You'll catch your death if you don't get dry and warm soon. Why don't you hurry off upstairs and I'll heat up your supper in the meantime. I managed to make a stew – well, sort of anyway – using this week's scraps and leftovers."

Mother shook her weary head. "I'm not feeling very hungry, dear. I think I'll head straight to bed and get a good night's sleep."

"But Mama, you've been working all day. Surely, you need to eat something?"

"You and Jane can have it, darling," she said, trying to put on a brave smile. Abbie watched her leave the kitchen, with slouching shoulders and tired feet that almost dragged over the floor. This wasn't the lively, energetic woman they used to know.

Abbie understood that Mama was still mourning for Papa. They all were. But this was more than grief, more than sadness for the loss of a loved one. Mama seemed to have lost the will to live. And that worried Abbie.

Working for Mr Yates in exchange for a laughable pittance was bad enough. But Mama was pushing herself hard by cleaning at several other addresses as well every day, so they would earn more money to repay the debt. Abbie was fearful that the added strain was beginning to break their mother.

She would talk to Mama about it, she resolved when the two girls were finally able to retire for the night. Yes, she thought as she laid down her head. They would talk and Abbie would convince Mama to take better care of herself.

The next morning, Jane and Abbie were the first to wake up in the stuffy little loft room that the three of them shared. Their narrow straw mattresses on the floor rustled as they stretched and got up.

"Time to rise, Mama," Abbie yawned. She reached over to give her mother a little nudge.

"Mama," she gasped at the first touch. "You've got a fever." She could feel her mother shivering underneath the thin blanket.

"I'll be fine," Mama croaked. "I'm just tired, that's all." With some effort, she sat up straight and threw aside her bedsheet.

"Shouldn't you stay in bed with a temperature like that?" Abbie asked.

"Can't. We have a lot of work to do today." Mother tried to stand up on her feet, but she wasn't even halfway when she swayed and fell back heavily onto her straw mattress.

"Mama!"

Abbie and Jane rushed over, fretting and fussing over their mother, who was blistering hot and drenched in cold sweat.

"It was nothing but a dizzy spell," Mama protested feebly. "Give me a moment to catch my breath and then I'll get up."

"No, you won't," Abbie ordered. "You're staying in bed this morning. I'll tell Mr Yates that Jane and I will be doing all the work today."

"But he'll be mad at us."

"Let him," Abbie answered firmly. "You're in no condition to be up on your feet all day. You need rest. Even a man like Mr Yates should understand that."

The two girls washed and got dressed in a hurry.

"I'll bring up a cup of tea and something to eat," Abbie promised. "After we've served breakfast for Mr Yates."

She fretted about the best way and the right moment to tell him her mother was sick. But in the end, Mr Yates provided the opening himself.

"Where's your mother this morning, Miss Lee?" he asked in his usual dour tone. "I haven't seen her in a while."

"She hasn't eloped, has she?" Percy quipped, earning him a reproachful stare from his grandfather.

"I'm afraid she's taken ill, sir," Abbie replied, ignoring Percy as usual. "I told her to stay in bed." She held her breath, nervous about how he would take it.

"Ill? What's the matter with her?"

"She got drenched in the cold rain yesterday. And this morning she had a fever."

"Disease," Mr Yates snarled irritably. "In my own home. We'll all be sick if we're not careful. I don't want to end up in my grave just because some silly charwoman caught a cold."

Abbie gritted her teeth. *That silly charwoman happens to be my mother, you despicable old man,* she grumbled silently.

"Surely, it won't come to that, sir," she said politely.

"We'll make certain that it doesn't," he replied vehemently. "You and your sister are forbidden from entering that room, Miss Lee. Until your mother has fully recovered. You can sleep in the kitchen in the meantime."

"But, sir! What about her meals? You don't expect my mother to starve, do you?"

"Of course not. Take up a tray with her food and leave it by the door."

"But what if she's too sick to get up?"

Mr Yates scoffed. "If she's hungry enough, she'll get out of bed."

Realising that it was useless to argue, Abbie simply inclined her head and left the men to their breakfast.

Back in the kitchen, she told Jane about the 'arrangement' Mr Yates had foisted upon them.

"That man has a lump of coal where his heart's supposed to be," her sister grumbled.

"At least coal can generate heat," Abbie scoffed. "I don't think he's capable of expressing any warmth whatsoever." She sighed and shook her head wearily.

"I've made breakfast for Mama," Jane said. "It's just some buttered toast with a bit of cheese and a pot of tea. But I'm assuming she won't have much of an appetite anyway."

"I'll take it up to the top floor for her. Let's pray she has the strength to stand on her legs and collect her tray by the door."

When she went up the stairs, Abbie heard Mr Yates leaving by the front door. *I hope he gets run over by a carriage,* she thought, instantly hating herself for wishing ill upon anyone – even someone as loathsome as Mr Yates.

And besides, she reminded herself, his death wouldn't benefit them at any rate. Just like they had inherited their father's debt, Percy was likely to inherit his grandfather's claim to that money.

Shaking off these useless reflections, she knocked on her mother's bedroom door. "Mama, I've brought you some breakfast. But we're not allowed to enter the room. Mr Yates is afraid we'll catch your cold if we do."

She waited for a response, and when none was forthcoming, she continued, "I'll leave your tray by the door, shall I?"

A painful moan was the only reaction from inside the room.

"Please try to eat something, won't you, Mama?"

Anxiously chewing her lower lip, Abbie had to keep herself from bursting into the room. Her mother needed rest, but that didn't mean she had to be completely isolated. Abbie would have fed her by hand if required.

"I'll have it later, sweetie," her mother's weak voice croaked.

"All right then." Abbie hesitated and wished there was anything more she could do. But there wasn't. "Jane and I will come up and check on you later."

She hovered by the door for a few more moments, and then went back downstairs. Their chores were waiting, she told herself bravely. Mama wouldn't want them to neglect their duties.

We'll make her proud of us, Abbie promised.

But when she reached the bottom of the stairs, suddenly, her emotions got the better of her. First, they'd been dealt the blow of Papa's debts, followed by the shock of his death in prison. And now, Mama had fallen ill.

Abbie fled to a quiet corner of the hall and buried her face in her hands. She would allow herself a few tears, but then she had to get on with her work.

"Miss Lee?"

No, not him. Not now.

Taking a deep breath, she quickly wiped off her tears with her sleeve and tried to straighten her shoulders.

"Apologies, sir."

"None needed," Percy replied softly. "I fully understand how all of this must weigh terribly on you."

His voice sounded almost warm and sympathetic. Abbie wasn't sure if she liked this apparent change in him.

"I'll be all right, sir." She took a step in the direction of the kitchen. "If you'll excuse me, I have to–"

"Miss Lee," he said, blocking her way. "If there's anything I can do, you'll let me know, won't you?"

"That's very kind of you, sir. But my family and I will manage." Holding her breath, she brushed past him. To her relief, he didn't try to stop her.

"I can solve your money problems, you know," he said. Involuntarily, she stopped in her tracks and turned round.

"How's that, sir?"

Grinning strangely, he closed the distance between them with a few long strides. "I could simply *give* you the money you need."

"It's a sizeable sum, sir." She eyed him with suspicion. What sort of trickery was he up to now?

"I know it is, Miss Lee. I'm well aware of my grandfather's business affairs. But I have my own funds. And I would be willing to support you financially."

"Support us?"

"Support *you*," he corrected her.

"In exchange for...?"

Slowly, he let his finger run over the lace trimmings on the edge of her maid's apron. "In exchange for, shall we say, certain courtesies on your part."

She blushed with shame and anger at the same time. *The outrageous nerve of that man,* she bristled. He really was an unseemly character.

"I'm not for sale, sir," she hissed.

"Everyone has a price, Miss Lee," he smiled arrogantly. "I simply haven't found yours yet."

Ending their conversation there and then, she huffed indignantly and stomped away from him.

"My offer stands, Miss Lee," he called after her, his tone confident and mocking. "You're free to take it up whenever you're ready."

Never, she swore. No matter how dire things might become, she would never sink that low. Some day, she would give herself to a man – it was the way of life. But she would choose to whom and when.

Chapter Ten

Two weeks later, Mama was still laid up in bed. Far from improving, her condition was only getting worse. Abbie was worried sick about her. And she had no doubt her sister Jane felt the same, even though they didn't talk about it much – for fear of upsetting each other even more.

Adding to their anxiety, Mr Yates continued to insist that they were not to enter their mother's bedroom. Privately, Abbie fumed and raged against his pigheaded stubbornness. But she obeyed his order nonetheless. Because if she were to go in and he found out about it, she was certain he would be perfectly capable of throwing them out on the street – including their bedridden mother.

What Mama needed was a doctor. Unfortunately, Abbie and Jane didn't have the money. And Mr Yates wasn't willing to pay for a physician out of his own pocket. Abbie knew, because she had asked him – politely.

"A waste of money," he had grumbled in reply. "The only thing your mother is suffering from is laziness."

Abbie had tried to protest, but he had cut her off rudely. "I've been in this business long enough," he had said. "And I know a poor excuse when I see one. This is just another way of you lot trying to weasel your way out of your legal obligations to me."

She had left it at that, knowing that she would have more chance of success if she argued with a brick wall. Mama would have to get better all by herself, without the advice of a doctor or the help of any medication. All that Abbie and Jane could do was hope and pray.

After the men had been served their breakfast, Abbie took up a tray for her mother, just like she had been doing every day for two weeks.

Trudging up the stairs to the loft, she became painfully aware of her sore limbs and her tired back. Even at this early hour of the day, she was already exhausted. She and Jane were trying to manage all the work between the two of them, including the charring jobs Mama used to do at other houses. Unfortunately, they had been forced to let go of a few of those customers. Which meant their meagre income had sunk even lower.

And sleeping on the cold, hard kitchen floor wasn't exactly conducive to a good night's rest either, adding further to their growing fatigue.

With a troubled sigh Abbie arrived at the top floor, where a tiny landing led to the small bedroom under the eaves. In the dim daylight that fell through the narrow skylight, she could see last night's supper tray standing by the door, untouched.

"Mama, you haven't eaten your food again," Abbie called out. "You really must try to eat something if you want to get better soon."

She knocked, hoping for at least a groan of acknowledgement from her mother.

"Mama?"

But there was no response. She knocked a few more times, until she could no longer resist the frantic urge to enter the room. With her heart beating forcefully in her tight chest, she opened the door and went in.

"Mama, are you awake?"

Still there was no sound or movement from the silent figure lying under the rough blanket.

"Mama," Abbie whispered as she paused by the side of the bed. Slowly, she reached out with her hand. But she hesitated when her hand hovered above her mother's shoulder. As if delaying the moment could somehow postpone the truth she was afraid to discover.

When she finally did touch her mother, the coldness underneath her fingers confirmed what her other senses had been telling her from the start...

Their mother was dead.

Abbie dropped to her knees, feeling raw and empty inside. Covering her face with her hands, she cried. With their mother dead, she and Jane were all alone. They had been such a happy little family not that long ago. But now Papa and Mama were gone, stolen from them by a cruel twist of fate.

If her father hadn't broken his legs, none of this would have happened. And the four of them would still be living in their modest yet comfortable home.

No, I mustn't think like that, Abbie admonished herself as she wiped away her tears. She was the eldest and, as such, she bore a responsibility towards her younger sister. Jane was all she had left.

Looking at her mother's dead body, Abbie made a solemn promise. "I swear I'll do anything it takes to look after Jane and myself. One day, we'll be happy once more. And we'll never be poor again."

But she would do it with respect for their own dignity and honour. Certainly not by accepting some shameful proposal from Percy or any other man.

"I'll be strong," she vowed. "For Jane's sake and mine."

Clenching her fists, she got up on her feet and stared down at her mother one final time.

"Goodbye, Mama. I hope you and Papa will be together in a better place."

Dazed by her loss, Abbie slowly went down the stairs, wondering who she should tell first: Jane or Mr Yates? Surely, her sister deserved to hear the tragic news before Mr Yates did? It would give them a little bit of time to cry, grieve and comfort each other.

Unfortunately, circumstances conspired against that plan. Because when Abbie reached the bottom of the stairs, Mr Yates was getting ready to leave the house. And the moment he saw her, a frown appeared on his brow.

He knows something's wrong, she thought.

"What's the matter, Miss Lee? I daresay you've been crying. That mother of yours not getting any better, is she?"

Abbie stopped and swallowed hard. She couldn't not tell him. "My mother is dead, sir."

A sharp clattering noise startled them both. Their heads turned towards the kitchen door, where Jane stood. She had dropped the large breakfast tray she had been holding, sending the dirty crockery crashing to the floor.

"What did you say?" the girl gasped in shock. "Is Mama... dead?"

As Abbie rushed over to her sister's side, she heard Mr Yates swear under his breath. It sounded like he was more upset about his broken china than he was about their mother's death. But Abbie chose to ignore his gross coldheartedness and took Jane's hands in hers.

"She must have passed away in her sleep, Jane. I went into the room this morning, because she wasn't answering when I called out to her. And that's when I found her."

"I should have liked to say goodbye to her… when she was still alive," Jane said unhappily. Her face hardened. "This is all his fault." She glared angrily in Mr Yates' direction.

"I beg your pardon?" the old man replied sharply. "I'm not to blame for your mother's death."

"Yes, you are," Jane shot back at him. "If we'd been allowed into the room, we would have been able to take better care of her. And then she wouldn't have died. But you didn't let us."

"Jane, dear," Abbie said, trying to calm her sister down. But Jane wasn't done with Mr Yates yet.

"You didn't even want to pay for a doctor," she continued, her voice shrill with bitter fury. "You could have easily afforded ten doctors, but you love your pennies too much, you mean old–"

"Jane, stop," Abbie said urgently. She could tell from Mr Yates' reddening face that he was about to have an angry outburst. And they would need his financial support if they wanted to give their mother a decent burial.

"Getting mad at anyone won't bring her back," she spoke soothingly. "I'm just as upset as you are, but we have to be brave now. It's what Mama would have wanted, too."

She could see her sister was clenching her jaw, eager to voice her grief and anger. But Jane wisely decided to keep silent. She nodded her head as she lowered her eyes and stared at the floor.

Abbie placed a soft kiss on her sister's forehead and then addressed their employer. "Mr Yates, might I kindly plead for your help, sir?"

"Bah," he scoffed sourly. "I suppose you want me to pay for the funeral, is that it?"

"We haven't got the funds, I'm afraid. We're still paying back the undertaker for Papa's burial and–"

"All right, all right, Miss Lee. I'll lend you the money to bury your mother." He threw a dark glare at Jane and added, "I wouldn't want to be called a mean old so-and-so again."

"Thank you, sir." Abbie sighed with relief. Mama would be spared the indignity of a pauper's burial. Abbie couldn't imagine much worse than being thrown in an open hole in the ground, together with a dozen or so anonymous drunks and wretches.

"But at this rate," Mr Yates grumbled, "I'm beginning to doubt whether your family's debt will ever be repaid in full to me."

"My sister and I will do our utmost to pay you back every single penny as quickly as possible, sir."

"You'd better, Miss Lee," he muttered as he finally shrugged into his coat. "At least you're both young. So there's less chance of you dying on me like your parents did."

He opened the front door and took one step outside. "Please make the necessary arrangements," he said over his shoulder. "But nothing too fancy of course."

As soon as he had left, Abbie and Jane fell into each other's arms.

"Oh, Abbie," Jane cried. "What will we do?"

"The same thing we always do, my darling. We keep going."

"But how–"

"I don't know yet. We'll find a way."

Jane looked up at Abbie. "I believe in you, sister dearest." Through her tears, she tried to put on a brave smile. "I believe in you, and I love you."

"I love you too, sweetheart," Abbie said as they hugged each other again. The tender warmth of Jane's body against her own was reassuring and comforting.

But I wished I believed in myself half as much as you seem to do.

Chapter Eleven

The days leading up to their mother's funeral passed by in a sad and confusing daze for Abbie and Jane. It was hard to believe that both their parents had passed away so suddenly and in such a short space of time. Even during their working hours, Abbie constantly found herself expecting to feel her mother's presence nearby or to hear her calming voice.

One time, in an absent-minded moment while she was busy preparing supper, she even asked Mama to pass her the jar of sugar, please. The empty silence she got in return was painful to bear.

The funeral itself didn't give the girls much comfort either. As Mr Yates had instructed, it was the simplest affair possible. Abbie and Jane were the only people present at the cemetery, together with a stuffy priest who delivered a short and dull eulogy, while two gravediggers stood waiting in the background, quietly smoking their pipes.

The only good thing about this brief and unreal period was the fact that Mr Yates left the girls in peace. He seemed to make an effort to be less gruff than usual – mostly by avoiding them as much as he could.

And even Percy refrained from making any more inappropriate comments or unwanted advances. Although he did still throw stolen glances at Abbie whenever they were in the same room, which never failed to make her queasy.

But this grace period was only temporary, Abbie knew full well. And it would probably end the moment they got back, she reckoned as she and Jane slowly walked the long way from the cemetery to Mr Yates' house.

"So what do we do now?" her sister asked after a while.

Abbie shrugged. "There's only one option, really."

"You mean we're staying with Mr Yates?"

"'Fraid so."

Jane sighed. "Must we?"

"What other choice do we have? Until we've paid off Father's debt, there's no chance Mr Yates will let us go."

"But it's such an awful lot of money. And now it's just you and me, so it'll take us even longer. It's not fair."

Abbie stopped and took her sister's hands in hers. "I know, sweetheart. And believe me, I don't like it any more than you do. But it's what we have to do. Mama and Papa wouldn't have wanted us to quit either."

"I guess you're right," Jane said reluctantly.

"We'll take it one day at a time. And we'll try to do something nice on Sundays. All right?"

Her sister nodded, not entirely convinced and visibly unhappy about the whole idea of spending the next three to five years of their lives in the service of Mr Yates and his horrible grandson.

Abbie smiled and gently squeezed Jane's hands, by way of encouragement, even though she shared her sister's anxious feelings about their immediate future.

The one thing Abbie was most afraid of however, was Percy. As long as Mother had been around, she had felt somewhat safe from his unwelcome attentions. But now she was on her own. Who would stop him from pressing his reprehensible claim?

As they walked on in silence, Abbie prayed for a solution to their problems. *Let Jane and I be free*, she begged looking up to the dreary sky.

She had no idea what this freedom would look like, or how they would obtain it. All she knew was that she wanted to be rid of the bonds that tied her to Mr Yates. One way or another.

When they arrived back at the house, they immediately changed into their work clothes and picked up their usual routine of chores again. And for once, Abbie was glad of their many household duties. Because hard and unpleasant as their work might have been, at least it took her mind off their troubles for a bit.

At the end of the day, long after the sun had set, they went up to their room. Strange, she thought with a sad smile, how a tiny room like theirs could feel so empty. She wondered how long that eerie feeling would last. And when it eventually passed, would that be a good sign? Or would it mean they had stopped caring?

Casting aside her brooding thoughts, she sighed and then looked at her sister. "I'll go and check downstairs if they still need something from us. Why don't you get ready for bed in the meantime? We can brush each other's hair when I get back."

Jane's face lit up. "The brush and I shall be awaiting your return eagerly," she quipped.

"I shall make haste then," Abbie replied with a little chuckle, before leaving the bedroom and closing the door. *As long as I have you, little sister dearest,* she thought cheerfully as she walked down the stairs, *I'm sure we'll be fine in the end.*

With a faint smile on her face and a mind filled with memories of happier timcs, she reached the door to the sitting room where Mr Yates and Percy were talking. She was just about to knock when she overheard Mr Yates mentioning their name. Her hand froze mid-air.

Holding her breath, she strained to listen to what the two were discussing.

"I'm telling you, Percy, the Lee family are more trouble than they're worth. First, the father breaks his ruddy legs and consequently dies on us. And now the mother has kicked the bucket as well."

"Yes, most vexing," Percy said, sounding somewhat bored with his grandfather's rant. "Luckily, we've still got the two girls. They're young and in good health, so they should be able to repay their parents' debt – eventually."

"No, I still say they're a bad investment. But those worries are over, my lad. Because I've decided to cut my losses."

"Cut your losses? How?"

Mr Yates let out an evil little snicker. "I've been talking to the innkeeper of The Blue Dove and he's agreed to buy the girls from me."

Abbie took a sharp intake of breath as a wave of panic washed over her. Buy them?! She didn't like the sound of that.

"The Blue Dove?" Percy asked. "Isn't that– How to put this politely? It's a house of ill repute, isn't it?"

"That's a nice way of saying it's a brothel, yes," Mr Yates laughed. "And the innkeeper has offered me a very fair price for the two wenches."

Abbie covered her mouth with both her hands. It was all she could do not to scream out in horror.

"Won't they mind?" Percy asked. "The girls, I mean. I can't imagine they'll go along with this arrangement. Not willingly."

"We won't tell them, of course," Mr Yates replied coolly. "We'll simply say I know someone who's looking for two charwomen and send them to The Blue Dove. Once they get there, it'll be too late for them."

"But how–"

"Oh, don't worry about the details, Percy. The owner and his wife have their methods to make a girl do what's required of her."

"I see."

"Don't look so glum, boy. All that matters is I've recovered a decent chunk of my money. By tomorrow morning, the Lee family will be off our hands for good."

Abbie had heard enough. They needed to get out of this house. Tonight.

Without making a sound, she rushed back up the stairs to their bedroom. Part of her wanted to panic, but there was no time for despair. She couldn't afford to be scared, no matter how sickening she found Mr Yates' vile plan to be. She needed to keep a clear mind and she needed to act.

Bursting into the small bedroom, she startled her sister, who was sitting cross-legged on the bed in her long nightshirt while holding the hairbrush in her hands.

"Abbie, what's wrong?"

"Pack your things, Jane. Only the bare minimum. We have to leave."

"Leave? Now? But why? It's late."

"I'll explain while we pack. Please hurry."

Abbie went to their creaky old wardrobe and started throwing a few pieces of clothing onto the bed.

Jane however was still too surprised by this sudden announcement. Not understanding the urgency of the situation, she stayed in the middle of the bed. "What happened? Is Mr Yates throwing us out?"

"Not exactly. He's going to do something much worse than that." Abbie continued with her hurried routine of inspecting and sorting clothes from the wardrobe. The ones she thought they needed went on a pile on the bed. The others she simply threw on the floor.

"Something worse than throwing us out?" Jane frowned. "Abbie, I don't understand. Do you mean he's sending us to prison, like he did with Papa? Or, wait... Please don't tell me he's sending us to the workhouse?"

Abbie grabbed one of their carpet bags and began stuffing it with the clothes she'd selected.

"The workhouse? That'd be a thousand times better than what that horribly wicked man has in store for us."

Jane gripped Abbie by the wrist. There was fear in her eyes. "Stop speaking in riddles, Abbie. Tell me what's going on."

Abbie paused and looked her sister square in the eye. No sense in hiding the truth from her.

"Tomorrow morning, Mr Yates is sending us to an inn where we'll be forced to–" She hesitated briefly, choosing her words, "– perform carnal acts with the guests."

Jane's eyes and mouth opened wide in shocked astonishment. "No," she gasped. "He wouldn't– Surely, not even he would be so... Would he?"

"Do you want to wait until the morning to find out?"

Jane shook her head and jumped off the bed. "No, you're right." She put her clothes on, then rushed over to the wardrobe and took out the other carpet bag. "What's your plan?"

"I haven't really got one, to be honest," Abbie admitted as they resumed packing. "I went downstairs and then I overheard Mr Yates telling Percy he'd sold us to an innkeeper. All I could think of was getting out of this house as quickly as possible."

"Can't we go to the police?"

107

"As if they've been much help to us in the past. No, running away is the safest thing for us to do."

"But where will we go?"

"Don't know yet." Abbie closed her carpet bag and lifted it off the bed. "Anywhere will do, as long as it's miles away from those two degenerate monsters downstairs."

Jane stuffed one more clean shirt in her carpet bag and closed it. "Won't they come after us?"

"They certainly will," Abbie replied. "Mr Yates loves his money after all. That's why we're leaving now – quietly and through the kitchen door. With any luck, they won't find out we're gone until tomorrow morning. And by then we'll be far away."

Jane nodded and tried to put on a brave smile. "Whatever you say. You're in charge, Abbie."

Seeing her younger sister standing there, clutching a worn carpet bag in their dingy room, Abbie felt a sudden pang of guilt. "I'm sorry you have to go through all this, Jane."

"It's not your fault. None of it is. And wherever we end up, I'm sure it won't be as bad as this place. Or the inn that Mr Yates has in mind for us."

Abbie reached out and placed a hand on her sister's arm. "I'll look after you, Jane. I promise.

I'll try my hardest to make our lives better again."

"I know you will, Abbie. And as long as we have each other, I don't mind a bit of hardship."

"Oh, come here, you." They hugged and then they each took a deep breath to steel themselves for what they were about to do.

"Let's go," Abbie whispered as she opened their bedroom door and cocked an ear. Judging the coast to be clear, she slipped out of the room and beckoned her sister to follow.

Deadly silent, they descended the stairs. As they approached the ground floor, Abbie could hear the voice of Mr Yates in the sitting room. It sounded like he was talking to Percy about his favourite topic – money.

Holding their breaths, they snuck past the sitting room door and headed for the kitchen. Only when they had made it there safely, did they dare to exhale.

"So far so good," Abbie whispered. "Be careful you don't knock anything over in here."

They tiptoed to the back door and opened it – slowly, to avoid making any noise. As they stepped outside, the cold air caused Abbie to shiver.

It also made her realise she hadn't the faintest idea where they would stay or sleep on their first night. They could look for cheap lodgings in the morning, but at this time of day she doubted any respectable hostel or boarding house would still be accepting guests.

Too late to worry about that now, she told herself. Worst case, they would have to keep walking all night. They could stop for a rest on a park bench every hour or so. But the more they stayed on their feet, the warmer they would be – and the more distance they could put between themselves and Mr Yates.

That last bit was the most important part, she thought with a stiff resolve as she and Jane began their long march in the freezing night. They would disappear in the underbelly of London, burn their bridges and keep their heads down. It meant they would need to live in a different part of the city, where nobody knew them. The sort of neighbourhood where people didn't bother to ask awkward questions.

They'd have to start all over again and find new charring work. Abbie knew it wasn't going to be easy. They would likely suffer hunger and poverty. But if that was the price they had to pay for freedom, then that's what she and Jane would do. Together.

Chapter Twelve

"Chin up, Jane," Abbie said with what she hoped was an encouraging smile on her face. "And remember, don't slouch. Keep your back straight and let me do most of the talking."

They were standing on the doorstep of the address where the owner was looking for a new charwoman, according to the advertisement they had seen in the newspaper.

"We want to make a good first impression," Abbie reminded her sister. *Because heaven knows we need the money.*

It had been three years since they'd run away from Mr Yates and his grandson Percy. Luckily, they had never again seen the pair of hideous men. So in that respect, their escape had been a success.

In every other way however, it had proven a formidable challenge. She and Jane were always skint, always hungry and, especially during the first two years, always on the run. Over half a dozen times they had upped sticks and moved to a different address. Just to be on the safe side.

They didn't own much, so the actual moving wasn't the hardest part. But each relocation meant they had to find new customers for their cleaning services. And this habit of starting all over again every time was beginning to wear on them. Abbie longed for some stability.

"I hope they take us on," Jane said. "This house looks nice from the outside. I wouldn't mind working here."

"Then let's pray that the people living here are equally nice," Abbie replied as she gave their modest clothes a final inspection. Satisfied their appearance was the best they could manage, she knocked on the polished front door and waited, nervously holding her breath.

A gentle-looking woman answered the door. She was in her early thirties, Abbie guessed. And judging by her elegant attire, she was probably the lady of the house herself. Certainly not a maid or the housekeeper.

"Yes?" the lady said, smiling at the two girls before her.

"Good morning, ma'am. I'm Abigail Lee and this is my sister Jane. We saw your advertisement in the newspaper. It said you were looking for a chargirl?"

"That's right, my dears," the lady replied warmly as she looked from Abbie to Jane and back. "Please come in, so we can talk."

Passing through a clean and tidy corridor, they were shown to the tastefully decorated drawing room. The furniture seemed only a few years old and every aspect about the room said its owners were fairly well off, but not in an extravagant or boastful manner. Abbie was beginning to think that her sister's first impression might have been right.

"How rude of me," the lady said. "I haven't introduced myself to you yet. I'm Bess Parker." She extended her hand with a smile and Abbie thought it would be very easy to like Mrs Parker.

Don't get ahead of yourself, Abbie. She has to like you *as well.*

"How do you do, Mrs Parker," Abbie said politely as she shook the woman's hand and bobbed a little curtsy. Next, Jane did the same.

"Please, sit down," Bess said, gesturing for them to take a seat on the sofa while she sat down in one of the armchairs opposite. "Would you care for some tea?"

"Oh, please don't bother on our behalf, ma'am," Abbie was quick to say. Most employers didn't even let you sit down on their fancy furniture, let alone offer tea. In the belowstairs kitchen, the cook might pour you a cuppa if she already had a kettle on the stove and she was the sociable type – but never the mistress of the house. And certainly not in one of the day rooms.

Somewhat awkwardly, Abbie and Jane sat down. Even so, they took care to only sit on the edge of the sofa. Because they knew it wouldn't do to appear too informal or relaxed.

"Very well then," Mrs Parker said. "Tell me about yourselves. Have you been chargirls for long?"

"For several years now, ma'am." Abbie tried to sound natural and confident, but she felt reluctant to share the finer details. No one needed to know about the sinister shadow of the past that still lurked over her and Jane.

"We've worked for a variety of families and households," she continued to explain. "But we've only just recently moved, so we're looking for new addresses that require our services."

"I must say you sound very eloquent for a chargirl, Miss Lee," Mrs Parker smiled. "None of the maids I've ever known were even half as well spoken as you seem to be."

Abbie blushed. She couldn't hide the fact they hadn't always been poor – nor did she want to. Was Mrs Parker merely paying her a nice compliment? Or was she suspicious of their motives and angling for more clues? The lady didn't strike her as the devious or sneaky type though.

"Our parents – may their souls rest in peace – insisted on giving us a proper education, ma'am."

"Oh, I see. You were orphaned?"

Abbie nodded and lowered her eyes, hoping this tidbit of information would be enough to satisfy Mrs Parker's curiosity.

"And now you and your sister work as a team?" Bess asked.

"We do, ma'am," Abbie replied, relieved that the conversation was moving onto safer grounds. "I realise your advertisement only called for one charwoman, but between the two of us, we can get the work done twice as fast."

"I'm certain that you can," Bess smiled. "And rest assured, with two small children in the house, there will be plenty of work for you." She gave a little girlish chuckle at this and Abbie found herself warming even more to the woman.

"Rosie and Philip are both sweet little angels, of course," Mrs Parker explained. "But they're at that age when they're capable of great mischief. The sort of mischief that tends to leave a dirty trail."

"Keeping your house clean would be our pride and joy, ma'am," Abbie promised her. Casting a few quick glances around, she added, "And a very beautiful home it is too, if I may say so."

"Thank you, Miss Lee. My husband's work keeps him rather busy, so I want our home to be a place where he can enjoy some much-needed peace and comfort."

"Is your husband in business, ma'am?" Abbie enquired politely. Whatever he did for a living, it was evident that it had made him a decent amount of money, she thought.

"Heavens, no," Bess laughed. "My darling Phineas isn't the business type. Mr Parker is a playwright and theatrical producer. And exceedingly good at it, too. You may have seen some of his plays, actually."

"I'm afraid we don't have much time to go to the theatre, ma'am," Abbie apologised, blushing. In reality though, as much as she wanted to, it was their lack of funds that prevented them from indulging in that sort of entertainment.

"Even though Abigail would make a great actress," Jane suddenly blurted out enthusiastically. "You should see her playing a princess–"

"Jane," Abbie interrupted quickly, blushing even deeper. "I'm sure Mrs Parker doesn't want to hear about that."

Bess giggled. "Or perhaps we should let you audition for one of my husband's plays instead."

Abbie threw her sister a brief warning glance. *Don't ruin it,* her eyes pleaded. Mrs Parker seemed like a very kind and pleasant woman, but they didn't have the job yet.

"All silliness aside," Bess said, "I need a charwoman rather urgently at the moment. Our previous maid has just left us on account of getting married. Do you have any family plans, Miss Lee?"

"None, ma'am," Abbie replied truthfully. "And I have no followers either," she added, using the polite word for boyfriends and lovers. She wasn't averse to the idea of love, but with all their worries, man trouble was the last thing she needed.

"That might change once you start working for me," Bess laughed. "All my maids seem to find love within a year of entering into service with me. It must be some bizarre talent I've developed."

Abbie and Jane laughed politely, but Abbie was more focused on the first part of Mrs Parker's little jest. *Once you start working for me,* she had said. Could it be?

"Anyhow," Bess went on, folding her hands together and placing them in her lap. "Back to the matter in hand. You seem like a pair of honest and sincere young women to me. And I'm usually a good judge of character."

She paused to smile at the two of them, and Abbie held her breath. *Please, please, please...*

"Therefore," Mrs Parker continued, "I would like to hire you both for six half days a week plus Sunday mornings, if that suits you."

Abbie felt like jumping up from her seat with joy. "That's splendid, Mrs Parker! Thank you so much."

"Thank you, Mrs Parker," Jane chimed in happily.

"Marvellous," Bess smiled. "I'd like you to start as soon as possible. Can you be here tomorrow morning?"

"We'll be bright and early, ma'am."

Agreeing on a wage was done in no time, since the amount that Bess suggested was slightly higher than what any of Abbie and Jane's previous employers had offered.

They bid their goodbyes and then the two girls were out on the street again. But how different the world felt to them. It was as if glorious rays of sunshine had come bursting through a heavy sky, chasing away the dark clouds that had hung over them.

"That was absolutely fabulous," Jane breathed ecstatically. "I say this calls for a celebration."

"Yes, it's wonderful. But let's not celebrate until we get paid, all right? I promise we'll go out for a spot of tea and some cake then."

"Always the sensible one," Jane teased. "I couldn't believe how nice Mrs Parker was, could you? And her husband works in the theatre world. How exciting!"

"That was very careless of you, Jane. Talking about our silly princess fantasies like that."

"Sorry. The words left my mouth before I realised it, I suppose. But Mrs Parker didn't seem to mind. I think she's an amazing woman."

"She's certainly remarkable, that's for sure," Abbie agreed. "I can still hardly believe our luck. After all these years..."

"Maybe our fortunes are beginning to turn," Jane said hopefully. "Maybe misery is finally getting bored with us."

"Perhaps," Abbie said cautiously. Or perhaps misery was toying with them like a cat who enjoys playing with the mouse it has caught – a game that rarely ended well for the mouse.

Chapter Thirteen

The next morning, Abbie and Jane arrived at the Parker residence shortly after the crack of dawn. The friendly cook let them in through the servants' entrance, and after a nice cup of tea, they launched themselves into their long list of chores, feeling more cheerful than they had in years.

By late morning, while Jane was washing up pots and pans in the kitchen, Abbie went to tidy up the family sitting room. She knew Mr Parker had left for a rehearsal at the theatre and she thought Mrs Parker and the children were upstairs. But just as she was carefully dusting off some delicate china ornaments with her feather duster, a little voice sounded behind her.

"Who are you?"

Abbie turned round to see a girl and a boy standing by the door, eyeing her curiously. It was the girl who had asked the question, and she had the sweet looks of her mother. The boy appeared a year or two younger and he gladly deferred to his older sister.

"Good morning," Abbie smiled. "I'm Abbie, your mama's new charwoman."

"I'm Rosie," the girl replied most politely. "And this is my brother Philip."

"Pleased to meet you both, Mistress Rosie and Master Philip."

The children giggled at being addressed in this way.

"Are you sure you're a charwoman?" Rosie asked.

"Positive. Why do you ask?"

"Because you don't sound or look like one."

Abbie tried not to laugh. "What's a chargirl supposed to be like then?"

"I don't really know." Rosie frowned and twitched her nose to one side, making her look even more adorable. "It's just that some of the previous ones we've had were much older than you."

"Fat and stupid too," Philip added.

"Philip," Rosie said sternly. "You mustn't say that sort of thing about people."

"But they were," the little boy insisted.

Abbie had trouble not to burst out in laughter. These divine little angels were loveable to the extreme. "Shouldn't you two be with your mama?" she asked. "Or upstairs in the nursery?"

"We gave Nanny the slip," Philip declared, proudly puffing up his chest over this daring feat.

"He spilled watercolour paint over the nanny's dress," Rosie explained. "When she went to clean herself up, we decided to come downstairs."

"And does your mama know you're down here?"

"No," Philip said, even more gleefully. "She was in her room, writing letters or something. We snuck right past her door."

"Surely, that was a bit naughty of you, wasn't it?" Abbie said, trying – and failing – to keep a straight face. These children had an admirably enterprising spirit.

"But we were getting so bored upstairs," Philip complained. "I like it when Nanny reads us stories. But she said we have to do other things as well. Boring things."

"Can you read, Miss Abbie?" Rosie asked.

"Yes, I can. My parents insisted that I learned to read and write."

"Now I know you're not a chargirl," Rosie stated.

"Why's that?"

"Because maids and chargirls can't read. Most of them can hardly spell their own name right."

"That's because they're stupid," Philip chimed in.

"Philip," Rosie protested. "I told you not to say such things about people. It's not nice."

Abbie laughed and then she bent forward towards the children. Lowering her voice, she

122

said, "You've caught me. I'm not really a chargirl."

Rosie poked her brother with her elbow. "Told you she wasn't."

"Can you keep a secret?" Abbie asked.

The children nodded, wide-eyed and holding their breaths.

"I'm actually a princess in disguise," Abbie continued. "I'm only pretending to be a charwoman, because I'm hiding from an evil old baron who was holding me and my sister captive."

The children fell into a giggling fit, loving Abbie's joke.

"I like to be a princess as well," Rosie admitted.

"Well, I don't," Philip grumbled.

"No, I bet you prefer to be a brave knight," Abbie said.

"That's right," Philip nodded vigorously. "But not one of those feeble ones. The sort who go around looking very clean and neat and do nothing but kiss pretty princesses all day long." He stuck out his tongue and pulled a disgusted face.

"I see," Abbie said, pretending to be impressed. "You want to be the kind of knight who slays dragons and fights villains, do you?"

"That's right," he replied with a sparkle in his eyes.

"Thank heavens for that then," Abbie sighed in relief.

"What do you mean?"

"Why, you have arrived just in time, Sir Philip," Abbie proclaimed, effortlessly slipping into her favourite role of the princess in distress. "The villagers have spotted a vicious fire-breathing dragon in the hills."

She handed Philip the feather duster and pulled Rosie close to her. "Here, o brave sir knight. Take this mighty sword and protect Princess Rose-Marie and myself. We beseech thee."

"What does 'beseech' mean?" he asked.

"It means we're begging you."

"Ah, right."

"Go forth, Sir Philip." Abbie pointed at the green velvet settee. "Ride to the green hills over yonder, slay the dragon for us and save the castle."

"Chaaarge," Philip roared, pretending to ride a horse while brandishing his feather duster as a sword.

"Such a brave warrior, don't you think, Princess Rose-Marie?" Abbie asked.

"Very fierce," Rosie agreed, before putting her hand over her mouth to stop herself from laughing.

"He's just the kind of hero we need to deliver us from evil." Abbie stared lovingly in the direction of their knight, who was doing battle with the settee. "So valiant," she sighed. "And so handsome too."

"Handsome?" Alarmed, Philip paused and threw Abbie and his sister a doubtful glare. "When I've defeated this dragon, you won't be wanting to kiss me or anything silly like that, will you?"

Rosie chortled, but Abbie reassured their hero. "I know you care not for such things, Sir Philip. So your rewards will be eternal fame and glory. Songs will be written about your bravery. And upon your return from the battlefield, everyone will cheer and shout–"

"Bravo," a voice exclaimed by the door.

Startled, Abbie spun round. Much to her embarrassment, she saw Mrs Parker standing by the open door. But the mistress was smiling and clapping her hands.

"Bravo," Bess repeated cheerfully. "What an excellent performance."

"I'm terribly sorry, ma'am," Abbie mumbled. She was mortified and couldn't bear to look at Mrs Parker, staring down at her own feet instead.

Rosie and Philip ran over to their mother's side, excited to share every moment of their grand adventure.

"Mama, Abbie told us she's a princess," Rosie said.

"And then she made me a knight," Philip declared proudly. "The kind who fights dangerous dragons."

"Oh my," Bess replied, greatly amused by her children's mirth.

"It's all my fault, Mrs Parker," Abbie confessed. "I dragged the children into this."

"They do seem to have that effect on people, don't they?" Bess sniggered. "But it was highly entertaining to watch, Miss Lee. I should tell my husband."

"Oh no, ma'am," Abbie gasped. "Please, don't." Her heart sank. They hadn't even been working in this house for a day, and already they were going to be dismissed. And it was all because of her silliness.

"But Phineas needs to hear about this," Bess insisted.

"Please, ma'am," Abbie begged anxiously. "It was a mistake. A momentary lapse of judgement. I promise it won't happen again."

Bess laughed. "Miss Lee, that's not what I meant at all. My husband is always looking for good actors for his plays."

Confused, Abbie looked up. "Ma'am?"

"It's true. You gave a stellar performance, Miss Lee. I know this was merely child's play, but you put heart and conviction into it. And when I tell Phineas about what I've just seen, he's likely to

126

offer you a small role in his next stage production."

Abbie was left speechless for a moment. Surely, this couldn't be real?

"Ma'am, I'm assuming you are ridiculing me. Which I thoroughly deserve. So once more, I would like to offer you my sincerest apologies. And if you want my sister and me to leave, we will – immediately."

"But I'm deadly serious, Miss Lee. I see great talent in you. And don't worry about your position. You'll be perfectly capable of combining your household duties here with your work at the theatre."

Next, Bess turned to her children. "As for you two," she said sternly, but with a benign grin on her face. "Back to the nursery, please. It was very naughty of you to deceive Nanny like that."

When the two young rascals protested, Bess shooed them along gently. "I'll have no more arguments from you, thank you very much."

"But if Miss Abbie is going to work for Papa," Philip complained bitterly, "then we won't be able to play with her any more."

"If you promise to behave," Bess replied, "I'll take you to one of the dress rehearsals during the daytime. Then you'll get to see Miss Lee on stage. How does that sound?"

Cheering loudly with delight, the children bounded up the stairs to their nursery, while

Bess and Abbie watched them until they had disappeared from sight.

"Dear, oh dear," Bess chuckled. "That was a rather memorable introduction to my beloved children, wasn't it?"

"They're absolutely adorable, ma'am," Abbie said. Clearing her throat, she went on, "And I do apologise for my behaviour."

"Nonsense. I'm grateful. As I said, I believe you're a woman of many talents, Miss Lee. And it would be a shame to let them go to waste."

"Thank you, ma'am."

"If my instincts about you turn out to be correct, then I'm certain you will make a fine addition to the cast of our next play."

"I'll try not to disappoint you or Mr Parker," Abbie said, her face flushing with an unexpected heat.

"Splendid," Bess replied. "I shall leave you to your work now. And this evening, I'll arrange everything with my husband."

Abbie felt completely flabbergasted after Mrs Parker had left the room. To make sure she wasn't dreaming, she pinched herself. The painful prickle of her skin confirmed this had really happened.

I have to tell Jane, she thought. Perhaps her sister would be able to make sense of it all. Because either this was the best thing that could have happened to them – or it would turn out to be a grave mistake.

Only time will tell, Abbie decided as she rushed to the kitchen, feeling just as excited as the Parker children had been.

Chapter Fourteen

The rehearsals were frantic and nerve-racking for Abbie. Not in the least because she also had her usual charring duties to fulfil. She would finish work and then hurry to the theatre. But she loved every moment of it, even though her part in the play was only a minor one.

Trusting his wife's judgement, Mr Parker had cast Abbie in the role of a washerwoman. During most of the play, she and two other extras were simply required to be present on the stage – to make things look more lively. In a couple of scenes however, Abbie had to deliver a few lines. Nothing complicated, just a witty comment on what the main characters were doing.

It wasn't much, but Mr Parker assured her that those lines were important. They lightened the mood, he said. And they had to be delivered in a way that sounded effortless and natural.

At first, she felt terribly nervous and self-conscious each time she had to speak on stage. And it showed in her acting. But with Mr Parker's encouragement, Abbie soon became more confident. She warmed to the role and delivered her lines with aplomb.

The other actors began to take notice of her too. They would nod in approval when her delivery was spot on. And she even received the occasional compliment from them, despite her lowly status as an extra.

"It's because they like you," the costume maker Mrs Roberts told her during a fitting session. "And who can blame them when you're such a genuinely nice person, dear."

"Miss Hawthorne doesn't seem to like me much though," Abbie replied, referring to the play's frivolous leading lady.

Mrs Roberts snorted derisively. "That one, puh. Pay no attention to her, my love. Penelope Hawthorne thinks the sun rises from her you-know-where," she said, giving a quick nod of the head towards her backside.

Abbie burst out laughing. She wouldn't have put it quite as colourful herself, but it was true. "She does seem rather full of herself, doesn't she?"

"It's one thing for an actress to be confident about her looks and abilities. But Miss Hoity-Toity is just plain arrogant. And it'll be her downfall eventually, mark my words."

Mrs Roberts fixed the final pins in Abbie's washerwoman costume and sighed as she stepped back. "It's a shame you never knew Miss Rebecca Sutcliffe. She had style, talent and charm aplenty. A very glamorous lady she was."

"Was she an actress?"

"The very best I've ever seen, love."

"And has she retired? Perhaps I should visit her. She might have some advice for a novice like me."

Mrs Roberts smiled ruefully. "She's dead, dear. What a sad tragedy that was. You should ask Mrs Parker about her some day. She used to be her assistant, years ago."

"I'm sorry to hear that," Abbie replied softly, sensing the sadness in Mrs Roberts. She knew what it was like to lose someone special in your life.

Meanwhile though, she had a play to prepare for. Abbie was determined to be the best washerwoman she possibly could. She vowed to make everyone proud, beginning with Mr and Mrs Parker, who had been so kind to give her this opportunity.

Finally, after weeks of rehearsals, the big moment arrived: opening night at the theatre. All day long, Abbie was a nervous mess. She couldn't eat and she had trouble concentrating on her work. The play was the only thing on her mind.

"Calm down," Jane told her in their small rented room, while Abbie was getting ready to leave. "Everything will be fine, you'll see."

"I don't know," Abbie replied with a plaintive groan in her voice. "What if I forget my lines?"

"You won't. You must have said them out loud over a hundred times by now."

"But never in front of a real audience. Suppose my voice fails me? I'll look like a proper fool then. People will laugh at me and think I'm a halfwit."

"No, they won't. They're going to love you."

"Oh Jane, I've got the jitters so badly. My legs are wobbly, my head is spinning and I feel like I might faint."

"That's because you haven't eaten anything today," her sister chuckled. "Shall I make you some buttered toast? You'll need your strength."

"My stomach is so tight, I'm afraid I won't be able to keep anything down."

"Then have some tea instead. We'll stir in an extra spoon of sugar."

Abbie relented and gratefully accepted the cup of strong brew Jane offered her. Duly fortified, they got dressed and headed for the theatre.

Backstage, they were met by a bewildering flurry of activity. Crew members hurried to and fro, while the main actors appeared to be lost in their private little dream worlds. Some of them were pacing around – going over their lines one final time, or laughing and talking nervously to anyone who came near them.

Abbie spotted Miss Hawthorne as well. The leading lady was consulting melodramatically with the stage manager. No doubt impressing upon the poor fellow how vitally important it was that the stage lighting did justice to her exquisite physique, Abbie sniggered to herself.

And in the dressing rooms, Mrs Parker was putting the finishing touches to the costumes. She had designed them herself, so naturally she wanted them to look perfect.

"It's hectic like an ants' nest in here," Jane said, gaping at the busy proceedings. "I'd better go and find myself a seat before all the good spots are taken. I'll see you after the performance."

After they had given each other a long hug, Abbie heaved a heavy sigh as she watched her sister escape from the madness behind the scenes.

Lucky you, Jane, she thought.

When it was her turn to dress, Abbie slipped into the modestly grey washerwoman's costume that Mrs Roberts gave her. And then there was nothing left for her to do but wait.

Feeling awfully overwhelmed by the frenzied chaos all around her, she found herself a spot out of everyone's way.

"Deep breaths, my dear," Mr Williams said. He was the actor who played the leading lady's sweet and elderly father. "Just take deep breaths and as soon as you walk onto that stage, those nerves will settle."

"I hope so, Mr Williams."

"Trust me. I was once in your position, decades ago. We all had to start out small. Even Miss Hawthorne, although I'm sure she'd rather not talk about her early years."

He winked at Abbie and laughed. His easy-going demeanour and friendly advice made her relax a little. She smiled and took a deep breath in and out, just like he told her to.

"Thank you, Mr Williams."

"You're welcome, my dear." He patted her amicably on the shoulder. "And now I believe it's nearly time for you and the others to take up your position on stage. Good luck."

With the stage curtains still closed, Abbie and a handful of actors got ready for the opening scene – a tableau as it was called, depicting Miss Hawthorne as a poor young woman from the slums. As everyone silently shuffled into place, they could hear the excited murmurs of the audience.

It's really happening, Abbie mused dreamily. *I'm going to be in a play.*

She drew in her breath, while her heart pounded madly in her chest. Then, just as she let out a long and slow exhale, the curtains opened – to the polite cheers of the spectators.

In her corner of the stage, Abbie felt a mix of excitement and dread. But as soon as the play got underway, she forgot all about her anxiousness and she became Cora, the perky washerwoman who's not afraid to speak her mind.

And whenever Abbie needed to say her lines, she did it with so much heartfelt gusto that the audience laughed and cheered – just as they were supposed to do.

On more than one of those occasions, the audience even shouted for encores. During the rehearsals, the more experienced cast had told her about this peculiar habit.

When the audience voiced their appreciation for a particular part of a scene or a dialogue, then the actors knew what was expected of them. Everyone would pause the play and simply repeat the lines or the action in question.

So that's what Abbie did as well. And she loved it. She relished the thrill of having every pair of eyes in the auditorium focussed on her. It made her feel... alive.

This is even more wonderful than I ever dared imagine, she thought after one of those encores. *I wouldn't mind doing this for the rest of my life. It's certainly much better than charring.*

When the play was over and the actors had taken their final bow, the curtains closed under the thunderous applause of the crowd. Buzzing with joy, everyone walked off the stage and into the wings. People smiled, laughed, clapped shoulders and hugged. A fair share of them came up to Abbie as well, congratulating her on a job well done.

Even Miss Hawthorne made an effort and offered her a limp hand at the end of a stiffly outstretched arm. *I guess she doesn't like it when a simple amateur like me gets asked to do encores,* Abbie said to herself with a grin afterwards.

Somewhere in the lively backstage throng, Jane's beaming face appeared.

"Abbie! You were brilliant," her sister said as they hugged each other tightly.

"I really enjoyed myself," Abbie smiled.

"You have a talent for this."

"So everyone keeps telling me," Abbie giggled. "But I never thought I'd be this good."

"Well, you were." Jane's eyes sparkled with pride. "I even thought you were better than that Hawthorne woman."

"That's because you're my sister," Abbie blushed.

"No, it's true. She's a stuck-up–"

"Hush, Jane. Here come Mr and Mrs Parker."

Abbie glanced at the couple, who were making their way towards her after they had spoken to the lead actors.

"Mr and Mrs Parker," she greeted them nervously. "Did you like the play? Did we do well?"

"Liked it?" Bess replied with twinkling eyes. "We loved it! Didn't we, darling?"

"We sure did," Mr Parker said with a big smile.

"And as for your performance, my dear," Bess continued. "Why, you were simply marvellous. Wasn't she, Phineas?"

"Frankly, I was amazed, Miss Lee," he said. "Are you sure you've never acted before?"

"You could say she's had some practice off stage," Bess chuckled before flashing Abbie a knowing grin. Then she slipped a hand in the crook of her husband's arm. "Darling, don't you think we should give Miss Lee a bigger part in your next production?"

Abbie gasped. Could it be that her wish of being an actress was coming true?

Mr Parker nodded. "Certainly. This play will probably run for several more weeks. But I've nearly finished writing the next one. Miss Hawthorne will get the lead again of course. Her character needs a maid however, and I think Miss Lee would be a great fit."

"Speaking of Miss Hawthorne," Bess said, "I think we should have an understudy for her part in our next production."

"What's an understudy?" Jane asked, barging into the conversation.

"That's someone who learns another actor's role, so they can jump in and play the part, should the original actor become indisposed," Mr Parker explained. "Do you really think that's necessary, darling?" he asked his wife. "We've never used an understudy before."

"I have this uncanny feeling we might need one this time," Bess said enigmatically. "Call it female intuition if you like."

"Ah, the most mysterious force in the universe," Mr Parker chuckled. "But who should we ask for the role? I'd rather not pay an additional actress just for the privilege of learning a part they'll most likely never play."

"Just ask one of our current cast members. Someone with not too many lines, so they can easily study Miss Hawthorne's part as well."

"Who?"

Bess fixed Abbie with a mischievous twinkle in her eye. "Miss Lee?"

"Me? Gosh, I don't–"

"She means yes," Jane blurted out. "She'd be delighted."

Abbie wanted to object, but Jane discreetly kicked her shin while simultaneously staring at her with big eyes and a broad smile. *Do it,* Jane's face seemed to say.

"Splendid," Bess laughed. "We'll discuss the details in the morning." She and Mr Parker took their leave, as they had plenty more people to talk to.

When they were gone, Jane grabbed her sister's arm. "Abbie," she said excitedly. "You're going to be an actress."

"It's only a small part, Jane."

"But it's a start. And you'll be taking over from that Hawthorne harpy if something happens to her. You could become a star, Abbie."

"Settle down, Jane," she chuckled. "I won't deny that I'm just as thrilled about the idea as you are. But the reality is that we're still chargirls first and foremost. That's our bread and butter."

Slowly, she began to push their way through the crowd towards the dressing rooms.

"Tonight has been magical," she admitted. "But tomorrow morning, it's back to charring and cleaning for us."

As much as she liked to dream of living the glamorous life of an acclaimed actress, they needed to keep their feet on the ground. She was nothing but a washerwoman in the background of this play. And in the next one she'd be a lady's maid, another small part.

But after that? The Parkers would probably tire of her, she guessed. And then she and Jane would continue to wash, clean and serve for other people. Fame and fortune just wasn't for them.

Chapter Fifteen

"She did what?!" Abbie couldn't believe her ears. "This must be some sort of childish jest. Intended purely to spite us?"

Sitting on the sofa, Mrs Parker let out an unhappy sigh. "I'm sure Miss Hawthorne meant to spite us all right. But I'm afraid it's not a jest. She really has left for Italy. Here, read the note she sent us."

Abbie took the letter that Mrs Parker handed her. It was written on expensive scented paper and in the sort of handwriting that tried very hard to show off just how gracious its author was. She read it – twice – and then gave it back to Mrs Parker, shaking her head in disbelief.

"An extensive cultural tour of Italy," she said, repeating the reason Miss Hawthorne had provided for her sudden departure. "With her wealthy fiancé."

"Yes," Mrs Parker replied wearily as she threw down the letter on the coffee table in front of her. "And she regrets to inform us that she doesn't quite know yet when she'll return to these shores," she said, giving a sarcastically mocking impression of Miss Hawthorne's snooty tone of voice.

So that was why Mrs Parker had summoned her, Abbie thought. When little Rosie came to tell her that Mama wanted to see her in the drawing room, Abbie had been worried that perhaps she had done something wrong.

But this was possibly even worse. Mr Parker's new play was supposed to open in a month's time. And now their leading lady had abandoned them on a whim.

"I'm not particularly surprised though," Mrs Parker said. "Our overly precious Miss Hawthorne never did like the fact that we made you her understudy." She smiled at Abbie. "Your talent was too much of a threat to her, I suppose. And that probably helped to hasten her decision."

"I'm sorry, Mrs Parker," Abbie mumbled, lowering her eyes. "It was never my intention to pose any threat to Miss Hawthorne."

"Miss Lee–"

"Perhaps if you took me off the play completely, she might be persuaded to come back in time for opening night."

Rosie, who had been sitting quietly next to her mama all the while, now tugged at her mother's sleeve. "But Abbie can play Miss Hawthorne's part, can't she?"

"Exactly, my sweetheart," Mrs Parker said. "This type of situation is exactly why your Papa and I picked Miss Lee as an understudy."

She turned to Abbie with a smile and a raised eyebrow. Abbie could have sworn Mrs Parker looked almost amused by the whole thing.

"You don't seem too upset by this development, ma'am," Abbie said.

"Why should I be, Miss Lee? We have you. You're the ace up our sleeve, so to speak."

"But I've never played the lead role before. I only had to say a few witty lines in Mr Parker's previous play and–"

"I've seen you at rehearsals, Miss Lee. And you'll do splendidly. I believe in you."

"Then you have more confidence in my abilities than I do myself – begging your pardon, ma'am." She took a deep breath and shivered. Even though she secretly dreamt of being an actress, now that her dream seemed to be on the verge of becoming a reality, she was petrified.

Mrs Parker grimaced and placed a hand on her tummy. Abbie thought her mistress had turned awfully pale all of a sudden.

"Is anything the matter, ma'am?"

"Please excuse me," Mrs Parker said as she rose to her feet. "I'm feeling queasy and I need to retire upstairs for a brief moment."

"Anything I can do to help, ma'am?"

"No, please stay here with Rosie, Miss Lee. I shan't be long. And then we'll talk more about the play."

Mrs Parker hurried out of the room, leaving Abbie alone with Rosie. The young girl didn't seem concerned.

"Don't worry, Abbie," she said, reading Abbie's face. "Mama has been having this queasiness for a while."

"Shouldn't she see a doctor then?"

Rosie giggled. "She's already been to see him. Several times. But she made me promise not to tell anyone."

Abbie frowned and sighed. "I suppose that's all right then. But to be honest, that's not the only thing on my mind. I'm even more worried about this business with Miss Hawthorne."

"Why?"

"Because..." She hesitated. But what use was there in hiding the truth from Rosie? Children could usually see right through that sort of thing. And Rosie was a particularly clever and sensitive girl.

"Because I'm nervous," she confessed. "Nervous and afraid."

"What are you afraid of?"

"Me becoming the lead actress in your Papa's play."

"And that frightens you? I thought you would have been excited."

"I am. In a way. But at the same time, I'm scared that I'll make a great big mess of it. If I botch this up, I'll ruin your Papa's play and then your parents will have every reason to hate me."

"That's not going to happen," Rosie said. "And you know it."

"But I'm not even a real actress. I'm just a chargirl who lives in a cheap and dingy rented room with her sister."

"What's that got to do with anything?" Rosie giggled. "Being poor doesn't change who you are."

"You're very sweet, Miss Rosie," Abbie smiled. How wonderfully simple the world could be in the eyes of a child.

"Mama used to be poor, you know," the young girl said. "Very very poor. Why, she couldn't even afford to rent a room. She had to sleep on the street."

Abbie stared at Rosie. She had never heard that story before. Was it true, or was this some sort of fairy tale that Rosie was making up on the spot? Nothing about the present Mrs Parker seemed to betray such destitute origins.

Appearing absolutely sincere, Rosie continued, "Luckily, a nice lady took Mama in and gave her food and pretty clothes. But then a mean gentleman became awfully jealous. And he even tried to blame a terrible murder on Mama. Thankfully though, Papa managed to save her in the end. And then they got married."

Rosie looked at Abbie with a happy smile on her face. "Isn't that a great story?"

"It is," Abbie agreed. "And did that really happen to your Mama? All those things you told me?"

"Yes, every last bit of it," Mrs Parker said as she suddenly re-entered the room.

Abbie jumped up, startled and more than a little embarrassed. "Mrs Parker, I–" She felt the need to apologise, but before she had a chance, Rosie cut in.

"Mama, Abbie said she's afraid she won't be any good as an actress. Because she's poor and all that. So I told her about the time when you were a lot poorer." She paused to consider something. A little uncertain, she asked, "Or was that too one of the things I wasn't supposed to have told her?"

Mrs Parker laughed. "No, that's perfectly fine, my darling. In fact, I think it's time we told Miss Lee about that other matter." She looked at Abbie. "The reason why I've been having these bouts of nausea."

"Please don't feel obliged, ma'am," Abbie hastened to say. "You don't owe me an explanation."

"May I say it, Mama?" Rosie asked excitedly.

"Of course you may, my precious," Mrs Parker replied.

"Mama is expecting another baby," the little girl blurted out, delighted to finally be able to share the secret.

"Congratulations, ma'am," Abbie beamed. Looking back, she realised the signs had been there. But she had been too busy to notice. And too preoccupied with her own fears and hang-ups.

"Never had any trouble with the first two," Mrs Parker chuckled. "But this third one appears intent on making up for it."

"That's because it's probably a boy," Rosie stated with great certainty. "Boys are always trouble."

Her mother laughed. "Speaking of boys, why don't you go upstairs to the nursery, darling? Check with Nanny if your brother has finished his nap yet. Then Miss Lee and I can have a chat in the meantime."

Rosie nodded and scampered away. Mrs Parker shook her head fondly as she watched her daughter go. Then she turned to Abbie.

"I think it's time I put your mind at ease, Miss Lee." She smiled warmly. "Your performance will be simply marvellous. I know it. I can sense it. Just like I sensed that Miss Hawthorne would cause us a big problem."

Abbie had heard that sometimes a woman benefited from heightened senses when she was expecting. But this did little to alleviate her self-doubt.

"That's very kind of you, ma'am. However–"

"You don't share my confidence," Mrs Parker finished the sentence with a grin. "Well, let me tell you, my dear, I have been watching you."

Abbie's body tensed. Of course Mrs Parker had seen her, since she spent so much time at her husband's theatre. Mrs Parker had designed the costumes and she kept an eye on many of the practical affairs behind the scenes. But the thought of having been observed by a woman so wise and creative made Abbie nervous. What opinion did she have of Abbie as an actress?

"I've already told you on numerous occasions that you have talent, Miss Lee," Mrs Parker said with that uncanny ability of hers to read Abbie's mind.

"So you have, ma'am."

"Talent alone however won't get you very far in life."

Abbie's shoulders slumped. *Here it comes – the damning verdict.*

"But you, Miss Lee, you have more than just raw talent. You have grit and determination. You work hard, in the hope of achieving something better in this world."

Surprised, Abbie stared at Mrs Parker, who was smiling fondly at her. "It's true, dear. And when talent and hard work come together?

Why, there are no limits to what you can accomplish."

"Thank you, ma'am." There was so much more Abbie felt she should say. But the right words eluded her just then, as a wave of emotions threatened to overwhelm her.

Softly, Mrs Parker placed a hand on Abbie's arm. "Those of us who have known true hardship will strive twice as hard to escape the nightmare. Believe me, I know."

Abbie nodded and stared at the carpet, fighting back her tears. She wondered if she should confide in Mrs Parker and tell her about their own background. How she and Jane had lost their parents and were still burdened with their late father's debt. It would feel good to get those fears and worries off her chest.

But in the end, she decided not to. Mrs Parker obviously thought the world of her. And she didn't want to risk losing that respect.

Better to let sleeping dogs lie, she thought. Everything would work itself out eventually. Wouldn't it?

Chapter Sixteen

The weeks flew by. Frenzied preparations were made to get everything and everyone ready for opening night. Somewhat to Abbie's surprise, no one in the cast or the crew seemed to mind that she was taking Miss Hawthorne's place as the leading lady of the play.

She even saw a few discreet smiles on people's faces when Mr Parker broke the news to the group that Miss Hawthorne had suddenly decided to abandon the production.

"Nobody's going to miss her," Mrs Roberts told Abbie. The theatre dressmaker seemed exceedingly happy with this unexpected change – even though it meant more work for her, since she now had to mend the costume to fit Abbie.

"But she was so lovely, wasn't she?"

"Lovely? Our Miss Hoity-Toity?" Mrs Roberts snorted. "Stuck-up is what she was, love. Always had her pretty little nose up in the air, looking down on everyone. Good riddance, I says."

"Still, she was a much better actress than I am. Won't the others think I'm an impostor? Heaven knows what they'll say about me behind my back."

Mrs Roberts shook her head. "I've told you before: they like you, dear. And they'll all be rooting for you when opening night comes along."

"Do you really think so?" Abbie didn't have any cause to doubt Mrs Roberts' words. Everyone had always been kind and supportive to her in the past. But she found it hard to place her trust in others. It was better to keep your guard up, she thought.

"I've worked in the theatre for decades," Mrs Roberts said. "And it's true there's a fair amount of rotten apples in the barrel. But Mr and Mrs Parker are different. And they've succeeded in gathering plenty of marvellous people around them."

With a warm smile and a soft pat on Abbie's shoulder, the dressmaker added, "You've landed in a good nest here, little duckling."

She chuckled and Abbie couldn't resist sharing in the laughter.

"Thank you, Mrs Roberts. Everyone is so nice to me." Abbie sighed. It was such a fitting image: the lost duckling being welcomed into a snug new nest. But it troubled her as well. Because the more appreciated everyone made her feel, the more her fear grew of being evicted from that safe and comfortable environment.

"Stop worrying, love," Mrs Roberts said, having spotted the frown on Abbie's brow.

"Have faith in yourself and in the good Lord, and all will be fine."

Abbie wanted to believe that. Desperately so. But the tense knot in her stomach stayed. And by the time opening night arrived, it was so tight that she could scarcely breathe.

As she and Jane stepped into the theatre through the back entrance, her throat felt dry while a metallic taste lingered in her mouth. How was she supposed to pull off a decent enough performance in a state like this? Part of her wanted to turn on her heel. Run away and start all over again, like they had done so many times in the past.

Don't be foolish, Abbie, she told herself. That wouldn't be fair on Mr and Mrs Parker or all the other people who depended on this production for a living. And it wouldn't be fair on her sister either, she thought. Jane needed this newfound stability as much as she did.

"You're trembling," Jane said as she helped Abbie change into her stage costume in the dressing room. "Are you cold? Or just nervous?"

"Just nervous," Abbie replied. "And if you tell me everything will be fine, I swear I'm going to scream."

"All right, I won't. Haven't you noticed though?"

"Noticed what?"

"All the smiling faces wherever we went? The people here are smiling at you, Abbie."

Abbie hesitated. Now that Jane mentioned it, yes, she had vaguely registered the smiles and the friendly looks that seemingly everyone gave her when they walked past her.

"That's just because they're all excited it's opening night," she argued.

Jane rolled her eyes. "Or maybe it's because they believe in you and they know tonight's performance is going to be special."

"Perhaps," Abbie said. She stared at her reflection in the mirror before she began to apply her stage make-up. "Do I look different to you, Jane?"

"You're still you, if that's what you mean. But you're stronger now. You can do this. You can make this a success."

Abbie nodded softly. If so many people had faith in her, then maybe it was all right for her too to have some faith in herself. Slowly and deliberately, she put on her make-up.

And by the time she was done, her transformation was complete – not just on the outside, but mentally as well. She smiled at the young woman looking back at her in the mirror. She was ready to be the leading lady.

"Miss Lee," Mr Parker called as he popped his head round the door of the dressing room.

"Kindly proceed to the stage, please. We're nearly ready to start."

He paused and added with a fond smile, "You look just like Mrs Parker and I had envisioned your character. Good luck."

"Come on," Jane said after he had dashed off again. She grabbed Abbie's hand and gave it a short, encouraging tug. "Time to show the world who Abigail Lee is and what she's capable of."

Overpowered by the nerves that were raging through her like a wildfire, Abbie was grateful that her sister led the way to the stage. In her current emotional state, she was afraid she might have got lost otherwise.

"This is as far as I go," Jane said when they reached the wings. "But the Parkers have given me a box seat with an excellent view of the stage. So I'll be close by and I'm sure I'll clap and cheer the loudest."

"Thanks, Jane."

"What for?"

"For... everything."

"You're my big sister, aren't you? I love you, Abbie."

"And I love you too," Abbie said as they fell into each other's arms and hugged.

"Positions, please," the stage manager's voice said from somewhere in the shadowy recesses.

With trembling legs, Abbie walked onto the stage, where Mr Williams was already waiting.

He was playing the trusted old family butler in this production, a role that fitted him marvellously.

"Ready for your debut performance as the leading lady, Miss Lee?" he smiled.

"Can anyone ever be ready for such a thing, I wonder, Mr Williams?"

"True," he chuckled. "But remember what I told you last time. Deep breaths."

Abbie nodded and immediately followed his advice while she took up her starting position: draped elegantly across the settee. Mr William stood by her side, holding a tray with a decanter of bourbon.

"Can you hear the waiting audience?" he asked with a twinkle in his eyes. "One can almost feel their excitement and anticipation emanating through those closed curtains."

"Oh please, Mr Williams. Don't say that. I'm nervous enough as it is."

"But they're your friends, Miss Lee."

"My friends?" Abbie briefly wondered if perhaps Mr Williams had been sampling that bourbon on his tray a little too much. "I don't even know those people. Most of them are perfect strangers to me."

"What I meant was you should *think* of them as your friends, my dear. Because just like a friend, they want you to succeed."

"And why is that?"

"They're here on an evening out. They want to see a nice play and enjoy themselves. And that's why every single member of that audience wants you to do well."

He chuckled and added, "Apart from one or two of those awful theatre critics, obviously."

"Curtains," the stage manager whispered from the wings.

Friends, Abbie thought as invisible crew members worked to open the heavy stage curtains. The audience clapped and cheered, and the butterflies in her stomach fluttered with a newfound excitement.

Let's give them a wonderful show, Abbie said to herself as she took a deep, steadying breath. She couldn't actually see people's faces, but in her imagination the audience consisted entirely of her friends. People like Mr and Mrs Parker, Mrs Roberts, and of course her sister Jane. All smiling at her.

Effortlessly, she slipped into the role she had been practising for weeks. Her nerves had evaporated and she felt ready to give the performance of a lifetime.

Abbie delivered her lines with perfect timing and poise. She spoke with such natural ease that people in the audience forgot they were watching a fictitious play, instead becoming completely enraptured by the story and its young heroine. They hung on every word she uttered, followed her every move.

It felt like magic to Abbie. And she was the principal enchantress, who weaved her benign spell over them. Having their full attention, sensing their eyes on her, making them go 'ooh' and 'aah', and causing them to laugh or cry at all the right moments – the effects were simply intoxicating.

When the performance ended, the audience rose to their feet and erupted into a wild applause. The other actors clapped and cheered for her as well. Abbie had never felt so proud and accomplished in her life.

And in her heart, an enormous sense of gratitude rose up toward Mr and Mrs Parker, for giving her the chance to be part of something so wondrous.

After numerous curtain calls, the cast rushed from the stage as a group, with Abbie in their middle. It seemed as if she was swimming in a sea of euphoric smiles and jubilant laughter as everyone backstage came pressing in closer to congratulate her.

Mr and Mrs Parker were there too, but Abbie was becoming so overwhelmed by it all that her mind barely captured what they told her.

"Get changed, Miss Lee," Mrs Parker smiled. "Hopefully we'll be able to talk when this madness around us has calmed down a bit."

Someone took her by the arm as the boisterous group of actors rushed to the dressing rooms, drunk on their triumph. And if someone had told Abbie that she was being propelled by the wings of an angel, she would have believed it. She felt ecstatic.

Chapter Seventeen

"That was incredible," Jane exclaimed joyfully when the two sisters found each other in the mad chaos of the dressing rooms.

"Did you like it?" Abbie asked. She was floating on a fluffy white cloud of delirious bliss.

"I adored it! You were divine. And the audience clearly loved you too. Did you hear the applause at the end? Like thunder it was."

Abbie let out a long and happy sigh. "Did that really happen, Jane? Part of me seems to think I'm merely asleep and all of this is nothing but a dream."

"Of course it really happened, you silly," her sister giggled. "Want me to pinch you to prove it to you?"

"No, that'll be fine, thank you," Abbie laughed. "Why don't you help me get out of this dress instead, so I can change?"

As Jane began to lend a hand, she said, "You realise this changes everything, don't you, Abbie?"

"In what way?"

"This could be the start of something big for you. We were just a pair of poor chargirls before. But now–" Jane paused to look Abbie in the eyes. "Now you're a proper actress. A leading lady who's going to be popular with the crowds."

"Let's not get our hopes up too soon," Abbie replied. She blushed modestly. Although, if she was honest with herself, it was a very tantalising thought.

"Whyever not?" Jane demanded. "You've got to have faith, Abbie. You saw and you heard how the audience reacted to you."

Abbie glanced around at the other performers, the bustling activity in the dressing room, and the scent of success and opportunity that seemed to hang in the air of the buzzing space. Maybe Jane was right. Perhaps it was time to start believing in herself and her talent more.

"You could be a star," Jane said with twinkling eyes.

"Do you really think so?" Abbie asked while she finished dressing.

"The Parkers would have to be out of their minds if they didn't give you more starring roles after this. And you and I both know they are anything but crazy. They're as clever as they are kind."

Abbie nodded. Her sister had a point there. For the first time in years, it began to feel like she could allow herself to dream again.

"And with fame, you'll soon have money, too," Jane continued excitedly. "Then we won't be poor any more. And we won't have to sweat and slave our days away. We could live somewhere decent and have nicer things." She grinned. "That is, of course, if you'll still want to have your baby sister around once you're famous."

Abbie laughed. "You cheeky rascal. I will *always* want you around. No matter what happens."

"Good, that's settled then. And now–" Jane gave Abbie a gentle nudge towards the door. "It's time for you to get out there and mingle with your new fans and all the important guests."

"What about you? Aren't you coming?"

"I'm going to help Mrs Roberts back here. I see the poor woman has a huge pile of clothing to sort out on her own. You have fun without me for a while. I'll join you later. Shoo."

They hugged and then Abbie left the dressing rooms, determined to find Mr and Mrs Parker first, so she could thank them properly.

She spotted them talking to a gentleman. A handsome gentleman, Abbie couldn't fail to notice. He was older than her, probably about Mr Parker's age if she had to venture a guess. And there was something wildly attractive about him. He had the most charming smile and he radiated a calm confidence. He seemed like a refined and cultured man, and he certainly dressed that way.

But there was more to him than that. Underneath his fine and smiling appearance, she sensed a looming power. A strength – both physical and of character – that lay there like a proud and nimble tiger, waiting to pounce when the need arose.

Little Rosie Parker had been standing with the group as well, but the girl now came dashing towards the dressing rooms.

"Rosie, who's that man talking to your Mama and Papa?" Abbie asked her.

"That's my Uncle Joe," the girl replied with a smile.

"I didn't know you had an uncle?"

Abbie thought Mr Parker only had two sisters, who lived somewhere in the country. And Mrs Parker had lost her parents and siblings at an early age.

"He's not really my uncle," Rosie explained. "But he's been Mama and Papa's best friend since before I was born. And that makes him part of the family, they always say. He's really sweet, you know."

And very handsome too, Abbie thought as Rosie skipped off to look for Mrs Roberts.

Keeping her eyes on this so-called Uncle Joe, Abbie slowly prowled closer to the chatting trio. They appeared to be engaged in a very friendly conversation, with lots of smiles and laughter. As Abbie came near, she caught a few words of what they were talking about.

"Your performances tend to draw the wealthiest crowds and the most eccentric people," the gentleman said to Mr and Mrs Parker.

Grasping the opportunity, Abbie decided to cut in. "Who's eccentric?" she asked with her most dashing smile. "Mrs Parker, won't you please do me the honour of introducing this kind gentleman to me?"

"But of course," Mrs Parker smiled broadly. "Mr Joe Thompson, please meet Miss Abigail Lee, our newest leading lady and soon-to-be star."

When Abbie and Mr Thompson exchanged their polite greetings, she was struck by the captivating power that shone from his glimmering eyes.

"Mr Thompson, you say?" she asked. "Why does that name sound familiar to me?"

"Perhaps," Mrs Parker replied, "because you've seen it on that great big plaque in our lobby."

"It was Mr Thompson who most graciously took it upon himself to find sponsors and benefactors to renovate the theatre," Mr Parker explained. "And that's why his name is mentioned on the commemorative plaque."

Abbie gasped in sheer astonishment. "Oh, my! Are you *that* Mr Thompson?"

"The very same," he replied. Like a true gentleman, he bowed, gently brought her hand to his lips and placed a tender kiss on it. From the grin on his face, she could tell he was as fascinated by her as she was with him.

"Are you a banker then, Mr Thompson?"

"Better than that, my dear. I get to play with other people's money."

"That sounds marvellously exciting, sir," she cooed. Abbie didn't know if it was due to the thrill of her stage performance that still had her in its grips, or simply because of his irresistible smile – but she felt fearless and more daring than she had ever been.

"You simply must tell me all about it," she said flirtatiously.

"I'd be happy to, Miss," he replied instantly. "Might I be so bold as to invite you to dinner? You must be starving after that exceptional performance of yours."

It took all of Abbie's acting skills not to betray the surge of glee that his invitation caused in her. *Steady,* she told herself. *Play it cool.*

"I must admit the stage takes quite a bit out of me," she replied. "But you liked it, did you, Mr Thompson?"

And did you like me, her eyes tried to ask him.

She thought she heard Mrs Parker suppressing an amused little cough.

"Stellar performance, Miss Lee," Mr Thompson said. "Simply and delightfully stellar."

"Why, thank you, Mr Thompson. Too kind of you, sir. Are you a great lover of the theatre?"

"I'm a lover of many of the finer things in life, Miss Lee. Theatre, art... beauty." Again he bore down on her with the full force of his mesmerising gaze.

"Oh, Mr Thompson. You sound like such a refined and distinguished gentleman. I feel like I could listen to you for hours."

"Then I suggest we dine at the Château d'Or, where we can discuss art, beauty and life for as long as we like."

"Château d'Or," Mrs Parker said. "Isn't that where you got Georgie a position as the chef's senior apprentice?"

"It is," Mr Thompson replied with evident pride.

"How is he getting along there?" Mrs Parker asked. "Is he enjoying himself?"

"Tremendously. I might just buy the restaurant for him once he's a bit older." He turned to Abbie with a smile and said, in that charmingly boastful way of his, "It's the least a man can do for a talented lad like him."

With a sudden sense of alarm, Abbie wondered if Georgie was his son. How foolish of her to think that a man like Joe Thompson could still be a bachelor. Of course he was married.

"Is he your son, Mr Thompson?" she enquired.

"No, Georgie is what you might call my ward. I've been looking after him since he was a little boy, haven't I, Mrs Parker?"

A silent nod from Mrs Parker confirmed this. But there was still that amused grin on her face as well, Abbie noticed. What did Mrs Parker know that Abbie didn't? Perhaps all wasn't lost yet.

"How generous of you, Mr Thompson," she said, feeling more hopeful again. "Haven't you got any children of your own then? A man like you must be married, surely."

Anxiously, she held her breath – and prayed that it didn't show. This was the moment of truth.

"Alas, no," he replied. "You might say I'm still looking for love, Miss Lee."

Abbie could have squealed with delight. Unable to hide how pleased she was, she quickly opened the painted fan she had in her hands. Thanking her lucky stars that she had kept hold of the theatre prop, she now tried to hide her smile behind it.

"You poor thing, Mr Thompson," she teased.

"I seek to bear my hardship with grace, Miss Lee."

When he kindly offered his arm, she duly slipped her hands around it – mirroring his smile but taking care to not appear too eager. Because even in the face of victory, a lady never forgot her manners.

When they said their polite goodbyes to the Parkers, there was no denying that Mrs Parker seemed to be grinning from ear to ear.

"Have a very lovely evening, Miss Lee," she said with eyes that sparkled like diamonds.

"I believe I will, Mrs Parker," she replied happily.

As Abbie and Mr Thompson stepped away from the other couple, she stole a sideways look at him. It was only a quick glance, but it was enough to set her pulse racing.

I've done it, she thought. *I've found my prince.*

He looked at her as well.

Now let's hope he doesn't turn into a frog the moment I kiss him.

Chapter Eighteen

"Do you have a chaperone, Miss Lee?" Mr Thompson asked. And with a smile, he added, "I wouldn't want to cause a scandal by taking you out to dinner without one."

Too late Abbie realised she hadn't thought of that. She had been too mesmerised by his charms. But he was right: a respectable woman couldn't be seen dining out with another man who wasn't a close relative of hers.

The fact that Mr Thompson had brought up this important detail himself only made her like him even more. It told her that he was a decent man and his intentions for this evening were honourable.

"Perhaps your mother?" he suggested. "If she's here tonight, she must be very proud of her daughter's performance."

"Both my parents passed away a few years ago, I'm afraid," she replied.

"I'm terribly sorry to hear that. Please accept my apologies. It was most insensitive of me to presume."

"Not at all, sir," she hastened to reply. She didn't want to ruin the mood now. "I could ask my sister. She's younger than me, but I suppose she will do as a chaperone, won't she?"

"I should think so too," Mr Thompson smiled. "She's currently in the dressing rooms helping Mrs Roberts. I'll go and find her."

"Please do. In the meantime, I must find my two young associates and tell them my plans have changed. Shall we meet up in the lobby?"

"That would be splendid. I'll join you there shortly."

With a little bow, he was off, but not before graciously kissing her hand again. Abbie was left feeling a little giddy. She had been invited – by a real gentleman no less – to have dinner in what sounded like a very fancy restaurant. It was almost too good to be true. Deciding she'd better hurry to find Jane before she lost her nerve, Abbie dashed to the dressing rooms.

"Jane, I need your help," she panted breathlessly.

"What's the matter?" her sister asked with some concern. "Is anything wrong?"

"No, it's nothing like that at all. Quite the contrary. I've just received a dinner invitation, but I need a chaperone. Will you do that for me, please?"

"Chaperone, me?" Jane laughed.

"I can't possibly ask Mrs Parker to come with me. Especially not in her current state. Please say yes, Jane."

"All right, all right. I'll be your chaperone." Amused, her sister frowned and tilted her head. "So who invited you then?"

"A very nice gentleman called Mr Thompson. Apparently he's best friends with the Parkers. Has been for years."

"Is he handsome?" Jane asked, grinning.

Abbie blushed. "Yes, rather."

"I knew it," Jane laughed. "You didn't waste time finding yourself a beau, did you?"

"It wasn't like that, Jane," Abbie protested. "He invited me. He's very kind and charming that way." Awkwardly, she added, "He also happens to be older than me. Quite a bit."

"Oh," her sister replied while her smile faded quickly. "Please don't tell me he's one of those?"

"One of those? What do you mean?"

Laying a hand on Abbie's arm, Jane lowered her voice. "I've heard stories in the dressing rooms this evening. About actresses who supplement their income by, erm, entertaining gentlemen. Rich and *older* gentlemen."

Abbie shook her head. "I'm not as foolish as that, Jane. And Mr Thompson strikes me as the honourable sort. In fact, it was his idea that I should bring a chaperone."

"If you say so, sister dearest."

"Besides, I once vowed that I would only ever give myself to a man on *my* conditions and of my own volition. Never out of material necessity."

Satisfied, Jane nodded and smiled. "Glad that's settled then. I must warn you though." She grinned. "I intend to be a very strict chaperone. There will be no flirting, no hand-holding and no funny business of any kind."

"Yes, matron," Abbie teased.

The girls laughed, linked arms and headed for the lobby.

"Good thing Mrs Parker gave us both nice new dresses for opening night," Jane said while they were on their way. "I feel like Cinderella now."

"Yes, about that," Abbie replied. "Let's not mention to Mr Thompson that we're charwomen. He probably thinks I'm a professional actress."

"I'm just the chaperone, remember?" Jane giggled. "My only job is to ensure you behave like a lady. I'll leave the conversation to you and Mr Thompson."

With a little flutter of excitement in their bellies, the two girls arrived in the lobby, where Mr Thompson stood waiting for them.

"This is my sister Jane," Abbie said. "She'll be my chaperone for tonight."

"Miss Jane," Mr Thompson greeted with all his usual warmth and charm. "I'm delighted to make your acquaintance."

"As am I, sir," Jane replied politely.

"Shall we be on our way?" he asked. "One of the doormen has hailed a cab for us. Miss Jane, is it acceptable if I offer my arm to your sister?"

"Perfectly, Mr Thompson," Jane said, trying hard to keep a straight face.

As they went outside, Abbie cast a quick glance over her shoulder at her sister, who grinned broadly and appeared to mouth the word 'handsome' while pointing a discreet finger at Mr Thompson.

Abbie smiled happily. What an adventure this evening was turning out to be. Even if the food at the restaurant would prove to be less than average, which seemed most unlikely to her, she was certain to remember this night fondly.

With a mind full of pleasant expectations, she let the gallant Mr Thompson help her get into the waiting hansom cab. Once they were all seated, the driver cracked his whip and they set off at a trot.

The ride was a pleasant one and Mr Thompson's conversation proved to be as interesting as she had hoped. Because even though he was evidently a very successful man, he wasn't the type to brag or boast about his wealth. And at no point did he make Abbie and Jane feel like they were any less than him.

Before she realised it, they had arrived at their destination for the evening. The carriage came to a halt in front of the restaurant and the three of them alighted. From the outside, the Château d'Or looked even more impressive than its name had led her to believe.

The moment they entered, the owner's face lit up with a beaming smile. "Mr Thompson," he said with a heavy French accent as he rushed over to greet them. "How wonderful to see you again, monsieur."

"Monsieur Joubert," Mr Thompson replied, equally amicable and with a perfect French pronunciation. "I apologise for not having booked in advance. You wouldn't happen to have a table for the three of us, would you?"

"For you, always, monsieur," Mr Joubert stated solemnly as if it was a matter of great personal pride. "Le Château d'Or would never turn away such an important and distinguished guest as yourself."

He snapped his fingers at a nearby waiter. "Étienne, show Monsieur Thompson and his guests to his table, please."

As they followed their waiter past several of the other tables, Abbie whispered, "This is a very fashionable restaurant you have chosen, Mr Thompson. If I didn't know any better, I would have sworn we were in Paris."

She spotted a string quartet playing a light classical tune over the subtle background murmur of civilised voices.

Mr Thompson chuckled. "Except that our Monsieur Joubert isn't French at all. He's really an Englishman who goes by the name of Robert Brown. Very kind and decent chap though."

The waiter led them to a quiet corner table, draped with a heavy white cloth and decorated with a vase of yellow roses. They all sat down, and Mr Thompson immediately ordered some champagne.

"Judging by Mr Joubert's respectful demeanour towards you," Abbie said, "I take it you come here often, Mr Thompson?"

"This certainly is one of my favourite restaurants, yes. I mostly come here with business relations." Grinning, he added, "Rarely with a female companion, in case you were wondering."

"I wouldn't dream to presume, sir," Abbie replied, matching his grin. "Whom you keep company with is entirely your own business. Although one would surmise that a man like you had the pick of the crop."

"I suppose I do. But I'm very careful in my choices and I tend to set a high standard."

"So does your inviting us here this evening signify that I meet those high standards of yours, Mr Thompson?" Abbie asked flirtatiously.

She heard Jane clearing her throat, but Mr Thompson didn't seem to be offended by her girlish coquetry. Instead, he chose to circumvent her question.

"The problem someone in my position often faces is that certain women are more attracted to a man's money than to his character."

"Then let me reassure you, Mr Thompson," Abbie replied with confidence. "Money in and of itself holds no particular attraction to me."

He smiled and they held each other's gaze for a few seconds, taking the other's measure.

"Your champagne, monsieur," Étienne announced as he arrived with a bottle in a silver bucket filled with ice.

After the waiter had uncorked the bottle and filled their glasses, Mr Thompson raised his glass and proposed a toast. "Here's to art, beauty and friendship."

Abbie had never tasted champagne before, but when she took her first sip, she loved its delicate sweetness and the fizzy sensation of its fine bubbles.

It didn't take long however for her to start feeling tipsy. Luckily, the fascinating conversation at their table engaged her faculties to the fullest and so she didn't think Mr Thompson noticed that the alcohol was having an effect on her. She was equally grateful to note that, being a true gentleman, he didn't seem inclined to force them to drink more than they could handle.

She soon found herself becoming increasingly entranced by his charms. Whether that was due to the champagne she wasn't sure. But one thing was certain: she had never met anyone quite like him. With each passing minute, she was beginning to like Mr Thompson more and more.

I wish this night would never end, she thought. *And I wish every day of my life could be like this.*

But then she quickly pushed away the pang of sadness that threatened to overcome the warm bliss in her heart. Gazing into his charismatic eyes, she took another sip of champagne.

At least I have this moment, she decided. And this moment would stay with her, forever.

Chapter Nineteen

Over the course of their exquisite dinner, Mr Thompson entertained the girls with stories of his life as a businessman and an investor. And just like she had come to expect from him, his stories weren't dull or tedious at all. At least not to her. She hung on his every word and she was genuinely interested in hearing about his business dealings.

Some of the finer details went over her head, but if she understood his explanations correctly, he made a lot of money by doing something quite ingenious. He found suitable investors for inventors, scientists and other people who had great ideas but lacked the financial means to turn their vision into reality. As the middleman, Mr Thompson received a tidy commission and a share of the profits.

Very clever, she thought. And most lucrative too, from the looks of it.

Over the years, Mr Thompson had invested some of his wealth in property as well. He now owned a considerable number of houses and buildings across the city and further afield, which he rented out to tenants.

Abbie wondered if perhaps he happened to be the landlord of some of the many tenements where she and her sister had lived in the past few years.

What an ironic coincidence that would have been.

But she immediately dismissed the notion. Theirs had all been cheap and rundown rooms located in crumbling, draughty buildings infested by rats and other vermin. Miserable hellholes unfit for human habitation. Mr Thompson wouldn't dream of renting out such properties, she imagined.

"You must forgive me," he said after they had finished their main course. "I'm probably boring you both to death with all my talk about business."

"Not at all," Abbie replied with a keen smile. "Jane, are you bored?"

Her sister shook her head. She hadn't said much at the table, but the radiant look on her face showed that she was thoroughly enjoying herself.

"Making money sounds so easy the way you tell it, Mr Thompson," Abbie said. "It's almost as if it comes natural to you. Did your parents teach you about the world of finance?"

It was a subtle way of asking if his family was rich. Accumulating wealth always seemed a whole lot easier for those who were born with a silver spoon in their mouth.

"No, I'm afraid not," he chuckled. "I come from very humble beginnings and I've had to work hard to get where I am today."

Abbie was relieved to hear it. If he had come from a wealthy family, any chances of her developing anything meaningful with him would have been non-existent. This at least levelled things up a bit more, even though he was still infinitely more well-off than her.

"Nothing wrong with hard work," Jane said with a knowing grin in Abbie's direction. "Wouldn't you say so, Mr Thompson?"

"Absolutely," he replied. "Money is so much more enjoyable when you've had to work for it."

Abbie nodded. She was convinced that Mr Thompson earned his money in an honest way, whereas plenty of people only appeared capable of gaining wealth by making others poorer.

"Is everything to your liking?" Monsieur Joubert enquired in his usual deferential style when he appeared by their table.

"Everything has been splendid so far, Monsieur Joubert," Mr Thompson replied. "The food, the ambiance, as well as the company." He smiled at Abbie.

"I am most pleased to hear that, monsieur. Most pleased. Can I interest you in some dessert perhaps?"

Abbie doubted whether she could eat anything more. Her clothes were beginning to feel awfully tight already. But Jane's ears pricked up at the mention of the word 'dessert'.

"I think we shall have your famous crêpes Suzette," Mr Thompson suggested. "They are simply delicious and quite a sight to behold, too."

"An excellent choice, monsieur," the owner said with a little bow. "I shall instruct the chef to send over the young Monsieur Georges himself."

"Is he the young man you mentioned earlier tonight, Mr Thompson?" Abbie asked when Mr Joubert had left them.

"The same," Mr Thompson replied.

"I can tell from your smile that you're very proud of him, sir."

"I most certainly am, Miss Lee. Georgie's start in life was quite possibly even harder than mine. For him to have reached his current position is a remarkable feat, as well as a show of his strength and character."

"With your help, as you hinted at," Abbie said.

"True, he's had some support from me. But as the saying goes, you can lead a horse to water but you can't make him drink."

"Who's George?" Jane asked. "Or Georgie?"

"He's my ward," Mr Thompson said. "My protégé, who I've been taking under my wing since he was a little lad. His real name is George, but we've been calling him Georgie for so long that the nickname has more or less stuck. It fits him perfectly though. He's a very kind and talented young man. You'll see."

A short while later, Georgie arrived at their table, pushing a serving trolley with a variety of bowls and cooking equipment on it.

"Good evening, Georgie my lad," Mr Thompson greeted him cordially. "How are you this evening?"

"I'm very well, sir. Thank you," he smiled. "Good evening, ladies."

Before Abbie could utter a polite reply, Jane thrust out her hand and cooed, "Enchantée, monsieur."

Blushing, Georgie politely took her hand in his and made a short head bow over it. "Enchanté, mademoiselle."

"Georgie, please meet the Lee sisters," Mr Thompson said. "Miss Abigail Lee and her younger sibling Miss Jane."

"Delighted to meet you both," Georgie said as the rosy blush on his cheeks slowly faded. Then he proceeded to make their dessert: crêpes Suzette as Mr Thompson had called them.

Abbie didn't know what to expect, but just like Mr Thompson had promised, it was rather spectacular to watch. Georgie started out by making what appeared to be thin pancakes using the finest butter, eggs, sugar, flour and milk. Then he prepared a runny sweet sauce from butter, sugar and orange peel, and he let the pancakes soak in it over his small portable stove.

"I don't know what exactly you're making, sir," Jane said, admiring his handiwork. "But it looks and smells delicious already."

"Wait until you see what happens next," Mr Thompson grinned.

Georgie poured a liqueur that smelled of oranges over his pancakes and when he shook his frying pan, its contents caught fire.

Abbie and Jane let out a little shriek in fright, but Mr Thompson assured them this was supposed to happen. "Georgie has the whole thing firmly under control," he smiled. A few moments later the flames died down by themselves.

"But surely," Abbie said, "those pancakes are ruined now?"

"Have a taste and you'll find out," Mr Thompson said with twinkling eyes as Georgie served them each a plate.

Using their fork and knife, Abbie and Jane sliced off a small corner and took a cautious bite. The sensation that hit their palate was amazing! It was sweet and buttery and slightly bitter all at the same time. And rather strong too, due to the liqueur Georgie had used.

"It's the most heavenly thing I've ever tasted," Jane declared. "Who knew setting flame to pancakes could be so good? You're an excellent chef, George."

"Thank you, Miss Jane," he nodded as he began to blush again. "But I'm not a chef yet. Only an apprentice."

"A very talented apprentice," Jane said.

"And he'll be a great chef someday soon," Mr Thompson added.

"You're all too kind," Georgie said with a short bow of the head, before taking his leave and wheeling his trolley back to the kitchen.

After they had finished their crêpes, tea was served in delicately hand-painted china cups. Made from the finest spring leaves and buds, it was simply divine and tasted nothing like the coarse powdery stuff Abbie and Jane were used to.

As she sipped her tea, Abbie realised with a start that the evening was drawing to an end. She had enjoyed her time at the restaurant so much that she had wanted it to last forever. But, alas, all good things had to come to an end.

Their meal over, Mr Thompson offered to escort them home. And the girls gratefully accepted since they were feeling too tired, and too full, to walk home. Nevertheless, Abbie asked the driver to stop at the corner of a nearby park.

"My sister and I will go the last bit on foot," she explained to Mr Thompson. "A short walk will do us good after all that wonderful food, I should think."

The real reason, obviously, was that she felt ashamed and didn't want him to see the modest boarding house where they lived.

"Of course," he replied graciously. "I've had a delightful evening, Miss Lee. May I hope that we shall be seeing each other again soon?"

Abbie blushed as a sudden heat rose up to her neck and cheeks. "I hope so too, Mr Thompson. Thank you for inviting us to dinner. It was truly a night to remember."

With that, they bade him goodnight, got out of the hansom and watched as the cab drove off, carrying him into the night. Then she and Jane crossed the quiet park, strolling side by side.

Stars twinkled in the dark sky above and the park appeared completely deserted at this late hour. But Abbie wasn't afraid. In the presence of Mr Thompson, all her fears and worries had melted away. She was truly and deeply content.

"That was quite a night, wasn't it?" Jane said, delight dancing in her eyes.

"Yes," Abbie sighed blissfully. A shame it was all over and that they would have to go back to their lives as chargirls again in the morning.

"Oh, dear," Jane giggled. "It sounds to me like someone is in love. This wouldn't have anything to do with a certain dashing gentleman, would it?"

Abbie blushed. Her heart was glowing with a happy, tingling warmth unlike anything she had ever experienced. Was this what it was like to fall in love, she wondered?

"He was charming, wasn't he?" she said. Intriguing, too. Mr Thompson had hinted at his simple background, but what was his real story?

"Very charming," Jane agreed.

"But I think I'm not the only one who's smitten," Abbie teased. "I saw the way you looked at Georgie, Jane."

Her sister didn't blush. "He was nice," she said with a smile.

It was too soon to tell, but perhaps, just perhaps, they had both found something special in the unlikeliest of places.

"Well, here we are then," Abbie said when they arrived at the doorstep of their simple boarding house. There was a bittersweet sadness to her voice. "Our fairy tale is over."

"Or maybe it's only just begun," Jane said.

Abbie smiled. "Wouldn't that be lovely?"

Chapter Twenty

Morning arrived far sooner than Abbie would have wanted. They had only had a few hours of sleep, but through years of routine, she woke up before daybreak. Painfully aware of the fatigue in her body, she sat up in bed and stretched.

Despite the lack of rest, her heart fluttered when she thought of the night before. Had Mr Thompson really meant it when he said he hoped to see her again soon? She knew she had to be careful with wealthy men, since they often had preconceived notions about actresses. But not once during their evening together had he struck her as that sort of despicable man.

Abbie sighed and rose from the small bed she shared with Jane. She was tired and her mind felt sluggish. But still she was excited to see what today would bring.

"Time to get up, Jane," she said as she threw aside the covers in an attempt to rouse her sleeping sister. But a disgruntled groan was the only response she got.

"Duty calls, sleepyhead," Abbie insisted.

"Just a few more minutes," Jane grumbled, tugging at the bedsheets. "Haven't we earned at least that?"

Abbie tutted and went over to the wash bowl to splash some cold water in her face. "We can't let the Parkers down, Jane. They pay us to char for them, after all."

Letting out a miserable moan, Jane heaved herself out of bed. "Alright then, if we must. I just hope this acting career of yours will soon earn us enough money so we don't have to work any more."

"That'll be quite some time still," Abbie said as she brushed her hair. "If it ever comes to that. So don't get your hopes up yet."

Jane picked up Abbie's evening dress, pressed it to her chest and twirled around. "Or maybe Mr Thompson will propose to you and we can all go and live in his big, fancy house. How many servants do you reckon he's got?"

"Are you sure you're awake? Or are you still dreaming?" Abbie laughed and snatched her gown from Jane. "Wash up and get dressed, please."

Moments later, the two of them stepped out into the street while the first faint signs of dawn became visible in the sky. And after they had bought a hot cup of tea from a street vendor, Abbie felt ready for whatever lay ahead. The day was her own and she was determined to make the most of it.

"You're very brave, my dears," the Parker family's kindly cook chuckled when Abbie and Jane came in through the servants entrance. "I was expecting you to show up much later than usual. What with yesterday being opening night and all that."

"See?" Jane said, giving Abbie a playful poke between the ribs. "I told you we could have stayed in bed a little longer."

"We shouldn't take advantage of Mr and Mrs Parker's kindness," Abbie simply replied.

"They wouldn't have minded," the cook laughed. "And I'm sure they'll be having a good lay-in themselves this morning. They didn't get home until very late last night. But they sounded very pleased with how the play went, that I can tell you."

"They were?" Abbie asked.

The cook nodded. "Oh, yes. They were full of praise for you."

Abbie beamed. All her hard work had paid off. But she didn't have much time to relish in her success. Because now the fires in the day rooms needed to be lit, there was cleaning to be done and once the family came downstairs, she would have to serve breakfast. Just like every other day.

As she went about her tasks however, her mind kept wandering back to the previous night and to Mr Thompson. Every time she thought of him, her heart beat just that little bit faster. He had been such a perfect gentleman.

Even when the Parkers finally took their breakfast towards the end of the morning, Abbie found it hard to focus on her tasks.

"You must be feeling terribly tired, dear," Mrs Parker said with a sympathetic smile.

"It's not too bad, ma'am." Abbie didn't want to tell the real reason for her absentmindedness, but she rather suspected that her blushing cheeks gave her away.

"I didn't get a chance to tell you yesterday," Mrs Parker said. "But it's perfectly all right for you to come in later the morning after a performance, you know."

"After all, we don't want to overburden our new star," Mr Parker chimed in, smiling. "I've arranged a short meeting with all the actors at the theatre this afternoon. To talk about yesterday's performance and to discuss a few practical matters. You're more than welcome to share a cab with me if you like?"

"That's very kind, sir," Abbie said while refilling his cup. "These things are still very new to me."

"You'll get used to it soon enough," Mrs Parker said. "Perhaps we should look at altering our arrangement somewhat, so you can focus more on the play. Do you think your sister would be willing to take on a bit more of your work here?"

"I'll ask her, ma'am," Abbie replied, making an effort to hide her excitement. One step closer to being able to give up her life as a charwoman! Only a small step, admittedly, but it was progress nonetheless. And she was sure Jane would see it like that as well.

When she arrived at the theatre with Mr Parker later that day, she thought she noticed a slight change in how people talked to her. She was one of them now. After her success the previous night, everyone saw her as a real actress.

"There's a surprise waiting for you in your dressing room," Mrs Roberts said as she gave Abbie's arm a playful squeeze.

"A surprise? For me? What is it?"

"Wouldn't be much of a surprise if I told you, would it?" the dressmaker chuckled. "All I'll say is you must have made quite an impression last night."

Abbie hurried to the dressing room. She gasped in excited wonder when she opened the door and saw a massive bouquet of flowers. They were so lush and beautiful – a vivid mix of lilies, roses, and peonies in a brilliant rainbow of colours. She picked up the bouquet and closed her eyes as she inhaled its sweet scent.

Opening her eyes again, she spotted the card that was attached to the flowers. With trembling fingers, she reached for it. The handwriting looked elegant and strong, perfectly reflecting the personality of the man who had written the note: Mr Thompson.

Her heart skipped a beat as she read his words. He thanked her once more for a most enjoyable evening spent in her delightful presence. And would she please consider doing him the honour of accompanying him on a stroll through the park on Sunday?

Abbie tenderly held the flowers close to her chest, her cheeks heating up as she thought of the man who had sent them. It all felt as if she was living in a dream. A sweet and wonderful dream – as opposed to the nightmare she and her sister had been going through these past few years.

She read the card several more times, until she was convinced she hadn't misunderstood Mr Thompson's note. But the invitation was plainly there, black on white, written in his own hand.

As soon as the meeting at the theatre was over, Abbie rushed to the exit, clutching her flowers. She was dying to tell Jane and to show her Mr Thompson's card. A Sunday stroll through the park meant her sister would have to be her chaperone again, but she knew Jane wouldn't mind.

She'll probably talk Mr Thompson into treating us to a sumptuous afternoon tea in some expensive cake shop, Abbie giggled to herself as she descended the stairs outside.

"My, oh my," a man's voice smirked from the shadows behind her. "Someone seems mighty pleased with themselves."

Abbie stopped dead in her tracks. She recognised that voice. She prayed it wouldn't be true, but as she turned round slowly, she saw his all too familiar mocking grin.

"Mister Percy," she croaked.

"Hello, Miss Lee. Did you miss me?"

She wanted to escape and get as far away from this horrible man as she possibly could. But his devilish eyes kept her nailed to the spot.

"That was very naughty of you," Percy grinned. "To run away from us in the middle of the night the way you did."

"Your grandfather was going to sell us to some seedy innkeeper," she shot back defiantly after she had recovered her wits.

"Hmm, yes," he replied with an unhappy pout. "I never quite liked that solution either, to tell you the truth. But you'll be pleased to hear my grandfather has passed away in the meantime."

"I didn't know. My condolences."

"It was a small loss," Percy shrugged. "He passed away shortly after you left, actually." Laughing, he added, "Must have been the shock of losing out on all that money you owed him."

Although she couldn't bring herself to mourn the death of the old Mr Yates, she resented Percy for treating the subject so lightly. It was disrespectful.

"Why are you here, sir?"

"To pay you my respects, of course," he sniggered. "The morning papers were waxing lyrical about this new rising star of the theatre, called Abigail Lee. So naturally, I had to come and see for myself if it really was you."

She cursed herself silently. This was one element of her newfound fame that she hadn't foreseen, much less counted on.

"You're mocking me, sir. What is it you want?" She was trying to sound strong, but her tone had no visible effect on the sarcastic smile that was plastered all over his face.

"I want to recover your old debt, Miss Lee. You didn't think I'd forgotten about it, did you? My grandfather might be dead, but I've inherited all his assets. Including the debt you inherited from your late father. Funny the way these things go, isn't it?"

He advanced towards her, fixing her with his menacing eyes. She felt her heart quicken, and a cold shiver ran down her spine. She was terrified. What would he do to her if she couldn't pay him back?

"Your debt has only grown these past several years, what with interests and all that. But I expect to be paid in full. Otherwise, I'll have no choice but to take measures."

He leaned in closer, his lips almost touching her ear. "Just imagine what the newspapers would say if they caught wind of this. It would be a shame to see your promising young acting career cut short, wouldn't it?"

Despite her trembling hands, Abbie took a deep breath, trying to keep her composure. She thought of the flowers, of Mr Thompson's invitation, of the wonderful life that lay ahead of her. She had to stay strong. She had to fight.

"I'll repay you, sir," she said with a straight back and her head held high. "I'm not in a position to pay back the entire sum at once, unfortunately. But I'm making a bit of money now, and I should be able to pay off my father's debt in monthly instalments. That is, if you are amenable to such an arrangement?"

Percy grinned. "But of course, Miss Lee. I'm not the unreasonable monster you take me for."

Ignoring his remark, she asked, "When would you like me to pay you the first instalment?"

"How about this coming Sunday? It's perhaps not a very Christian thing to conduct business on the Lord's Day, but I appreciate that you have work to do during the week."

Abbie hesitated. Mr Thompson had invited her to the park on Sunday. Would she refuse him, of all people, just so she could give Percy some of his crummy money back?

"Miss Lee? Is Sunday an issue for you?"

"No," she replied quickly. "No issue at all, sir. Shall we meet here by the theatre at four o'clock?"

That should still give her enough time for her stroll with Mr Thompson, she reasoned to herself.

"Splendid," Percy beamed. "I shall be looking forward to our meeting." He smiled and tipped his hat to her. "Good day, Miss Lee."

Abbie watched him go, her heart pounding in her chest. She wasn't sure what to make of Percy's sudden reappearance, but she knew one thing.

Her old life had just come back to haunt her.

Chapter Twenty-One

"Look at those flowers," Jane exclaimed when Abbie entered their small rented room. "They're simply stunning. Where did you get them?"

"Mr Thompson had them delivered at the theatre for me," Abbie replied flatly.

"I knew it," Jane squealed excitedly. "He really has taken a fancy to you." She paused. "So why the sad face?"

Abbie sighed. When she left the theatre, she had been so eager to get home and share with Jane the thrill of receiving Mr Thompson's flowers as well as his invitation.

"It's Percy Yates," she said gloomily. "He's tracked us down again. And he wants his money back."

Jane gasped. "Oh, no. What do we do now?"

"I've arranged to meet him on Sunday. He's agreed to be repaid in instalments."

"That's good, I suppose. But what about his grandfather? Does he still want to send us to–" Jane stopped, unable to utter the words.

"The old Mr Yates is dead."

"Hurray for that then."

"Jane, that's not very nice of you."

"What that dreadful man had in mind for us was far less nice than the worst names I could call him. So now it's just Percy then, is it?"

Abbie nodded and stared at the flowers she was still holding in her arms. So beautiful, so delicate and so serene. *I wish I could be one of them,* she thought sadly.

"Did he give you any trouble?" Jane asked.

"Not more than usual. You know what he's like: grinning and smirking all the time." *Like a fat tomcat playing with the scared defenceless mouse he's caught.*

"Don't let him intimidate you, Abbie. Men like him get pleasure from other people's fear."

You don't know half of what Percy Yates gets pleasure from, my sweet angel, she thought ruefully. Abbie had never told Jane about the amorous advances he had made towards herself.

"Just when we believed we'd turned a page," Abbie sighed. "And things were finally looking up for us." She laid down her flowers on the table. "How foolish of me to use my real name in the theatre. I should have known better. I should have made up a stage name."

Jane came over to Abbie's side and placed a gentle hand on her shoulder. "We can't keep hiding forever, Abbie."

"Can't we? Part of me thinks that perhaps it would be best if we ran away again. Like we've done in the past. Just disappear and start over in a new place. Maybe we should leave London altogether. What do you think, Jane?"

She looked at her sister with helpless, pleading eyes.

"I think you should stop thinking that way," Jane answered resolutely. "We've done enough running already. We can handle this – together."

"I suppose you're right."

"Of course I'm right. And I wonder..." Jane tilted her head and tapped the side of her face with her index finger.

"What?"

"I wonder if we could challenge Percy's claim in court. After all, strictly speaking, it's not our debt. Father owed that money to the old Mr Yates. And they're both dead. So it doesn't have anything to do with either us or Percy."

"We've been over that before, Jane. Debts and claims are passed on to the heirs, remember?"

"I still think a good lawyer might be able to help us."

"And how do you suggest we find such a lawyer?" Abbie asked. "Let alone pay for one."

"We could ask Mr Thompson. A well-connected businessman like him is bound to know a good legal expert or two."

"No," Abbie replied with a forceful urgency that surprised them both. "I don't want him to know about the debt. He shouldn't even find out that we're charwomen. Let him think we're a pair of decent, properly educated middle-class girls."

"Which is precisely what we are," Jane argued. "If it hadn't been for Father's accident, and all the ensuing nastiness, you and I would have been sitting in the old drawing room at home – playing the piano, learning French or doing some other perfectly middle-class thing."

Abbie smiled meekly. Her sister was right again. Without Father's misfortune, none of this trouble would have happened.

But then I wouldn't have met Mr Thompson either, she thought. Could that have been the purpose of fate's outrageous twists and turns? To allow her and Mr Thompson to cross paths?

And if so, was he worth the challenges, the grief and the fear she and Jane had been through?

With a slight blush, she admitted to herself that he probably was. His charm had an almost magical effect on her. When she was around him, she forgot about her own problems and she felt like she could take on the world.

How sweet life would be – not just for her and Mr Thompson, but for Jane too – if only everything worked out between the pair of them.

Lost in her rosy musings, Abbie's hand reached out and touched one of the pretty flowers lying on the table.

"He's invited me for a stroll through the park on Sunday, you know," she said.

"Who? Percy?!"

"No, Mr Thompson." Abbie blushed, embarrassed that her sister had caught her daydreaming. She showed Jane the note he had written. "This came with the flowers, too."

Jane's face lit up with a smile while her eyes darted over the elegant words on the card. "Well, that settles it then," she said as she handed it back. "There's no chance in hell we're running away now. He loves you, Abbie!"

Abbie blushed even deeper, only this time with delight, as a wave of excitement washed over her. She had been attracted to Mr Thompson from the moment she laid eyes on him. But she hadn't yet dared to hope that her feelings were reciprocated.

To hear it from Jane's mouth however was a confirmation that she wasn't imagining things. Why else would he send her flowers and express his desire to see her again so soon?

After the rude awakening of her encounter with Percy Yates, her spirits lifted once more and she felt hopeful about their future. And in that moment she allowed herself to acknowledge the truth: she was madly in love with Mr Thompson.

It was like a heavy burden had been lifted from her shoulders, and despite all the hardship they faced, Abbie felt truly happy for the first time in ages. She realised that it was worth it – every single bit of sadness and worry – to feel such blissful joy at having finally found someone who made her heart flutter with excitement and anticipation.

Whatever happened from here on out, she would have no regrets – because she had surrendered to the beauty of being in love.

"So I take it you'll be needing a chaperone again this Sunday?" Jane said as she wrapped an arm around Abbie's shoulder and smiled. "Because you will be accepting Mr Thompson's invitation, won't you?"

"Yes, I will." She looked at those beautiful flowers of his again and a rush of determination coursed through her veins. Yes, she would have a lovely afternoon with Mr Thompson. And in doing so, she would prove to everyone – but mainly to herself – that she wasn't going to let anyone stand in the way of her dreams.

Especially not someone like Percy Yates.

No matter how hard she had to work for it, she would make sure he got all of his money back. And then he would disappear from her life forever. The sooner the better.

Chapter Twenty-Two

Arm in arm, Abbie and Jane walked through the city streets, heading towards the park where they would meet Mr Thompson. The pavement of the tree-lined avenue that led to the park was packed with people, all out on their leisurely Sunday stroll.

Looking round, Abbie thought she saw nothing but elegantly dressed ladies escorted by their husbands, chaperones or maids. The rich splendour of everyone's attire made her feel even more anxious than she already was.

"We must look like a pair of country bumpkins in these old dresses," she said under her breath. "Whatever will Mr Thompson think of me when he sees me dressed in this?"

Since charwomen like them couldn't afford to buy the latest fashion – or even anything new for that matter – they were forced to make do with what they had: cheap hand-me-downs that had been worn by two or three previous owners.

And that's why, over the course of several evenings, they had each been mending and altering an old dress in order to make it more presentable. But despite their best efforts, she couldn't help but feel that the end result was still far too simple for the occasion.

"Don't worry," Jane said. "You look radiant. All you need to do is mesmerise Mr Thompson with that pretty smile of yours. Then he won't even notice what you're wearing."

Abbie laughed. "If only it were that easy." Letting out a sigh, she said, "I'm worried Mr Thompson will see right through us and figure out we're not who we pretend to be."

"Surely, the clothes you wear and the amount of money in your purse don't change who you are?"

"You know what I mean, Jane."

"Don't you think you'll have to tell him the truth at some point?"

"Of course... eventually. But not just yet." She wanted to be certain first that he loved her for who she really was – not for who he thought she might be.

As they reached the park entrance, Abbie adjusted her bonnet, pulled her shawl tighter around her shoulders and pinched her cheeks to make them seem rosier. She wanted to look her best for Mr Thompson. Love ran deeper than mere appearances, she knew that. But it didn't hurt to help the process along by being a bit more pleasing to the eye.

"There he is," Jane said shortly after they had passed through the gates. "Over by that large tree."

When Abbie spotted him in the distance, she felt a rush of nerves and she took hold of Jane's hand for support. Her sister smiled and gave her hand a gentle squeeze.

"You'll be all right, Abbie. Just think of it as another part you're playing: the beautiful young daughter from a well-to-do family who's going to have a pleasant and innocent rendez-vous with the man of her dreams."

Abbie gave a short, nervous giggle. "I suppose that might work."

Just like she had expected, Mr Thompson was dressed impeccably, wearing a smart grey suit and a top hat. And it seemed he had bought flowers again: a small yet artfully arranged bouquet of dainty little flowers – clearly not something he had picked up for a few pennies from a random flower girl on the street.

Taking a deep breath to steady her nerves, she reminded herself to stay calm and not let her anxiousness show on her face. *Princess Abigail gracefully approaches her noble knight in shining armour,* she told herself.

Their eyes met, and she was pleased to register the fond smile that appeared on his handsome face.

"Miss Lee," he said warmly as the two girls drew near. "And Miss Jane. What a delight to see you again." He politely shook their hand, holding Abbie's for just a fraction of a moment longer than was required, while their eyes exchanged glances that seemed to convey more meaning than words could have done.

"I have brought you these," he said as he presented her with the flowers.

"Thank you, Mr Thompson. They are lovely." She held them close to her nose, as she knew you were supposed to do with these so-called tussie-mussies. When she inhaled, their fragrant scent caressed her senses.

"They're not even half as lovely as you are, Miss Lee."

She blushed lightly. "And thank you for the flowers you had delivered to the theatre for me. You spoil me, sir."

"Just a small token of my appreciation." He proffered his arm to Abbie. "Shall we take a stroll through the park? And afterwards, I know a charming little place where they serve the most excellent cake. If you are so inclined?"

"You've spoken the magic word, Mr Thompson," Jane said. "If there's cake at the end, then I'll gladly follow you as my sister's chaperone for however many tours round the pond you both care to make."

They all laughed and set off in good spirits, with Abbie's hand resting snuggly in the crook of his arm. Being this close to him sent a little thrill through her body. And with every step they took together, she found herself wanting to spend more and more Sundays like this.

How easy it is to fall head over heels in love with this man, she thought while butterflies kept fluttering in her stomach.

Their conversation flowed effortlessly, since Mr Thompson turned out to have a wide variety of interests. "Please do tell me if I blather on too much, Miss Lee," he quipped at one point. "I would hate for you to think I'm one of those people who love the sound of their own voice."

"I know the sort of person you're alluding to, sir," Abbie replied with a smile. "And let me assure you that, in my opinion, you aren't like them at all. I'm quite enjoying our conversation, to tell you the truth, and I feel I could listen to you for hours."

Quite conveniently, letting him do most of the talking also relieved her of the need to reveal too many details about herself. She wasn't ashamed of her past, but she was frightfully worried what Mr Thompson would say if he found out how she and Jane had ended up in their present circumstances.

He'd probably want to get as far away from me as possible, she thought. A successful businessman like him surely wouldn't choose to be around a woman as deeply in debt as she was? Little would it matter to him that the debt wasn't originally hers.

Oh, that wretched Percy Yates, she grumbled silently. Why had he picked this Sunday for their meeting? She should have insisted on a different date. She should have stood up for herself more. All she wanted was to enjoy her time with Mr Thompson this afternoon. But instead, she found herself thinking about Percy and the trouble he represented.

"You're becoming rather silent, Miss Lee," Mr Thompson said, interrupting her brooding thoughts. "I take full responsibility, of course. Having been so engrossed in our conversation, I failed to notice that our walk was beginning to tax your physique."

Abbie started to protest, even though she knew she couldn't possibly tell him the real reason for her silence. But he smiled affably and said, "Perhaps it's time for some refreshments?"

"An excellent idea," Jane agreed from behind them. "I don't know about you two, but all this walking in the fresh air has given me a bit of an appetite."

"Then cake it shall be," he replied. "I'm a man who keeps his promises."

"You're also a man with great taste, sir," Abbie said once they were seated in the tearoom he had chosen. "This place is every bit as charming as you claimed it would be."

"As I told you the evening you and I first met, Miss Lee, I do appreciate the finer things in life." The twinkling gleam in his eyes as he looked at her was enough to make her blush from her neck to the top of her head.

Abbie stole a sideways glance at her sister, to see what she made of the remark. But Jane was too busy gazing intently in the direction of the cake trolley at a nearby table.

Soon their own order arrived, and it didn't disappoint. "I'm quite beginning to like this chaperoning business," Jane said jokingly after she had devoured her piece of cake to the very last crumb.

"I'm glad to hear that, Miss Jane," Mr Thompson smiled as he politely dabbed the corners of his mouth with his napkin. "Very glad as a matter of fact."

"And why is that, sir?" Jane asked.

"Because," he replied, letting his gaze wander towards Abbie, "I hope we shall have need of your services as a chaperone more often."

Abbie held her breath. She sensed his eyes on her and she willed herself to look at him with an innocent expression on her face – as if she didn't know what he was going to ask next.

"Miss Lee, I realise this is most unconventional, perhaps even a little forward of me. But as you have no surviving parent or guardian, I can only direct my humble request at you directly."

With a slow nod, she begged him to proceed.

"Over these past few encounters of ours," he continued, "I have grown fond of your unique talents as well as your character. And I think it fair to say that I have great respect for your intelligence and wit."

He paused and his eyes took on an even gentler quality as he readied himself to ask the big question. "Therefore, if you consent to it, I would like to ask if I may have the honour of courting you?"

Abbie felt her heart swell with emotion. She had not expected this kind of attention just yet, but here it was – an earnest request from a most remarkable man. She swallowed hard and tried to focus on what he had said, instead of getting carried away by his good looks or charming ways.

When she finally found her voice again, she spoke in a soft tone – barely more than a whispering sigh. "Yes, Mr Thompson. I give you my permission to commence our courtship."

The words might have been formal, but there was no denying their sincerity or the intense feelings behind them.

"Thank you, Miss Lee," he beamed. "You've made me very happy."

"I can confidently make a similar statement, sir."

Unsure of what more she could say, a blissful silence fell between them. How she longed to feel his touch right now. She wanted nothing more than for him to sweep her up in his arms and hold her... forever. But she knew they weren't even allowed to hold hands while sitting at that tearoom table.

The sound of Jane politely clearing her throat made Abbie come out of her reveries. "I hate to ruin this wonderful moment," her sister said. "But I believe we'd better be on our way. It's past three o'clock already."

"Is it?" Abbie responded, somewhat startled. The prospect of having to see Percy Yates instantly banished all romantic thoughts from her mind. "Heavens me, we don't want to be late."

"Shall I hail a cab and accompany you both home?" Mr Thompson asked.

"Most kind of you, sir. But no, I think Jane and I will walk. It's not very far."

That was a lie of course, but it would be hard to explain to him why they wanted to go to the theatre. Nor did she want Percy to see her emerging from a carriage with Mr Thompson in it. She needed to keep those two parts of her life strictly separated. Because she was terrified it would spell absolute disaster if ever either man learned of the other one's existence.

Rising from their seats, Abbie and Jane said a quick thank you and a hurried goodbye. She hated to leave him like this, but she knew that the longer she waited the more conflicted she would become.

"Adieu, Mr Thompson," she said, trying to put tenderness rather than sadness in the sentiment.

After one last lingering look at him, she turned round and headed for the door with Jane right behind her. But in her aching heart, a tug of war was going on – a struggle between love... and fear.

Chapter Twenty-Three

"I feel like such a coward," Abbie bristled as she and Jane walked to the theatre at a brisk pace.

"Why?" her sister asked.

"Oh, for so many reasons. And not only am I a coward, I'm stupid too. A spineless weakling. Jellyfish have more backbone than I do."

"Abbie, stop that." Jane placed a firm hand on Abbie's arm and brought the two of them to a sudden halt. "Why are you talking about yourself like this?"

"Because it's true," Abbie replied hotly. She could feel tears burning behind her eyes and she didn't know if she cared enough to hold them back.

"I honestly don't understand," Jane said. "Mr Thompson declared his love for you back there. He asked if he could court you. And you accepted. I thought you'd be over the moon."

"I am. Or rather, I was – when he asked me. Oh Jane, this should be one of the happiest days of my life so far. But now we have to go and see Percy. And it feels like leaving behind an angel in sunny paradise to visit a goblin in the filthy pits of hell."

"Surely it's not that bad?"

"Have you forgotten what Percy's like? With his mocking grins and sneering sarcasm?" *Not to mention his unwanted advances,* her mind added. "He's impossible to put up with on any other day. But it'll be twice as grim after such a perfectly lovely afternoon."

She dropped her shoulders and sighed. "And the worst thing of all is that I have only myself to blame. I should have arranged to meet him some other time."

"You're being too hard on yourself," Jane said. "This appointment with Percy Yates is strictly business. We say a polite hello, you give him his money and then you arrange a date for the next payment. Done."

"If you say so," Abbie replied. She admired her sister's optimistic view of the matter, but she wasn't convinced it was going to be as straightforward as that.

"I do say so," Jane insisted. "Come on, let's go." Grabbing Abbie by the hand, she smiled and then they started walking again.

Torn between hope and doubt, Abbie's mind was a blurry jumble of thoughts and emotions. Part of her wished their meeting with Percy would be as quick and uneventful as Jane predicted. But she knew Percy Yates.

You have to be strong, Abbie, she told herself. The man was like a bloodhound: if he caught a whiff of her fear and uncertainty, he would only feel more impelled to torment her.

When they arrived at the theatre, he was waiting for them – casually leaning against one of the stone columns at the top of the stairs outside. The moment he saw them coming, Percy's face split into a wide grin and Abbie felt her heart sink.

"If it isn't the fairytale princess and her beloved baby sister," he greeted them. Moving unhurriedly, not unlike a prowling predator, he descended the stairs.

"Mr Yates," Abbie nodded with a straight face. "I see you remember my sister Jane."

Smiling smugly and refusing to be rushed, he cast an appraising gaze over their simple Sunday dresses. "And I see I should be thankful my money isn't being squandered on frills and fancy dresses."

Abbie could feel her temper beginning to boil up as her face flushed red with anger. Luckily, Jane was having better luck at keeping her composure.

Her sister stepped forward and gave Percy a stern look. "We're here for business, Mr Yates," she said firmly. "Let's get down to it."

Percy chuckled. "Business, eh? Of course. But why rush things? It's been so long – years in fact. Don't you want to tell me what you've been up to all this time?"

"No, we don't," Jane replied. "Unless you'd rather have stories instead of your money?"

"You know me, Miss Jane," he grinned. "I like to have it all in life." He turned to Abbie and gave her a sly wink. "What do you say, princess? Shall we go grab ourselves a cuppa or something stronger, and reminisce about old times?"

"As my sister already pointed out to you, Mr Yates," Abbie replied frostily, "we're here for business." She riffled through her purse and took out the money she had put aside for him.

"Your first payment," she said, holding it out to him. "As promised."

"Thank you," he said. When he took the money from her, his fingers brushed against her hand – slowly and, she had no doubt, deliberately.

His eyes lingered on her for a little while, gauging her reaction. But she resisted the urge to shiver and eventually he looked down at the money to count it.

"It's not much," he said. "But I suppose it's a start. A token, let's say, of your renewed commitment to fulfil your obligations to me."

Abbie didn't reply. If that was what he wanted to call it, then so be it. She steeled herself and kept her gaze trained on his face, unflinching and unyielding.

"It's going to take you a long time to repay the full amount though," he said, pocketing the money. His lips curled up in a malicious grin as he stared directly at her. "On the bright side however, this way we'll have many more of these happy moments to look forward to."

Fed up with his games, Jane stirred. "If you're quite done with the chit-chat, Mr Yates? You've had your first instalment. When would you like the next one?"

"You've grown feisty, my dear girl," he chuckled. "Not quite the cool-headed princess like your big sister, are you?"

Abbie quickly intervened, bringing the conversation back to the matter at hand. "I think we agreed on monthly payments?"

"We did indeed," he replied. "So shall we say the same place at the same time in four weeks?"

Before Abbie had a chance to reply, Jane spoke up first. "No," she said adamantly.

"No?" Percy laughed, amused by her determined tone.

"We shan't be meeting you on a Sunday any more," Jane said, standing her ground. "We have other and better things to do on Sundays."

For the first time, a glimmer of anger briefly flashed across his face. It was gone in a heartbeat, but Abbie had spotted it. Not wanting the situation to get out of hand, she racked her brain for an excuse – any excuse.

"What my sister is trying to say is, well, we're usually frightfully busy on a Sunday. So another

216

day of the week would probably suit us better for these payments."

"Frightfully busy," he repeated with a mocking snarl in his voice. "What with? Dressed in your Sunday best, no less. Out man-hunting, are you?"

Abbie's cheeks flushed with embarrassment as images of Mr Thompson's sweet smile and handsome face came to her mind. She was feeling exposed and vulnerable, but she didn't want to give Percy the pleasure of seeing her squirm.

"Would a Friday or Saturday be convenient for you, Mr Yates?" she asked calmly.

"Ho-ho," Percy taunted. "I seem to have touched a nerve there, Miss Lee. Don't tell me you're on the prowl for a husband?"

"No, she isn't, you foul-mouthed bully," Jane blurted out angrily. "As a matter of fact, she doesn't need to 'prowl', as you so rudely called it."

"Decided she's going to join a nunnery, has she?" Percy laughed, clearly enjoying his barbs.

Jane lifted her chin, trying to look down on him. "Not that Abigail's future is any of your business, but my sister happens to have excellent prospects."

"Does she now?" One eyebrow raised, Percy regarded Abbie with keen interest. "Lots of suitors swarming round the new rising star of the theatrical world then?"

Panic gripped her. "Jane is exaggerating. It's true my success as an actress has attracted a moderate amount of attention. But nothing momentous." She threw her sister a warning glance. This encounter needed to end – before Percy could pry any more details about her personal life out of them.

"Certainly nothing that would prevent me from paying you back," she added. Her heart was still racing, but she refused to show her discomfort. Instead, she forced a polite smile onto her lips and tried to sound pleasant. "Friday or Saturday in a month's time, sir? The choice is yours."

"Saturday will do me nicely, thank you."

"That's settled then," she nodded while her frantic heartbeat slowly began to drop. "Any other matters that require our consideration?"

"No, I think that's enough excitement for one day," he said, regaining his old familiar grin. "We'll pick up where we left off next time we meet." He tipped his hat to them and gestured that they were free to leave.

Abbie gave him a curt nod before leading Jane away from him, her back straight and her head held high – despite the turmoil inside her mind.

They had only walked a few yards when he called after them. "Miss Lee?"

She froze and looked back over her shoulder. "Yes?"

"My grandfather left me his house in his will, so my address is still the same." He paused, enjoying this power to keep her waiting. "Just wanted to let you know. Should you wish to rearrange our appointment due to any other pressing social duties that might arise."

"Most considerate of you, sir," she acknowledged politely. *Obnoxious cad,* she added silently before walking away.

Jane didn't say a single word to Abbie until they were three streets further and they were sure Percy wasn't following them.

"I'm sorry, Abbie. That was foolish of me."

"Yes, it was."

"Are you mad at me?"

Abbie sighed. "No, of course not." She stopped to give her sister a hug. "Percy is dangerous and cunning that way. He taunts and teases his victims to provoke them."

"I nearly told him about Mr Thompson," Jane frowned. "Do you think he suspects anything?"

"You've aroused his curiosity, that's for sure."

"Me and my big mouth."

"What's done is done. But you also managed to wipe that smug grin off his face, if only for a little while."

"Yes, I did, didn't I?"

They giggled, gratefully allowing the tension to ease out of their bodies.

"Let's go home," Abbie smiled as she linked arms with Jane again. "We need to be up bright and early tomorrow morning."

Chapter Twenty-Four

Abbie woke up before the crack of dawn the next morning. Reluctantly, she dragged herself out of bed. Her mind and body felt heavy with exhaustion from the emotional ups and downs she had been through the day before. Between the joy of Mr Thompson asking to court her and the dread of Percy Yates trying to stick his nose in her personal affairs, it was hard to imagine it had all happened in the same afternoon.

"Morning," Jane croaked as she too got out of bed, even more slowly than Abbie. Her sister had never been any good at rising early.

"Morning, my angel. Did you have a good night's rest?"

"Could've done with a few more hours."

"Nothing new there then," Abbie teased before splashing some ice cold water in her own face.

"How about you? I bet you must have had some sweet dreams... seeing as you're practically the future Mrs Thompson."

"We're not quite there yet," Abbie cautioned. Although she had to admit she liked the idea. "It's only a courtship."

"But that's the first step, isn't it? Next, he'll be proposing to you. And once you're engaged to be married, well, then there's nothing Percy Yates or anyone else can do about it."

Abbie smiled weakly. "You make it sound so easy. I wish it really was that simple."

"Why wouldn't it be?"

"Because–" She sighed and began to dress. "Well, for one thing, we're not sure if Mr Thompson will love me enough to want to marry me. He might decide he doesn't like me very much, once he gets to know me better."

Jane made a derisive laughing noise. "You don't honestly believe that, do you? The more he gets to know you, the sooner he'll want to make you his wife."

"But then there's the issue of our debt. I really should have that cleared before I can marry Mr Thompson. It wouldn't be fair on him otherwise. The trouble is it's so much money. It'll take me several years to pay it all back."

"So tell him."

"I can't."

"Why not?"

"Jane, please. He'd think I was some sort of money-mad Jezebel who chases after men only to lay her hands on their fortune."

"If Mr Thompson really loves you – and he does, believe me – he will understand. Especially when he hears you're not to blame for the debt. Father's the one who got himself into a whole pile of money problems, remember?"

"Papa did it with the best of intentions, Jane."

"I'm sure he did, but that's beside the point. All I'm saying is this: I think you should seriously consider telling Mr Thompson the truth."

"Noted," Abbie replied, wanting to close the matter. "Now please get dressed. Or we'll be late at the Parkers."

It was all right for Jane to say Abbie should come clean with Mr Thompson – the man didn't even know yet that they made a living as charwomen. He still thought she was an actress.

However much she loved Jane, this was one instance where Abbie believed her sister was being overly optimistic.

They quickly finished dressing and left the boarding house together, buying two small bread rolls from a street vendor they passed. The rolls were still warm inside when they sank their teeth into them, and the girls enjoyed this simple pleasure while they walked.

Inside the more stately homes, the respectable members of the upper crust were still sound asleep. But out on the streets, the city was coming alive. As Abbie and Jane continued their walk towards the Parkers, they saw the growing crowds – the people who were up early to do the hard and menial work that kept London running.

There were the street sweepers with their long-handled brooms, forever combating the dirt and the grime that always seemed to cover every surface in a city teeming with factories, horses and many thousands upon thousands of people.

Hawkers were setting up stalls on every corner, with some of them already busy shouting out what they were selling and why their goods were the best.

Men pushed heavy carts, while women and children carried baskets piled high with whatever the city needed to thrive and survive.

And through this hustle and bustle, Abbie and Jane made their way to work – two tiny specks in a vast ocean of humanity, as if they were a pair of ants scurrying about and only concerned with doing their own part.

When they arrived at the Parkers, the cook gave them a hot cup of strong tea, just like she did every morning. And then they each got cracking.

Abbie diligently worked through the tasks that needed doing, trying not to let her mind wander too far away from her duties. But as she scrubbed and mopped and polished, her thoughts invariably drifted back to the hours she had spent with Mr Thompson.

The faintest of smiles appeared on her lips as she recalled the way his eyes sparkled when he laughed, and how gentle and caring he had been. A contented sigh escaped her when she realised how deeply connected she felt to him, despite their differences in age and social standing.

While her hands busied themselves with her chores, in her head she was free to picture herself going on walks with him, attending concerts and recitals together, or merely sitting in the quiet comfort of his home... as a happily married couple.

The hours passed quickly this way. And since it had been her sister's turn to serve the family at breakfast, Abbie had more or less lost track of time when she entered the parlour to do some dusting.

Blissfully distracted by her daydreams, she was surprised to bump into the mistress of the house.

"Begging your pardon, Mrs Parker. I didn't know you were here. Shall I come back later to do the cleaning?"

"Not at all, Miss Lee," Bess smiled. "Don't let me keep you from your work."

"Thank you, ma'am," Abbie said as she began to carefully pass her feather duster over the various ornaments that graced the room.

"And how have you been getting on with our dear old family friend, if you don't mind my asking?" Mrs Parker enquired politely.

"Mr Thompson, you mean?" Abbie blushed.

"Yes, I never got the chance to have a private chat with you after he asked you out to dinner the night of your debut as our leading lady. Did you have a pleasant evening?"

"We did, ma'am. Mr Thompson is a perfect gentleman and a fine conversationalist."

"He is rather adorable, isn't he? I must say I was very happy, for both of you, as I watched you leave together."

"Were you, ma'am?"

"Of course I was. Why do you ask? You sound surprised, Miss Lee."

Avoiding Mrs Parker's quizzical gaze, Abbie cast her eyes down to the floor. "It's just that, well, since Mr Thompson is such an old friend of yours, and very affluent to boot, and with me being just a chargirl– I wasn't sure how you would feel about the matter, ma'am."

When Mrs Parker laughed, it sounded like music; a delicately soft melody that danced in your ears and made you smile. "My dear Miss Lee! First of all, Mr Thompson is wise enough to make his own decisions. He doesn't require my blessing for anything. Secondly, you're not just a charwoman. You're an up-and-coming artist."

Before Abbie could interrupt and humbly point out the vast gap that remained between herself and Mr Thompson, Mrs Parker pressed on.

"And thirdly, you seem to forget that I wasn't exactly born into this life of comfort." She vaguely gestured at their tastefully decorated home. "I know better than most people that material wealth or background don't make the true mark of a person. It's what's in someone's heart that matters."

Abbie nodded. Mrs Parker was such a sweet and charitable woman. She didn't seem to have any prejudices or disparaging opinions in her entire being.

"I trust that the old rascal has been on his best behaviour in your company?" Mrs Parker asked with a slightly mischievous chuckle.

"Oh yes, ma'am," Abbie hastened to assure her. "Mr Thompson has been most generous and faultlessly gracious at every occasion."

"Ah, so there has been more than one occasion then, has there?" Mrs Parker's eyes twinkled with the intensity of an excited yet innocent child.

"Yes, ma'am. In fact–" Abbie blushed. No sense in keeping the news from Mrs Parker, she decided. "Only yesterday, Mr Thompson asked if he could court me."

"And you said yes," Mrs Parker blurted out, virtually bobbing up and down in her seat. "Didn't you?"

"I did, ma'am," Abbie replied, smiling shyly.

Forgetting her manners as a lady for a brief moment, Mrs Parker let out a little squeal of delight. "This is so wonderful! Congratulations, Miss Lee. I must tell Phineas as soon as he comes home this evening. He too will be very pleased to hear this."

"Thank you, ma'am."

"You do realise what this means though?"

"Ma'am?"

"If Mr Thompson snaps you up and marries you, I'll lose you as a maid," Mrs Parker quipped.

Now Mrs Parker was jumping to premature conclusions too, Abbie thought. Just like Jane had done. She sighed, inwardly. Everyone was so happy for her – everyone but herself. She felt too burdened by the debt she owed to Percy.

"You seem a bit cheerless, Miss Lee," Mrs Parker said sympathetically. "Anything troubling you?"

Perhaps... An urge took hold of Abbie. Perhaps this was a good moment to confide all her fears and worries to Mrs Parker. It would be so good to get that weight off her chest.

"Mama," little Rosie Parker wailed as she burst into the room. "Philip got angry with me and then he threw all my dolls on the floor. Just because Nanny said my drawing was very pretty."

"Oh dear," Mrs Parker said patiently. "I suppose I'd better come up to the nursery to help you make peace again."

She rose from her seat and turned to Abbie. "We can continue this conversation later if you like, Miss Lee."

"It's fine, ma'am," Abbie lied.

Mrs Parker studied her for a short moment, before Rosie took her mother by the hand and led her out of the room.

So close, Abbie mused with some regret.

Or maybe it wasn't meant to be. Maybe this had been a sign that she was supposed to keep her problems to herself and solve them on her own, without any help from others.

She stared at nothing in particular for a while, until she remembered the feather duster in her hands. Admonishing herself for having entertained foolish notions, she resumed her work.

She – and she alone, she vowed – would have to find her way out of this mess.

Chapter Twenty-Five

On their next day off, Abbie rose early. Even Jane, the habitual late sleeper, didn't complain and as soon as she had opened her eyes, she jumped out of bed – much to Abbie's astonishment. The reason they were both so excited was simple: Mr Thompson had invited them to join him on a visit to the National Gallery.

Abbie had been both delighted and impressed when she received his note at the theatre. By showing an interest in beautiful paintings, Mr Thompson had once more revealed a fascinating side of his personality.

"What do you think, Abbie?" Jane asked while she hurriedly brushed her hair. "Will he buy you flowers again?"

"A gentleman like him? I'd say it's highly likely. He's got remarkably good taste, too."

"Who knows," Jane teased enigmatically. "Maybe this time he'll have brought you something... a bit different."

"Such as what, you jesting little clown?" Abbie smiled, knowing her sister was working up to one of her jokes.

"Oh, such as... an engagement ring! On one of those soft velvet pillow cushions."

"You absolute ninny," Abbie said, shaking her head.

"And he's going to drop down on one knee in the middle of Trafalgar Square and propose to you," Jane went on. Grabbing a large pillow from their bed, she played out the scene like a very bad actor. "'O, my dearest Miss Lee,' he'd say, 'Please marry me. We'd be the happiest couple on earth. And we'll have a dozen or so darling babies.'"

They burst out laughing, as Abbie took the pillow from Jane and playfully hit her sister over the head with it. "You should audition for Mr Parker," she said. "I'm certain he'd hire you on the spot."

"Of course he would. And then I too could meet a wealthy gentleman and fall in love."

"Really?" Abbie teased. "I thought you'd already fallen in love. With Mr Thompson's ward. What's his name again?"

"Georgie," Jane replied as a dreamy smile spread across her blushing face.

"Why, Jane dear," Abbie laughed. "I do believe your flushing cheeks betray you."

Her sister pulled a face and stuck her tongue out at Abbie, before taking the second pillow and starting a harmless pillow fight.

Their nervous smiles and giggles continued all the way to Trafalgar Square, where they stopped to gape at Admiral Nelson's column.

"It's enormous," Jane said breathlessly. "I'd heard it was tall, but this..."

"Impressive, isn't it? Let's go and take a closer peek."

"Careful, Abbie! I don't like the look of those lions."

"They're statues, you silly," Abbie laughed, taking her sister by the hand and pulling her towards one of the lions guarding the base of the monument.

"Are you sure they're not real?"

"Yes, they're made of stone. Here, touch it." Reaching up to the plinth, Abbie placed Jane's shaking hand on the lion's paw.

As soon as she felt the cold hard stone, Jane relaxed and sighed in relief. "I knew that, of course," she said in an all too obvious attempt to save face.

"Taking in the sights, are you?" a familiar voice behind them asked affectionately.

Smiling, Abbie spun round. "Mr Thompson, how lovely to see you."

"Good morning, Miss Lee," he beamed while tipping his hat, first to her and then to her sister. "Miss Jane."

"I was just proving to Abbie that the lions aren't real," Jane declared with an angelic expression on her face.

"Well, I never!" Abbie blushed, worried that Mr Thompson would think they were behaving like air-headed debutantes.

"I'm pleased to find you both in such high spirits," he laughed. "Hopefully, the gifts I have brought will keep the peace between the two of you."

With a polite little bow, he presented flowers to Abbie. They were even prettier than his first two bouquets.

"You surpass yourself on each occasion, sir," she said, breathing in the wonderful aroma.

"And this is for you, Miss Jane," he continued, handing her a small colourful paper bag tied with a bow ribbon.

"Thank you, Mr Thompson. That's very thoughtful of you." Jane pulled on the ribbon and peered into the bag. "Sweets," she exclaimed wide-eyed. "And chocolate bonbons."

Abbie's hand went up to her chest. She guessed this sort of confectionery had cost him more money than she and Jane made in a month's worth of charring.

"To make up for the tedious task of being our chaperone," Mr Thompson smiled warmly.

Jane tried to mumble something, but she had already popped a bonbon in her mouth.

"What my sister is attempting to say, I have no doubt," Abbie quickly translated, "is that you're a very kind and generous man, sir."

Jane nodded eagerly and eyed the rest of the bag's contents with great appreciation and anticipation.

"Shall we go inside?" Mr Thompson suggested. "Before Miss Jane runs out of sweets?"

Once they had entered the gallery, Abbie's jaw dropped. She had never seen anything like it before. It was like stepping into a completely different world, full of colour and light that filled her with wonderment.

Mr Thompson showed them around to his favourite pieces: paintings of serene landscapes, vivid historical scenes, and portraits that made you feel as if the person on it was alive and staring back at you.

"You'll let me know, won't you," he said after a while, "when you grow tired of looking at all these stuffy blotches of paint on canvas?"

Abbie could tell he was joking. "Let me assure you that I haven't enjoyed myself this much in a long time, sir. You always have the best ideas for these outings of ours."

"High praise indeed. Aren't you afraid I'll run out of inspiration soon?"

She gazed into his eyes and smiled, "A man of your tastes and abilities? Never."

Graciously accepting her compliment, he laughed softly and she swooned at the little dimples that appeared on his kind face.

As they moved on to the next room, walking side by side with Jane close behind them, she stole a quick sideways glance at him. It took no effort whatsoever for her imaginative mind to pretend they were husband and wife—Mr and Mrs Thompson, out on a delightful cultural excursion. Afterwards, they would have a bite to eat and a spot of tea in one of the many fine establishments where the staff knew them well and greeted them like the esteemed guests they were.

And then, in the evening, they would sit peacefully at home and talk about the splendid day they'd had together. Until, finally, the time came to retire to bed.

Blushing at her romantic daydream, Abbie discreetly cleared her throat and started paying attention to the paintings again.

"Do they look happy to you, Miss Lee?" Mr Thompson asked suddenly.

Pushing aside the last remnants of her little fantasy, Abbie blinked. "Pardon?"

"The couple in this portrait," he clarified, pointing at one of the paintings in particular. "Do they strike you as happy? With each other, I mean."

Abbie looked at it more closely. The painting depicted a man and his wife, standing in their reception room and holding hands.

"They certainly look well-to-do," she said. "I'm not sure if I'd call them happy though."

"They were indeed wealthy. He was a rich Italian merchant living in Flanders in the 15th century."

"His facial expression is so... vague."

"Yes, a bit smug, isn't he?" Mr Thompson chuckled softly.

"His wife seems shy. Or modest perhaps," she said, squinting as she studied the pair. "But she does appear to be proud of her husband, in a humble way. Which I find rather endearing."

"You two would look so much happier in a painting like that," Jane piped up from behind them. "Better dressed, too."

Abbie turned a deep crimson red with embarrassment. She fully agreed with Jane's sentiment, but it was just typical of her younger sister to blurt out such awkward statements.

Mr Thompson didn't seem bothered by it at all however. "I wouldn't mind commissioning a portrait of my wife and myself," he smiled, with a distinct twinkle in his eyes. "But I would need to get married first, of course."

He looked at Abbie and as they held each other's gaze for a while, she wondered if he was taking her measure. Was he trying to determine if she would make a suitable wife? And did *she* believe she could be all that he was looking for?

Before Abbie could find an answer to those questions, Mr Thompson interrupted the moment of quiet contemplation. "I don't know about you, but my head is slowly beginning to spin." Breaking off their eye contact, he gestured at the pieces on the wall. "From looking at all these paintings, most likely. Shall we go for a cup of tea? I know a quaint little place nearby."

"Sounds like a splendid idea," she said. Even if he had suggested a visit to a sewage pumping station, she would have followed him gladly. As long as they could spend more time together, the details didn't matter to her. But tea certainly was lovely.

They left the marbled art palace and crossed Trafalgar Square, heading towards the busy Strand.

"Abbie," her sister suddenly whispered. "Over there, on the other side of the street." There was urgency and panic in Jane's voice. "Isn't that you-know-who?"

Abbie looked in the direction Jane indicated with a nod of her head. She gasped and held her breath. It was Percy Yates! And he had spotted them too.

"Anything the matter?" Mr Thompson asked, seeing Abbie and Jane's fearful reaction.

Abbie shook her head and tried to smile as she quickly looked away from Percy. But it was too late. Mr Thompson glanced in the direction in which the girls had been staring. And at that exact moment, Percy smirked and raised his hat to the three of them in a smug and sarcastic salute.

"Who's that man?" Mr Thompson asked, sounding genuinely baffled. "He seems to know you."

Using all her acting skills, Abbie shrugged and feigned ignorance. "Must be a theatre lover who's seen me on stage." Keeping up the charade, she smiled and nodded politely in Percy's direction – as if he was nothing but an anonymous admirer whose greeting she wanted to acknowledge casually.

Inwardly however, her nerves were shot to pieces. Mr Thompson seemed content to let the matter rest, although she thought she detected a hint of doubt in his face. His smile felt more contrived, less natural, to her.

As they continued on their way to the café, Abbie glanced over her shoulder a couple of times. But there was no more trace of Percy. Had he vanished in the crowd? Or was he following them – intent on causing all sorts of terrible mischief?

Her heart raced while fear and paranoia consumed her. She tried to remain calm, but her mind was filled with a myriad of possibilities. Percy could be trailing them, hidden from view by the busy traffic. Maybe he was observing their every move and waiting for an opportunity to pounce.

And of course he knew about her budding relationship with Mr Thompson now. He wasn't stupid; he could put two and two together. Was he somewhere behind them – mere yards away – plotting to sabotage her newfound happiness?

A cold sweat broke out on her forehead, while her stomach turned and twisted into a hard knot of anxiety. She wanted to escape, as fast as possible. Even if it meant more lies.

Putting a hand to her temple, she stumbled a few steps. She looked up at Mr Thompson with an apologetic smile. "I'm sorry," she said in a small voice. "But I feel unwell all of a sudden... I think I should go home."

Mr Thompson's expression softened and he immediately took her by the arm with concern. "Of course," he said gently. "We'll get you into a cab straight away."

He hailed a nearby carriage and helped her inside, after which Jane climbed in as well. Mr Thompson stayed behind and generously handed the driver an ample amount of coins, instructing the man to take his lady friends home.

"I'm sorry our time together had to end like this," Abbie told Mr Thompson with a faint voice.

"As am I, Miss Lee. But please, don't fret. Miss Jane, kindly take good care of your sister."

"I will, sir," Jane replied.

He tipped his hat to them and the hansom set off. Through the small window, Abbie gazed back at Mr Thompson until their carriage rounded a corner. Then she buried her face in her hands and broke down in tears.

Chapter Twenty-Six

Abbie cried all the way back to the boarding house. When they got out of the carriage, her eyes were red and swollen. But at least the sobbing had stopped. When Jane moved to go inside, Abbie stopped her. She didn't want to risk their landlady seeing her in this dreadful state. The ensuing questions would have been too awkward.

"What must he think of me?" she said, her voice hoarse from all the tears she had shed.

"Who?" Jane asked, putting her arm around her sister. "Mr Thompson?"

"He must think I'm a liar and a fraud," she replied, wiping away fresh tears with a trembling hand. "I'm sure he'll never want to see me again after today's disaster."

"There, there, now," Jane said comfortingly. "It wasn't all that bad."

"But he saw Percy waving at me. Lord knows what he'll make of that. Oh, why did Percy have to turn up there and then?"

"I don't—" Jane froze mid-sentence and gasped, staring at a point behind Abbie's back. "Speak of the devil. It's him!"

Abbie spun round, only to see Percy descending from a hackney cab. The usual mocking smile appeared on his face when he saw their frightened looks.

"Trouble in paradise?" he asked.

Abbie scowled at him. "What do you want? And why are you here?"

Percy chuckled and swept his hat off his head in a theatrical gesture as he bowed low. "I only wished to check up on you, my dear Miss Lee. To ensure that you made it home safely," he said cheerfully, straightening back to his full height.

Then he glanced around in wonder, as if he was missing someone. "I didn't expect to find you here alone. Has your charming companion deserted you? After all that distress you seemed to suffer? Tsk tsk, most insensitive."

Glaring at him, Abbie felt her stomach churn with anger. "Were you following me?"

"Back there at Trafalgar? No, *that* little encounter was pure luck, I assure you. Gentleman's honour."

"You're no gentleman," Jane grumbled. "And you have no honour."

"Tut-tut, Miss Jane. That's no way for a young lady to speak to anyone. Least of all to someone to whom you still owe such a large debt."

"Is that what this is about?" Abbie asked. "Money? Our next payment isn't until three weeks."

"I have decided to alter our arrangement," he grinned.

"You can't do that!"

"Yes, I can. I can do whatever I want, Miss Lee. You were the one who fled from your legal obligations years ago. I'm doing you a great service and I'm being very lenient by agreeing to these instalments."

"So what is it you want from us today?"

"Assurances, Miss Lee. That is all."

"What kind of assurances?" She could tell from the smirking expression on his face he was up to something.

"Seeing how easily you ran away from your gentleman friend got me thinking."

"So you *were* following me!"

"At that stage, yes. I admit I was intrigued when I spotted you with your companion. So I decided to observe you from a distance. A bit rude of me perhaps, but such is human nature."

He flashed a haughty grin at her, daring her to make a comment. But she refused to take the bait.

"Where were we?" he continued. "Ah, yes. Watching you abandon your gentleman companion stirred a grave concern in my mind."

"And that is?" Abbie gritted her teeth. She hated how he was taking pleasure in drawing out the moment.

"What's to stop you from fleeing from *me*? After all, you have wriggled out of your duties before and you could very easily do so again."

"Mr Yates, I promise you–"

"A woman's promises are as empty as they are meaningless," he replied coldly. "I need assurances."

"So you keep saying. But you have yet to tell me what they are."

The wicked grin returned to his face. "I have decided that the only way for me to feel more secure about our arrangement... is if I were able to keep a closer eye on you."

"By following me around even more, you mean?" She didn't bother to hide the sarcasm in her voice.

Percy merely chuckled in response. "Miss Lee, that would be far too inconvenient. I have a business to run, don't you remember? No, what I am suggesting is far more... permanent."

He paused and slowly took a few steps in her direction, his eyes never leaving her face. Abbie glanced at Jane, who had grown pale as she watched the exchange between them.

"I propose," Percy continued, "that you come stay with me in my house. As a maid, naturally. That way, you will be under my watchful eye at all times and I will know precisely what you are up to."

He said it as if it was nothing more than an innocuous suggestion. But his words were dripping with wickedness while his eyes glinted with sinister delight.

"We can iron out all the details later," he added indifferently. "For now, let's just say it would be wise for you to accept this offer."

The veiled menace in his voice was unmistakable and Abbie felt a chill run down her spine.

He's jealous, she thought. He had seen her with Mr Thompson, and this was his crude attempt to sabotage their relationship.

"You're such a shallow and obvious man, Mr Yates. It's plain to see why you're doing this."

"Is it now?"

"Yes, you want to prevent me from socialising with others." Abbie knew she was playing with fire, but his shocking offer had emboldened her. "You're clearly envious of the brief moment of happiness that you witnessed between me and–" At the last minute, she swallowed Mr Thompson's name "–this other person."

"That's where you're wrong, Miss Lee," he snapped a little too quickly, proving that she had hit a nerve. "My reasons are purely business-related."

Liar, she snorted silently in her head.

"In light of your past actions," he explained, "I feel I need some sort of collateral, so to speak, living under my roof."

Sticking out his chin, he reverted back to his previous arrogant demeanour. "Unless, of course, your fine gentleman friend would be willing to be your guarantor."

"No," she gasped involuntarily. Immediately, she cursed herself for betraying her feelings with her impulsive reaction.

"No," she repeated, more sedately as she cast her eyes to the ground. "He doesn't need to know about any of this."

"I thought so," Percy smiled, revelling in his apparent victory.

Abbie balled her fists. She wanted to scream in frustration. She felt like lashing out at this cowardly villain, who took so much pleasure from abusing the power he held over her.

But before she could say or do anything, Jane stepped forward. "If it's collateral you want, Mr Yates, then surely, I'm the better candidate."

"Jane, no!"

"Explain," Percy said, ignoring Abbie.

"As an actress, my sister makes a lot more money than I do. So from a financial point of view, it would be unwise for her to go into service for you."

Abbie wanted to interrupt her again, but Jane held up her hand and pressed on.

"Furthermore, with me living under your roof, you are assured that my sister won't do anything rash or foolish. She would never run away and leave me behind."

"Jane, this is madness," Abbie protested. "Besides, think of the scandal it would cause. You're not a little girl any more, you're a young woman. You can't go and live in a bachelor's home."

"Wrong again, Miss Lee," Percy smirked. "I'm a married man these days. Perfectly respectable. So the presence of my dear wife in the house should be enough to circumvent any gossip."

Abbie stared at him. He was married?

"Be that as it may," she said after she had regathered her wits. "I still find this idea wholly unacceptable."

"Personally, I think it's the perfect solution," he grinned darkly. "I thought it would have been fun to keep you close by my side. But it will be even more entertaining to watch you squirm and agonise over your baby sister."

"Why you evil man," Abbie growled, every muscle in her body straining with the desire to pounce on him. Only the soft touch of Jane's hand on her arm held her back.

"Please," her sister said quietly. "You know it's the only way."

Abbie didn't want to hear it, but she knew Jane was right. This was their best option. She looked at her sister, and though her face showed no emotion, Abbie could feel the tension underneath the surface.

But there was something else as well: a strength in Jane's gaze that reached out to Abbie and filled her with a resigned sense of calm.

"Very well then," Abbie said tersely, mustering up as much courage as she could find within herself. Her heart heavy with worry, she turned to Percy. "I will agree to your proposal, on one condition: you must let me visit my sister whenever I please."

Percy nodded. "Certainly. You may visit her as often as you wish. In fact, I encourage you to do so."

Of course you would, she sneered in her head. They both knew it was Abbie whom he was really after.

"We'll need to pack some of Jane's things," she said. If she focussed on practical matters, then perhaps she could keep the grief at bay for a little while longer.

"Take as much time as you need," he replied. "I'll wait here outside for you."

Under his pretentious and conceited gaze, the girls entered the boarding house. As they went up the stairs to their small room, their legs felt slow and heavy while the creaky wooden steps seemed steeper than usual.

The two sisters didn't speak much as they began packing, Abbie's mind a jumble of conflicting emotions. She remembered all too well the incidents with Percy she had been through years ago, as well as the perils she had barely managed to escape.

And wife or no wife, she was terrified of what might happen to her sister in Percy's house.

"Jane," she said slowly, "I feel I must warn you. Percy can be... dangerous. And no matter how obligated you might feel towards me, you should never let him pressure you. Do you understand?"

"It's all right, Abbie," Jane smiled. "I'm not afraid of him. I can handle this."

Abbie's heart bled. Her sister was so young, so innocent. "This is a bad, bad, bad idea," she said, shaking her head. "I can't let you go through with it."

Jane closed her bag and looked at Abbie. "It's the only choice we have. It's far from perfect, I know. But it's the lesser of two evils."

Evil, Abbie shuddered. Yes, it most certainly was that. Then, with a sigh, she opened her arms and gave her sister a long, sorrowful hug. She could feel fresh tears welling up in her eyes, but she fought them back with all her might.

Jane pulled away and gave her a tremulous smile before turning towards the door. Their hearts weighed down by sadness, they descended the stairs and emerged onto the street, where Percy was waiting for them.

"Cheer up," he grinned. "You look as if you're going to your own funeral."

Pretending not to hear, Abbie turned to Jane and took her sister's hands in hers. "Be brave and stay strong, my love," she said softly, trying to smile through the tears blurring her vision. "I will come visit you as soon as I can."

Jane nodded bravely, touched Abbie's cheek and tenderly wiped away the tears that had been there. "Everything will be fine."

I pray to God you're right, Abbie thought as Jane picked up her carpet bag and went over to Percy.

"We'll need to walk to the nearest avenue to get a cab," he said, not bothering to offer to carry her bag.

Abbie's eyes followed them until they disappeared around the corner and she felt a lump form in her throat as reality sunk in: Jane was gone now, off to an uncertain future.

No matter how hard she tried, Abbie couldn't shake off a deep feeling of dread pervading her heart and soul. She felt a weight pressing down on her chest, like a heavy burden that seemed impossible to bear.

I've lost my baby sister. And it's all my fault. I failed to look after her.

With one last deep sigh of sorrow, Abbie turned away from the street and trudged back up the stairs to their empty room where all that remained were memories.

She threw herself onto the bed and cried until she fell asleep.

Chapter Twenty-Seven

Staring cheerlessly at her own reflection in the mirror, Abbie felt an emptiness that she never knew existed – and it scared her. She was alone in her dressing room at the theatre, getting ready for her performance that evening. In the corridor and in the adjoining rooms, she could hear the nervous hustle and bustle of the other actors and the crew members. Somewhere nearby, a woman laughed.

Normally, all those noises would lift Abbie's spirits and make her feel alive with excitement. But without Jane by her side, she found it impossible to experience any joy.

Suddenly the door swung open and the familiar voice of Mrs Roberts greeted her. "Ah! Here is our star performer," the dressmaker exclaimed merrily. "Do you need a hand with that costume of yours, dear?"

"Yes, please," Abbie replied, forcing a weak smile onto her lips. Jane had always been so good at helping her to get dressed. But now that she was gone, Abbie didn't even know where to start.

"How's your sister doing?" Mrs Roberts enquired politely as Abbie slipped into her costume. "I haven't seen her in a while."

Abbie felt her chest tightening. She knew people would be asking questions about this, since she and Jane had been almost inseparable. So she had prepared a lie. She just hoped she could deliver it without blushing.

"Jane's away. Not for long, hopefully just a couple of weeks."

"Oh? Where's she gone off to then?"

"Somewhere in the countryside. She was asked to help with cleaning up one of those old manor houses that haven't been lived in properly for years. I forgot the name. But I hear they might ask her to stay on for a bit."

Abbie hated herself. She thoroughly disliked telling a lie, and she liked it even less when she had to do it to good people like Mrs Roberts.

If the kindly dressmaker had any suspicions that Abbie might be lying, her face wasn't showing it. "Well, in that case, I hope they're paying her decent money," she said. "Wouldn't want to be working in one of them old crumbling houses myself. Cold and draughty they always are."

Someone knocked on the open door. Sitting in front of her mirror, Abbie couldn't see who it was. But Mrs Roberts turned round and half-gasped.

"Mr Thompson, sir. Fancy seeing you down here."

There was a note of disapproval in her voice: it wasn't appropriate for a gentleman to enter the dressing room of an actress. Even when the gentleman in question was an old and important friend of the Parkers.

"No need to raise the alarm, Mrs Roberts," he quipped. "I'll remain right here in the doorway."

"Very well, sir," she said, giving a slight nod of the head. "Anything we can help you with?"

"I came to see Miss Lee." He turned to Abbie and they looked at each other through the mirror. "I wanted to make sure you were all right. You haven't been answering any of my notes recently."

She broke off their eye contact and stared at her hands, which lay folded in her lap. "Yes, I am fine, sir. My apologies if I have caused you any concern."

"No, there's no need for you to apologise, Miss Lee," he said cordially. "Although I do admit I was beginning to worry somewhat."

"I'm sorry to have been the source of your distress, sir." What else could she say? She wanted to tell him everything. About Jane and Percy. And how that troublesome jealous man had taken her beloved sister away from her. But she couldn't. Not without revealing the full scale of her problems to him.

Mr Thompson cleared his throat, breaking the uncomfortable silence that had descended upon the dressing room. "I'm glad to see you are well. And since I am here now, might I invite you to a matinee this coming Sunday? There's a performance of some of the best arias at the Royal Italian Opera House."

"That's very kind of you, sir." She paused. What she was about to say caused her almost as much pain as when she had watched her sister being led away by Percy. "But I'm afraid I have to decline your offer."

When she glanced up briefly, she caught the surprise on his face.

"I– I see," he stammered, trying to hide the crack in his warm joviality. "Is it because you don't like Italian opera?"

Abbie opened and closed her mouth. How was she supposed to talk herself out of this terrible mess?

"We could visit an art gallery instead if you prefer," he suggested hastily. "Or if you'd rather be out in the open air, we can go boating on a lake. And afterwards I'll take you both to Gunter's. They have the best ices and sorbets in the whole of England." Smiling broadly, he added, "Your sister will love it."

Abbie hesitated and began to fidget with the folds of her dress. She wanted nothing more than to spend Sunday afternoon with Mr

Thompson, but she knew that wasn't possible. Not without Jane acting as their chaperone.

Finally, she lifted her gaze up to meet his eye and managed a weak smile of appreciation. "Thank you for all your kind suggestions, sir," she said softly. "Unfortunately however, none of them appeal to me at this time."

Another lie. The dreadful sense of guilt about deceiving him stung her heart like a cold steel dagger.

But Mr Thompson wasn't giving up that easily. Chasing the frown from his forehead, he smiled and said, "Then perhaps you would care to make your own suggestions? Whatever you'd like to do and wherever you'd wish to go, I am more than happy to oblige."

Abbie winced inwardly. Why was he making this so hard? She had hoped to avoid him or to fob him off with some simple pretext. But she should have known better. A man with so much character and passion in him was never going to let himself be deterred by feeble excuses.

There was only one way out. It was desperate – and glaringly foolish – but, under the pressure of the moment, her frazzled mind couldn't think of anything else.

"Perhaps," she started saying, her voice weak and hesitant, "it would be better if we didn't see each other for a while."

For a few heartbeats, there was complete silence in the room. Abbie sensed that even Mrs Roberts was holding her breath. She looked at Mr Thompson, whose face had turned ashen. An expression of shock and disbelief stared back at her.

I've broken his heart, she thought. Abbie felt sorry for him, even as she hated herself for being the one responsible for his pain. She wished she could somehow undo the damage that had been inflicted.

But it was too late for regrets. The treacherous words had left her mouth and they hung heavily in the air like a thick mist, refusing to be dissipated.

"It has nothing to do with you, sir," she said, trying to fill the silence and soften the blow. "It's just that... my circumstances are different now. Things have changed since–"

"Is it that man?" he interrupted suddenly. "The one we saw at Trafalgar Square?" There was a coldness to Mr Thompson's voice, and Abbie suspected he would make for a fierce and formidable enemy in any dispute.

"The one who waved his hat to you," he continued in the same icy tones. "And whom you claimed not to know?"

The accusation was out in the open – a harsh reminder of Abbie's duplicity. And like an impenetrable wall of mistrust, it stood between them.

She racked her mind for an answer. Would she tell him more lies? Or did he deserve to hear at least a shred of truth in the wreckage that she had created?

"He is involved, to some degree," she admitted timidly. Deeply ashamed and embarrassed, she couldn't bear to look him in the eye. She wanted to apologise and make him understand. But how? She struggled to find the right words, anxious to cause more hurt by choosing the wrong ones.

"No need to explain yourself any further, Miss Lee," he said, cutting through her mental anguish. "I see how matters stand between us." Stiffly, he straightened his back while clenching his jaw.

"No, you don't understand," she hastened to say as it suddenly dawned on her: he probably thought Percy was a rival suitor – or worse, another man she had been associating with behind his back.

"I understand perfectly, Miss Lee." The look he threw at her was so frosty, it made her shiver. "All that remains is for me to wish you adieu." Then he turned his head to Mrs Roberts and nodded politely at the dressmaker. "Good day, ma'am."

Maintaining an air of calm dignity, he disappeared from the open doorway and vanished from Abbie's life. She wanted to call after him and beg him to come back. But her breath caught in her strained chest. And she doubted he would have listened to her anyway.

A soft hand came resting gently on her shoulder. "I hope you know what you're doing, love," Mrs Roberts said with a sorry look in her eyes.

"I don't," Abbie replied in a low murmur. "And that's the trouble. It feels as if everything is spiralling out of control."

Tears welled up in her eyes and threatened to spill over, but she refused to give in to them. "I've been such a fool," she whispered.

"Sometimes life takes us down unexpected paths, my love," Mrs Roberts said. "But not every decision is final. And not every deed is irreversible."

She gave Abbie's shoulder a little squeeze. "In the meantime, you have a performance to give. They'll be waiting for you," she said, inclining her head towards the open door.

Abbie nodded. Taking a deep breath, she steeled herself and made her way to the stage. She thought she wouldn't be able to perform. Not in her present state of mind. But the moment she opened her mouth and began to deliver her lines, a strange power surged through her veins.

Her profound heartache lent her words an urgency that seemed to fill up every corner of the theatre, transporting the audience into an emotional realm where laughter and sadness came together and formed one giant, turbulent stream.

The story of love and loss was something that had now become eerily familiar to her. This wasn't just a role in a fictional drama any longer. It was as if she were living it for real as the play progressed. Each word felt like a confession of sorts, an outlet for everything she had been suppressing inside herself.

By the end of her performance, everyone in the audience was in tears – from joy or sorrow, Abbie wasn't sure. She savoured the rapturous applause before leaving the stage.

And as she wandered silently through the euphoric backstage chaos, she harboured a faint glimmer of hope that she would run into Mr Thompson. With any luck, her dramatic performance had softened his heart.

But he was nowhere to be seen.

I've lost him.

He and Jane had been the only bright sparks in the sea of darkness that was her life. And one by one, they had been ripped away from her – all due to the same heinous man.

Chapter Twenty-Eight

The closer Abbie got to Percy's house, the more her stomach turned and twisted into a hard, sickening knot. She didn't want to go, but it was time for the next payment. Which meant she would see Jane again. And that's what kept her going, no matter how much she dreaded having to face Percy's obnoxious grins and smirks.

When she turned into his street, a swell of painful memories flooded her mind. There was her father's accident, resulting in him being sent to prison by the old Mr Yates. There was their plunge into poverty and the death of both her parents.

And of course there was Percy, with his constant smugness and his unwanted romantic advances towards her. The mere thought of him made her skin crawl.

Ignore all that, Abbie, she told herself. *Focus on Jane. She's who matters most.*

Pausing in front of the house, she took a deep breath and knocked on the door. Who would be coming to answer it, she wondered while she waited? She couldn't imagine that Percy would bother. Not when he had a domestic servant to do that sort of trivial thing for him.

Fully expecting to see her sister, a smile spread across her face when she heard the key being turned in the lock.

But her smile vanished the instant the front door opened. Before her, wearing a plain and frayed dress, stood a pale and haggard woman whose frightened eyes first darted nervously up and down the street before coming to rest on Abbie.

Must be Percy's maid, she thought. *I'm surprised he hasn't fired her yet, now that he has Jane working for him for free.*

"What d'you want?" the maid asked quietly, as if she was afraid to speak up. She could have been Abbie's age, but she looked so grey and scraggy it was hard to tell how old or young she really was.

"I'm Miss Abigail Lee. I've come to see my sister. And to pay Mr Yates his next instalment." Abbie tried not to stare at the woman's visibly swollen belly. Pregnancy clearly did nothing to soften her emaciated appearance.

"You'd better come inside then," the woman said, her voice barely more than a whisper. She stepped aside and Abbie walked in.

"I'll tell Percy you're here."

"I would like to see my sister first if that's all right," Abbie replied boldly. *What sort of maid refers to her master by his first name,* she frowned?

Unless...

"Fine by me," the woman shrugged. "She's in the kitchen."

"Thank you. I still know my way around, so you don't need to show me to the kitchen," Abbie said over her shoulder as she started moving to the back of the house.

When she opened the kitchen door, she saw Jane standing by the range. Her sister glanced up and her face brightened instantly.

"Abbie!"

Abbie smiled and quickly crossed the room in three strides. She threw her arms around Jane and hugged her tightly. When she pulled away, she could feel tears welling up in her eyes.

"It's so good to see you again," Abbie said softly, trying to keep her voice steady despite the emotion that was rising inside of her. "How have you been?"

"I'm well," Jane replied with a reassuring smile. "But what about you? Your face looks drawn."

"That's only because I've been worried sick about you. Tell me, how's Percy been treating you?"

"He's been surprisingly polite and very reasonable. In all fairness to him, we've worked for people who were a lot more difficult to deal with."

Abbie raised her eyebrows in surprise. "Let's hope he stays that way then. And what about his wife? How is she?"

"Do you mean to say you haven't met her yet?" Jane asked. "But then who opened the door for you? Percy?"

This time, Abbie's eyebrows shot up even higher. "Was that his wife?" she whispered. "Good heavens, I thought she was the maid."

"It's an easy mistake to make," Jane smiled ruefully. "Poor Alice. He's just awful to her, you know."

"How so?" Abbie asked, her heart sinking.

"You've seen how she's dressed. And that's nothing compared to how he talks to her. He belittles her all the time and treats her worse than the lowliest kitchen skivvy."

"How does she react?" Abbie asked, afraid of what the answer may be.

"As little as possible. Because as soon as she utters a single word that displeases him, he gets angry and starts shouting at her. It's really quite heartbreaking to witness."

"But you say he's been polite to you so far?"

"Oh, yes. As mean and as horrible as he may be to his own wife, he's always friendly and nice to me. He's probably feigning it all, maybe even doing it on purpose – just to torment her."

"And she's–?" Abbie left the word unspoken, gesturing instead with her hands to suggest a round belly.

"Yes, she is," Jane nodded sadly.

Suddenly, they both started at the sound of a weak voice by the kitchen door. "Miss Lee?" Alice spoke up timidly. "Percy says he'll see you now."

"Certainly, Mrs Yates," Abbie replied quickly.

"He's in his study." Assuming that Abbie would find her way, Alice turned around and disappeared into the gloom of the corridor.

Almost as if she's a ghost, Abbie mused with pity.

"I'll come and see you again before I leave," she promised Jane.

Bracing herself for her encounter with Percy, she slowly went to his study and knocked on his door.

"Enter," he said, smiling broadly from behind his large desk as she came in. "Ah, Miss Lee. Welcome once more to the Yates residence. Brings back memories, I bet?"

"One or two, yes," she replied, stony-faced. Wanting to seize control of the conversation, she opened her purse and took out the money she had brought for him. "Here's this month's payment, sir."

With a grateful nod of the head, he accepted her money and laid it down on his desk, after which he reached for a heavy ledger by his side.

"Please, sit down," he gestured. "I need to add this to your record and then I'll write you a receipt."

"That's all right," she said, preferring to remain standing. "I don't need a receipt." The sooner she got out of there, the better.

"I insist," he smiled affably.

Fidgeting while she watched him scribble a note in his ledger, the urge to fill the silence was too strong for her to resist.

"Jane tells me you have been treating her fairly and politely," she said. "I suppose I ought to thank you for that."

"You don't have to thank me for treating someone in my home with civility, Miss Lee. It's only natural."

Except when it's your own wife, Abbie thought sceptically. Poor Alice was dressed in rags and received worse treatment from him than if she had been a scruffy dog straight off the street.

"Here we are," he said as he finished writing out her receipt and handed it to her. "That's yours."

"Thank you, sir."

"I have been thinking, Miss Lee. Why don't we change to weekly instalments? Smaller amounts, naturally. That way, you can come visit your sister more often."

"That's very thoughtful of you, sir," she replied, fingering the slip of paper in her hands.

It wasn't like him to be this courteous. Still, if he was giving her the opportunity to see Jane every week, she wasn't going to say no. "I gratefully accept your offer."

She inclined her head to him and was about to turn around and leave, when he lazily leant back in his seat.

"And of course, there is an easier way to repay your late father's debt in full."

"Which is?" she asked, eyeing the door.

He rose to his feet and strode towards her. His eyes were like two pieces of coal, burning with an intensity that made Abbie take a step back.

"You can stay here with me," he said in a low voice. "Share my bed and I will forgive your father's debt – all of it."

Abbie's stomach lurched in disgust even as she felt the blood rush to her face. "That kind of arrangement is completely out of the question," she said sternly, meeting his gaze with unwavering conviction.

His features hardened and he stepped closer until only a few inches separated them. He ran a finger along her jawbone and she closed her eyes while her breathing became more shallow. His touch felt like ice to her.

"Have it your way," he whispered. "I'm sure you'll come to your senses sooner or later."

His finger disengaged itself from her face and she heard the rustle of his suit when he went back to his desk. Slowly releasing the breath she had been holding, she opened her eyes again.

"I'll see you next week then," he said as he sat down and pretended to casually study the heavy ledger in front of him.

Without saying another word, Abbie hurried out of his study. There was no doubt that he had carefully prepared this trap for her. And she had walked into it with her eyes wide open.

I have to stop being such a fool around him, she grumbled to herself while her feet rushed back to the kitchen.

"That didn't take long," Jane said with a happy smile when Abbie came in. "So I guess Percy didn't give you any trouble?"

"None at all," she lied convincingly. No need to upset Jane with the unpleasant truth. If Percy treated her sister correctly, then he could be as nasty to Abbie as he wanted for all she cared.

Putting on a brave face, she gave Jane a long hug.

"When's the next time I'll see you?" her sister asked.

"Next week," Abbie replied excitedly, pushing away all thoughts of Percy. "I'm paying in weekly instalments now, so I can see you more often."

"That's wonderful," Jane beamed.

"Isn't it just?" Seeing how blissfully unaware her sister was of the looming menace only served to make their goodbye more painful to Abbie.

"Ah, Mrs Yates," Jane said when Percy's wife entered the kitchen. "My sister was just about to leave. Can you show her out, please? I've got this stew to keep an eye on."

"Sure," the woman said in that sad and forlorn tone of hers.

After giving Jane one last quick peck on the cheek, Abbie followed Alice to the front door. Nothing about this poor woman suggested she was the mistress of the house, Abbie thought. But she felt embarrassed for having assumed that Alice was a maid nonetheless.

"I must apologise, Mrs Yates," she said when Alice opened the door for her. "If I had known sooner that you are Percy's wife, I would have addressed you with the respect that you're due."

Abbie blushed and added, "I'm afraid I wrongly assumed you were a domestic servant."

"Nah," Alice grinned weakly as Abbie stepped outside. "He treats those much better than me."

The door closed, leaving Abbie standing on the pavement with horribly mixed feelings. She was relieved to be out of the house, with its oppressive presence, but deeply unhappy about having to leave Jane there.

As she made her way down the street, Abbie couldn't shake off a feeling of dread and foreboding concerning Percy and her sister.

Despite his promise to take good care of Jane, Abbie knew all too well that she could be walking right into another trap by trusting him. But what other choice did she have?

Chapter Twenty-Nine

After another crippling day of scrubbing, cleaning and cooking, Abbie trudged home along the dirty roads, her shoulders heavy with exhaustion. Each day was beginning to seem longer than the last, and without Jane, there was no one to share the load.

She could have worked fewer hours. And common sense told her it would most certainly be the wiser choice. But then she would earn less – and Jane would be stuck at Percy's for even longer.

Working hard was the only way she saw out of their problems. No matter how much it drained her mind and body of precious energy and cheer.

At least the play is still going strong, she comforted herself. The audiences loved her and the newspapers continued to praise her heart-rending performance.

If only they knew, she thought glumly. No one was aware of the very real tragedy that she faced. And nobody suspected the true source of the impressive sadness she managed to pour so effortlessly into her role.

Yet despite her success on stage, Abbie couldn't help but feel like she was slowly sinking deeper and deeper into a really dark place. She carried the weight of responsibility for two people's lives: her own and that of her sister.

And if, for whatever unfortunate reason, Abbie's payments to Percy were to stop, heaven knew what that man would do to Jane.

"Good evening, Miss Lee," a friendly voice said when she arrived in front of the boarding house where she rented a room.

Startled out of her gloomy thoughts, she looked up at the young man who had been waiting for her.

"Georgie," she said. They had only met Mr Thompson's ward once, at the expensive restaurant they had gone to after her debut as the leading star. But the chef's apprentice had made a lasting impression and she recognised him instantly.

"What brings you here?"

And how did he come to know where she lived?

"I'll gladly explain everything," he replied with an apologetic smile. "But I think it would be better if we went indoors. Someplace where we can talk quietly? Perhaps I could offer you a drink and something to eat?"

She searched his face for any sign of malice or trickery, but of course there was none.

Georgie was the sort of young man who wore his heart on his sleeve. And his face only spoke of genuine concern.

"There's a decent chop house nearby," she said, suddenly remembering that she hadn't had a proper meal since breakfast.

They engaged in smalltalk on their way over to the eatery, starting with the weather and swiftly moving on to mutual enquiries about their work life – the theatre for Abbie and the Château d'Or for Georgie.

But this did little to alleviate the awkwardness that clearly troubled them both. She was dying to know what the purpose of his visit could be. And whether he had come of his own volition or if someone, possibly Mr Thompson, had sent him.

Judging by the exaggerated eagerness with which Georgie talked about mundane trivialities, she guessed he was aware of her unspoken questions.

Luckily, she didn't have to wait long for an explanation. Because once they were seated and had placed their order, Georgie blushed and cleared his throat.

"You must be wondering why I showed up on your doorstep unannounced, Miss Lee."

Abbie simply nodded and remained silent, inviting him to continue.

"The truth is your sister has sent me a letter."

"A letter?" she gasped. "How?"

"Since she didn't know where I live, she sent it to the Château d'Or, addressed to me."

Abbie smiled: Jane was clever like that. But how had she managed to get it past Percy? He would never allow her to send a letter to someone without him reading it first. Had she secretly sneaked out of the house? That would have been foolishly risky of her.

"Did she bring the letter herself?"

"No. But she didn't send it through the post either. Someone delivered it for her: a rather shoddily dressed woman."

Percy's wife maybe? Perhaps Jane had bribed Alice to run this little errand for her.

"She didn't want to tell me where Jane was," Georgie said. "But I did succeed in weaselling the address of your boarding house out of her."

"What did the letter say?" Abbie asked anxiously.

"Here," he replied, producing a folded piece of thin, crumpled paper from his pocket. "You're welcome to read it for yourself."

She quickly scanned the letter, just as the waiter brought their food to the table.

Thank heavens, she sighed in relief when she had read it: Jane hadn't revealed the grittier details of their plight. Her sister mostly wanted Georgie to know that she was doing well, and that circumstances beyond her control were preventing her from having much of a social life.

The letter did mention a great financial burden for which neither she nor Abbie were responsible, but which they were legally obliged to carry nonetheless.

Who would've thought Jane could be so subtle with words, Abbie half-smiled to herself.

The letter ended with sweet words of affection, as well as the explicitly stated hope that they would be able to meet in person soon.

Abbie sighed as she gave back the piece of paper to Georgie, who carefully refolded it and tucked it away in his pocket.

Almost as if it's a cherished treasure, she remarked.

The thought pained her. Because it reminded her once more that she wasn't the only one to be so adversely affected. Jane and Georgie, together with the budding feelings they had for each other, were a victim of Percy's petty cruelty, too.

"I wanted to write back," Georgie said. "But there's no return address on the envelope, unfortunately."

Abbie tried to smile at him. "Probably an oversight on Jane's part," she lied. The real reason, obviously, was that Jane wouldn't want him to send her any letters at Percy's address.

"Miss Lee?" Georgie began. She could tell he was working up the courage to ask a difficult question. "Is Jane– Well, what I mean to ask is... Are you sure everything's all right?"

She hesitated.

"Yes." *For now anyway.* "Why do you ask?"

He shrugged and blushed. "Something about the tone of your sister's letter, I suppose. Maybe I'm merely imagining things, but I rather got the impression she was asking for my help."

Abbie lowered her eyes, unable to lie to his face. He didn't deserve to be involved in this mess. "My apologies, Georgie. I'm sorry if Jane has troubled your mind."

"No, not at all," he hastened to reply. "Well, to be perfectly honest, yes, I am a bit worried."

He dabbed his mouth with his napkin and straightened his shoulders. "I won't hide from you that I find myself thinking about Jane rather a lot. I have great affection for your sister, Miss Lee. And I would love to be of service to you in any way I can."

He's so adorable, she thought with a bittersweet feeling as she studied his young and sensitive face. Abbie was convinced that he and Jane could make each other very happy. If only fate would give them a chance.

"And I must admit," Georgie went on after a brief pause, "I have another reason for wanting to see you."

Quickly, she stared down at the table again, having a pretty good idea what his reason was... and whom it involved.

"If this is about Mr Thompson–" she said softly.

"I admire and respect him more than words can describe, Miss Lee. I wouldn't go so far as to say he's like a father to me, but I certainly think of him as the older, caring brother I never had."

When Abbie glanced up, his sincere face showed the passion and conviction behind his words.

"Without him," Georgie said, "I would probably have been sitting in a dingy prison by now, rotting away for life. Either that, or something worse."

Abbie suppressed the urge to shiver as she pictured this sweet and innocent young man dangling by the neck at the gallows. Mr Thompson had been Georgie's saviour. Could he be hers as well?

"So you see, Miss Lee, I owe him my eternal gratitude." Georgie grinned and added, "Even though he's usually the first to dismiss those kinds of sentiments."

"That sounds like Mr Thompson all right," she said as a memory of his handsome smiling face came unbidden into her mind.

"Please forgive me for asking, Miss," he said hesitantly. "But these difficulties you and Jane are currently facing– Are they in any way connected to your recent rupture with Mr Thompson?"

Right on the mark, Abbie winced inwardly. How was she to respond? She could hardly tell him the truth – could she? But she wasn't a very good liar, and lying to someone as kind as him felt twice as wrong.

"Apologies if my question was too direct," Georgie said with flushing cheeks. "It's just that the episode has left the man devastated."

Abbie looked up, intrigued by this information. After their break-up, she had assumed that Mr Thompson must believe she was some sort of harpy. And that he would have moved on, happy to be rid of her. He had been so cold and distant when they parted ways. But now Georgie made it sound as if Mr Thompson was heartbroken.

"He hides it well, of course," Georgie said. "But I know him and I can clearly see the tell-tale signs."

"I had no idea," she whispered sadly. Torn and confused by conflicting feelings, she looked at him, her eyes begging him to tell her what to do.

"I realise it's no business of mine, Miss. And I wouldn't know what the best course of action might be. But I do know that he loves you."

Love.

The word almost sounded like an accusation to Abbie. Mr Thompson had loved her – and she had ruined it. Was there any hope left for them, she wondered? Georgie seemed to think so.

But even if the young man was right in his appraisal of Mr Thompson's feelings, what was she supposed to do about it? She couldn't expect Mr Thompson to come to her. So it was up to her to put matters right. But did she have the courage? If she wanted to make amends, she would need to tell him everything.

And Abbie wasn't sure if their love was strong enough to withstand the cold and ugly truth that lay at the root of all her problems.

"Thank you, Georgie," she said eventually. "Thank you for seeking me out and for... sharing your concerns with me."

"As I said, Miss Lee, I care for the people involved. And I would like nothing more than for everyone to be happy – yourself included."

She nodded and smiled faintly. "I need time to think. Please promise me you won't mention anything to Mr Thompson."

"You have my word, Miss. In the meantime, if there's anything I can do – anything at all – please let me know."

He slid a card across the surface of the table towards her. "This is his address. In case you'd like to write him a letter."

With a grateful nod, she picked up Mr Thompson's card and tucked it away safely after reading the name and address on it.

When they had finished their meal, they said their goodbyes before each going their separate ways. Abbie returned to the boarding house, made her way up to her room and dropped onto the bed. Her eyelids felt heavy, yet sleep was elusive due to the thoughts swirling around in her head.

What will the morning bring, she thought gloomily. More misery? Or would she see the right path to take? Maybe if she had a good night's rest, things would cease to appear so bleak to her desperate mind.

But all she could do was lay in bed and let the tears run silently down her cheeks, until eventually exhaustion won out and sleep overtook her.

Chapter Thirty

The next morning, Abbie awoke to a grey and dismal day. She had hoped that all the answers she needed would be there, as if they had been waiting for her all night. But no such luck. All she felt was an overwhelming sense of dread and foreboding.

She pulled the covers up around her neck in a futile attempt to ward off the coldness of the room. The tiny space she called home felt emptier and more isolated than ever before. Abbie was alone in her misery, with only her thoughts for company, and those seemed intent on tormenting her further.

He loves you...

Georgie's words kept echoing through her troubled mind. Maybe it was true... Maybe Mr Thompson still cared for her as much as she did for him. Would he still love her though, once he found out the truth about her past? Or was it too late for them?

Abbie knew that if she wanted a chance at redemption, then she had to set things straight between them. But how would he react when he heard what she needed to tell him? Her mind kept whirling in circles as she tried to make sense of it all.

"Enough," she said out loud. "Time to go to work."

Flinging off the blankets, she marched to the wash bowl and splashed cold water onto her face in an effort to regain some kind of control over herself and her tumultuous emotions.

She dressed quickly and hurried down to the street, where she bought a bread roll and a cup of tea from a stall on the corner. Normally, the tasty bread and hot tea provided a bit of comfort on these cold, early mornings.

But not today.

Today, the weight of confusion kept pressing heavily upon her heart. She felt as though she was standing at a crossroads with no idea which direction to take.

"Morning, my lovely," Mrs Parker's cook smiled when Abbie walked in. The woman's jovial nature seemed unshakeable.

"Morning, Cook." Her own voice sounded noticeably flat in comparison.

"Oh my. Someone needs a good cup of tea, methinks."

"Thanks, but I've already had some. Maybe later."

Even though she had plenty of work to do, Abbie spent the day in a daze; lost in thought and consumed by worry. As time passed, she found herself becoming increasingly desperate for an answer that seemed to be so far out of reach.

Several times, she thought about the card Georgie had given her. Writing a letter to Mr Thompson would certainly be easier than facing him in person. But how could she properly explain herself? How could she make him understand her plight and, ultimately, forgive her?

In her head, she started to compose the letter over and over again.

'*Dear Mr Thompson...*'

No matter how hard she tried, the rest always ended up sounding wrong – too cold or too sentimental, or simply lacking the words to express her feelings.

All she wanted was to tell him how much she loved him and how truly sorry she was. But her mind kept refusing to create the perfect phrase, as if it knew that no amount of words could ever be enough to make up for her mistake.

Exhausted and dejected, Abbie eventually let out a deep sigh and gave up on the idea. Maybe she would try again in the evening when she got home. If she wasn't feeling too tired.

"Don't forget to pass by Mrs Parker before you leave," the cook told her late in the afternoon.

With a hint of alarm, Abbie looked up from the piece of apple crumble she was tucking into. "Why? What does she want to see me for?"

Cook rolled her eyes and chuckled, "Because it's Saturday, love. And that's when we get paid."

"I'd forgotten what day it is today," Abbie said, blushing with embarrassment.

"I thought you were a little more distracted than usual. Good thing I reminded you, eh?" Laughing, the woman turned round and continued washing up the last of her pots and pans.

When Abbie had finished her piece of cake, she stood up and went to find Mrs Parker. *Saturday,* she mused. That meant tomorrow she would be visiting Jane again. And face Percy, too.

She tried not to think of him as she knocked on the door to the sitting room.

"Come in," Mrs Parker called from inside.

"I've finished for the day, ma'am," Abbie said after she had entered the room.

"Thank you, Miss Lee." She picked up the neat little pile of coins from the small occasional table by her side and handed them to Abbie. "Your wages for this week – well deserved as always."

"Thank you, ma'am," Abbie said, bobbing a polite curtsy as she slipped the coins in the pocket of her apron.

"It can't be easy for you, doing all the work on your own," Mrs Parker said with just the right amount of empathy in her voice.

"It isn't. But I manage."

"How is your sister by the way? Will she be back soon?"

Abbie had told Mrs Parker the same lie she had used to explain Jane's absence to others: her sister was away, helping to clean an old manor house in the country.

"I'm afraid she's not likely to come back anytime soon, ma'am. She's been asked to stay."

"That's a shame. Where did you say she was?"

"Somewhere up north. But I couldn't possibly tell you where exactly. I was never any good at geography and I always get those shire names mixed up."

Staying vague about these details made her nervous. But she had no other choice, since she didn't want to run the risk of accidentally exposing her deceit. The Parkers had friends all over the country. And if Abbie put a real name to Jane's fictitious workplace, they might have heard about it. And then her carefully constructed lie would come tumbling down, like a house of cards.

But all this lying made her hate herself. It wasn't right to lie to someone as nice as Mrs Parker.

"You must miss her awfully," her mistress said.

"I do," Abbie replied. *No need to lie about that one.*

"So who's your chaperone now your sister isn't around?"

Abbie blushed and stared at her feet. "I haven't got one."

"But then how do you arrange to meet with Mr Thompson?" If it had been anyone else, Abbie would have thought they were prying. But not Mrs Parker. She looked genuinely stumped.

Abbie hesitated what to say. More lies? Or could she afford to tell the truth for a change?

"I've–" She forced herself to breathe in and out, despite the tightness in her chest. "I've had to rupture my association with Mr Thompson."

Mrs Parker's eyes widened with shock. "Oh, Abbie. I'm so sorry to hear that. What happened?"

Fighting back her tears, Abbie opened her mouth and then closed it again, not sure how to explain without revealing too much.

"You don't need to tell me if you don't want to," Mrs Parker spoke softly. "I understand it's probably still painful for you. Was it something Mr Thompson did or said? Because I'll give him a very stern talking to if–."

"No, ma'am," Abbie replied, shaking her head without daring to look Mrs Parker in the eye.

286

"He's not to blame in this matter. The fault is entirely mine."

"I see." When Mrs Parker looked at Abbie, there wasn't a trace of blame or judgement in her eyes. Her face conveyed only kindness and compassion.

I don't deserve to work for someone as wonderful as her, Abbie scolded herself.

"If there's anything I can do to help..." Mrs Parker said cautiously. The tenderness in her voice made Abbie's heart swell with gratitude and with regret at the same time.

"Thank you for your kindness, ma'am. But I'm afraid there's nothing to be done."

It was tempting to take Mrs Parker up on her offer, but the guilt about her lies and her secrets was beginning to feel like a crushing weight. And was it her imagination, or did the air in the room seem hot and stuffy all of a sudden?

"I should go home now," she said.

"Of course. Get some rest. Enjoy your day off tomorrow."

Abbie nodded and took her leave. After gathering her things in the kitchen, she made her way home – her shoulders slumped with despair. She was alone and adrift in a sea of memories, no longer knowing what was right or wrong and feeling completely powerless to change anything about it.

When she entered her room, her head was spinning and her stomach was growling with hunger. But she couldn't find the energy to make even the simplest of dinners. So instead, she curled up in bed and prayed that she would doze off quickly. Because the sooner she fell asleep, the sooner morning would come.

And tomorrow, she would see Jane again.

Chapter Thirty-One

After attending church, Abbie started her journey towards Percy's home, still wearing her Sunday best. The sky above her showed a promise of sunshine, but she wasn't in the mood to take much notice. To her, the pleasant morning felt like no more than a masquerade – overshadowed by the apprehension that came with having to meet Percy again.

Trudging along the cobblestoned streets, the soft fabric of her Sunday dress rubbed against her skin. *I should have changed into something simpler,* she thought.

Then again, even if she wore filthy rags, Percy would find some other excuse to pay her an unwanted compliment, filled with innuendo.

Forget about that. He's not important, she reminded herself. Jane was the real purpose of her visit. Handing Percy some money for her next instalment was just a minor detail.

Nevertheless, her hands were clammy and her legs felt weak when she arrived in front of Percy's house. Willing her jittery heart to remain calm, she knocked on the door and waited.

The grey face that appeared looked just as sad and gloomy as the previous time. "Oh, it's you," Alice mumbled.

"Good morning, Mrs Yates. I've come to see my sister."

And to pay off another tiny part of my debt to your miserable husband, she added in her mind.

"She's in the kitchen," Alice said listlessly as she opened the door wider to let Abbie in. "You know the way, don't you?" Without waiting for an answer, she closed the door behind Abbie and disappeared – to wherever it was she spent her days.

Abbie shook her head. It was hard not to pity Alice. The poor woman clearly wasn't happy. How on earth had she and Percy got married? It was a mystery to Abbie.

Still, rather her than me.

All those thoughts vanished from her mind however, the minute she entered the kitchen and saw her sister.

"Jane," she smiled, opening her arms and pulling her sister into a fond embrace. Closing her eyes, Abbie savoured the joy of being reunited and the pleasure of sensing her sister's warmth against her. Everything felt right when they were together.

"How have you been?" Jane asked, pulling away to look at Abbie with a gentle smile adorning her face. "How was your week?"

"Georgie came to see me," Abbie replied, coming straight to the point.

"He did?"

"You sound surprised. Weren't you expecting him to pay me a visit then?"

"Well, no. Not really."

"So why did you write him a letter?"

"I don't know," Jane shrugged. "I just felt like writing to him when I realised how long I'll be stuck here."

"But you–"

"I know what you're going to say, Abbie: I volunteered for this. And I still stand by my decision. But that doesn't mean I like the prospect of spending the next few years of my life working for Percy and living under his roof."

Abbie nodded, understanding how Jane felt. "I don't blame you. And I'm not sure if I'd be able to cope much better myself."

Filled with sorrow and guilt over what Jane had to endure on her behalf, Abbie paused and looked around the dismal kitchen before continuing in a more resolute voice: "But we'll get through this together, you and I."

Tears gathered in Jane's eyes as Abbie embraced her once again. They remained like that for what seemed like an eternity – two sisters clinging to each other in desperate need of mutual comfort and strength to carry on through their struggles.

When they finally let go of each other, they both wiped the tears from their eyes. "I should go see Percy now," Abbie said.

Jane smiled, despite her sadness. "Yes, I suppose you should. See you next week?"

"I'll be counting down the days," Abbie replied, trying to put a reassuring tone in her words. Giving her sister one last peck on the cheek, she left the kitchen and headed for Percy's study.

Alice hadn't said whether that was where he would be, but Abbie knew he was expecting her and she guessed he had heard her coming in earlier. In her mind, she pictured him at his large wooden desk, waiting.

It wouldn't surprise me if he actually practises that smug expression of his when he's alone.

She reached the threshold of Percy's study and knocked. "Come in," he said from within.

When she entered, the scene was just as she had imagined it: he was seated in his chair with a smirk on his face and an air of superiority.

"Miss Lee, how wonderful to see you. I trust you are well?"

"Well enough, thank you." Determined to keep their meeting as short as possible, she took his money out of her purse and carefully deposited the coins on his desk. "This week's payment, sir."

"Marvellous," he beamed. When his lips curled up in a smile, she was reminded of a monster predator baring its sharp teeth right before sinking them into the soft flesh of its prey.

He gestured at the chair on the other side of his desk. "Please, why don't you sit down while I write your receipt?"

"I'll remain standing up if it's all the same to you, sir," she refused politely yet firmly. "I won't be long."

"As you wish," he said with a slight nod of the head. He pretended to look for the ledger that was right by his side, and then he made a bit of a show of taking his expensive pen and dipping it into his crystal inkwell. His movements were slow and almost theatrical, and Abbie was convinced he did it to taunt her and to draw out the moment.

Let him have his little fun, she told herself while she stood and watched him scribble his notes.

"Have you had a chance to consider my offer yet?" he asked casually and without looking up from his writing.

"Your offer, sir?"

The grin reappeared on his face as he fixed her with the full force of his ominous gaze. "My solution to your money problems, Miss Lee. Wiping out your entire debt could be such an easy thing to do."

Her cheeks flushed with shame and anger when she remembered his so-called solution and the scandalously degrading act it involved.

"I gave you my answer last time, sir," she said, trying to sound strong and in control of her emotions. "And it shall remain the same today and every other day. I will never agree to such a proposal." Her heart was racing, but her voice was calmly defiant.

"That's a shame," he said evenly as he put down his pen and leant back. "I suppose I'll have to accept your refusal then."

"That's right, sir."

"Terrible shame," he repeated. Something in his tone however said that he didn't feel quite as upset about it as his words suggested. "But, fortunately, there's still another member of your family."

Abbie gasped in shock. "You wouldn't—"

"Why not?" he grinned maliciously. "Since you refuse me, you leave me no other choice but to turn my attentions to your lovely sister." He chuckled and said, "If I can't have the main prize, then I'll have to settle for the younger princess."

"But you're married," she growled, horror-struck and disgusted to her core.

"A mere technicality," he smiled. "People have accidents, you know. Even in the safety of their own home. They could tumble down the stairs for instance, and break their foolish neck."

Abbie thought she would be sick if she had to listen to much more of his dark threats. *He would do it though,* she knew. A ruthless man like Percy would be perfectly capable of murdering his own wife.

"It would save me the trouble of becoming the father of a child I never really wanted as well," he said, confirming her suspicions. "And then I would be free to take Jane as my new wife."

"Jane would never want to marry you," she bit back.

"I can be very persuasive when I need to, Miss Lee. How do you think I hooked my darling wife? In fact, your sister reminds me a bit of what poor Alice used to look like... before she became such a dreadful wretch."

Bile rose up in Abbie's throat. Was there truly no limit to Percy's depravity?

"Here's your receipt," he said haughtily, holding the slip of paper out to her. Gingerly, she took it from him – as if he were the devil handing her a receipt for her immortal soul.

"I advise you to reconsider my offer," he sniffed. "I'll expect your final answer next week."

Abbie nodded and left his study without uttering any further word. Her throat simply felt too constricted to speak.

As she hurried towards the front door, she passed by Alice: Percy's hapless wife was standing silently in the half-open doorway of one of the downstairs rooms.

How much had she heard, Abbie wondered briefly?

Not bothering to ask, she pulled open the heavy front door and fled outside. The air was filled with the usual stench of factory smoke and human industry – but those odours smelled a thousand times better than the stink of evil and sin that reigned in the house behind her.

She had never felt so lost, so alone, so confused – and so horrified. If she didn't give in to Percy's vile desires, he would try to defile Jane, her pure and sweet baby sister.

And he'd succeed too, she thought. There wasn't a doubt in her mind about that. Either he would find a way to trick Jane into it; by appealing to her sense of duty towards Abbie maybe.

Or, if his treacherous wiles failed him, he would simply force himself onto her.

I can't let that happen!

But what was the alternative? Accept his offer and give herself to him? Even if she could bring herself to stoop to such immoral depths, she knew it wouldn't solve her problems. It would merely create new and even bigger trouble.

Plodding on with heavy feet while her mind raged against the injustice in her life, her heart ached. Tears threatened to pour out, yet she fought against them, not wanting her inner turmoil to be known.

You're a fool, Abbie. A ludicrous, silly fool.

There was only one way out of this quagmire.

Only one person in the world could help her now – one man who would be able to rescue her sister from Percy's wicked clutches.

She didn't know if he would be willing to receive her. Let alone listen to her. But she had to try. She needed to swallow her ridiculous pride and see him.

For Jane's sake.

Abbie searched her purse for the card Georgie had given her, and then went looking for a hansom cab.

Chapter Thirty-Two

As the coach trundled down the street to where Mr Thompson lived, Abbie's heart raced with trepidation. Eyeing the ornate houses that lined the avenue, she winced and anxiously wrung her hands, feeling more inadequate than ever before.

She had always known that a wealthy man like Mr Thompson would be enjoying a life of luxury. But to actually see the grandeur and the elegance of this neighbourhood made her realise just how different his world was to her own. It seemed a million miles away from the poverty and hardship that were part and parcel of her daily existence.

The hansom cab stopped in front of the address on the crumpled card she was still holding in her hand. After she had paid the driver, she took a deep breath and walked up to the front door.

The heavy brass lion's head that served as a door knocker stared at her, looking imposing and regal – and she was afraid it might come alive and bite her hand off if someone as lowly as her dared to knock at this door.

Pull yourself together, girl, she chided herself. If a lion-shaped brass door knocker frightened her, then what chance did she have of facing Mr Thompson?

She knocked and waited. A house of this size and scale would have several servants, no doubt: maids and footmen and others – perhaps even a butler – to help the household operate smoothly and efficiently.

Would they recognise one of their own, she wondered? Abbie was wearing her Sunday dress, but that wouldn't fool the trained eye of an experienced footman.

Involuntarily, she held her breath when the highly polished door opened. The prim lady who appeared in the doorway wore a modest but tasteful dress. And she was looking Abbie up and down. "Yes?"

"Good afternoon, ma'am." Abbie guessed the woman would be the housekeeper – the first hurdle she needed to overcome. "My name is Abigail Lee and I was wondering if I might see Mr Thompson."

"Is he expecting you?" The housekeeper's tone said they both knew that he wasn't.

"No, he's not and I'm awfully sorry for showing up on Mr Thompson's doorstep unannounced. But he knows me well, and I won't take much of his time."

"Wait here," the housekeeper said, one eyebrow raised in disapproval at such a social faux-pas. "I'll enquire if Mr Thompson is receiving any visitors on this Sunday afternoon."

The door closed and Abbie was left standing outside, alone with her fears and doubts. Had she made the right decision? Or was coming here simply foolish of her? Was she naive for believing that Mr Thompson would want to help her – after she had broken his heart by keeping secrets from him?

I suppose I'll find out soon enough, she thought as the door finally opened again.

"Mr Thompson will see you in his study, Miss Lee," the housekeeper said. Her voice was polite if not exactly friendly: the woman clearly frowned upon unexpected visitors showing up on a Sunday.

And for all Abbie knew, the entire household might have been aware of who she was and what she had done to their employer.

"Miss Lee to see you, sir," the housekeeper announced after they had entered the opulent study. Mr Thompson was standing by the fireplace, giving Abbie a cool and indifferent look.

"Thank you, Mrs Harrison," he said. "You may leave us now."

"Certainly, sir. Shall I send in some refreshments?"

"No, that won't be necessary. Miss Lee shan't be staying long."

Was that his guess… or a promise, Abbie wondered? Had he only let her in to have the pleasure of humiliating her and turning her out? She swallowed. If that was what he wanted, then she would play along and let him have his revenge. Sacrificing her dignity was a small loss compared to the danger Jane's life was in.

"Well then," he said, after Mrs Harrison had left the room. "What brings you here?" He remained standing by the fireplace, like a victorious general receiving a broken opponent who has come to surrender. She noted that he didn't invite her to sit down, despite there being several chairs in the spacious study.

"Apologies for disrupting your peace on a Sunday, Mr Thompson."

"The damage has been done, Miss Lee. Please state the purpose of your visit."

So cold, so distant.

"I have come to seek your help, sir," she said, making every effort to sound humble and deferential.

"Have you now?"

It pained her to hear him speak to her like that. This wasn't the same Mr Thompson she knew and loved. Was he intentionally making it hard for her? Or had she been sorely mistaken about him?

"I realise I have no right to ask for your assistance, sir. But this isn't in regard to myself; it's about my sister Jane."

"Your sister? Explain." Was she merely imagining it, or had some of the frostiness just left his voice?

Abbie took a deep breath. What she was about to say next could cause him to fly into a rage. "Jane is in grave danger I'm afraid." She paused, but she knew she could no longer postpone the inevitable. "And it involves the man we saw in the street that time we visited the National Gallery."

She waited, and when Mr Thompson didn't respond, she thought that perhaps he didn't know who she was referring to.

"The one who waved at me? And who—"

"I remember perfectly who you mean, Miss Lee," he replied with a vehemence that startled her. "What about him?"

She lowered her eyes. "This man – Percy Yates is his name – he has forced Jane to work for him as a maid. And now he's threatening to... have his ways with her."

"So you did know him?"

"Yes, sir. I did."

"He wasn't some anonymous theatre lover who admired your work, like you claimed he was?"

"No, sir. He wasn't. And I'm terribly sorry—"

"Oh, I'm sure you're sorry, Miss Lee. Good Lord, you have some nerve, don't you?" His previous air of detached indifference had now vanished completely. And instead, he started pacing angrily in front of the fireplace.

"I find it all a bit rich," he said, his words dripping with resentful passion. "First, you toy with a man's heart – and heaven knows with how many other men's feelings. And then, when one of your undoubtedly many suitors makes it plain that he prefers your sister over yourself – why, then you come whimpering to me."

Abbie opened her mouth to protest, but his bitterness hadn't abated yet. "What is it that you want from me, exactly?" he sneered. "Do you expect me to seek out this man? Cause a big scene? Shall I challenge him to a duel perhaps, Miss Lee? Would that give you pleasure, my dear lady?"

She shook her head in denial. "No," she said ardently while fighting back her tears. "That's not what I want. And it didn't go at all the way you think it did."

"Then enlighten me," he snapped. "Tell me what really happened. If you even know what the truth is. Or have you spun a web of lies so thick you can't tell fact from fiction any more?"

"Stop it," she begged, unable to contain the tears any longer. "I will tell you everything you want to know, but please, Mr Thompson, no more anger."

Her heart simply wouldn't withstand his wrath much longer. Not from him. He had always been so kind and charming to her. Georgie had been right: she had hurt Mr Thompson badly with her betrayal.

"Start talking, Miss Lee," he growled. "The truth this time."

"My sister and I are terribly in debt: a burden that we've inherited from our late father. We never knew about his financial difficulties until it was too late. He died in debtor's prison."

"And how does Percy Yates come into this?"

"His grandfather was the money lender who sent Father to prison. When he died, Percy inherited the business... and our family debt. He's been pursuing us ever since."

"You said he was after your sister?"

Abbie nodded, but she was too ashamed to look up and kept her eyes glued to the floor instead. "Jane volunteered to work for him as a housemaid, to repay our debt. And I've been paying in weekly instalments as well."

Through her faltering and tear-filled breath, she continued with the more unpleasant side of her story, despite the hurtful shame it caused her.

"He's after more than money however. It's me whom he really wants. I keep refusing him, but today–"

Thinking of what Percy had told her almost made her burst out crying. But she had to press on. For Jane.

"Today, he threatened to visit his unwholesome desires upon my sister if I didn't relent. He even said he'd push his wife off the stairs and force Jane to marry him."

"He's married?" Mr Thompson asked in disbelief.

"He is, but poor Alice is dirt to him." Abbie looked up and gazed into his eyes, with every ounce of strength and faith she had left in her.

"Please, Mr Thompson. I understand if you can never trust me again. I've lied to you and I'll regret that forever. But I'm begging you, sir. For the love of all that is holy, won't you help my sister?"

She stepped over to him and took hold of his sleeve, pleading.

"I don't care if I have to do the most soul-crushing work in the grimmest of places for the rest of my doomed life – as long as Jane can be kept safe from the wickedness of men like Percy Yates."

She shuddered and gazed up at him. He held her sister's fate in his hands now, and the power of a single decision could change the course of their lives forever. Her heart ached with fear, her courage dwindling with every second that he stared down at her in unyielding silence.

Finally, he blinked and let out a sigh. "Very well, Miss Lee. I will help you to save your sister."

As relief washed over her like a foaming wave crashing on the rocks, her legs gave way and she threw herself at his feet, crying hot tears of joy.

"I'm doing it for Miss Jane's sake, mind you," he cautioned her even as he gently pulled her back to her feet.

"Thank you, sir," she sniffled, her face soaked with tears. "From the bottom of my heart, I owe you a lifetime of gratitude."

"No, you don't, Miss Lee. I have very strong opinions on this sort of injustice. No girl or woman should ever be preyed upon by men abusing the power they hold over their victims."

Reaching into his pocket, he gave her his pristinely white handkerchief. "And your sister happens to be a particularly bright and blameless person."

Abbie dried her tears. "She's more dear to me than life itself."

"Is she with him now?"

"Yes, that was one of Percy's conditions: Jane has to live under his roof."

"Then we mustn't waste any time." He took a few purposeful strides towards the door of his study and opened it with vigour.

"What will you do?" Abbie asked.

Mr Thompson grinned. "We're going to pay Mr Yates a little visit." Sticking his head in the corridor, he called out, "Bill, Tom, Georgie! In here, lads."

In the room next to the study several pairs of feet were heard stumbling about and then they came rushing through the corridor and into the study: Mr Thompson's two young associates and his ward.

Seeing Abbie's startled confusion, Mr Thompson explained, "The four of us were in the midst of a friendly game of cards when you showed up."

Georgie smiled at Abbie, making her blush. *They probably heard every word of our argument,* she thought with some embarrassment. But the three young men all seemed excited, sensing that something was up.

"What's the word, Joe?" the eldest of the three asked. Abbie guessed that he was the one called Bill.

"We're all going to accompany Miss Lee, and pay a social call to a rather unpleasant gentleman. But first, we're going to change into our street clothes."

Much to Abbie's surprise, a thrilled grin appeared on the young men's faces. "Just like old times then," the one next to Bill said gleefully.

"That's right, Tom," Mr Thompson replied, placing one hand on Tom's shoulder and the other on Bill's. He turned round to Abbie and smiled.

"I confess I'm itching to meet this infamous Percy Yates of yours, Miss Lee."

Chapter Thirty-Three

A short while later, the four men returned to the study after changing into well-worn tweed flat caps and plain-looking clothes that had been mended and patched in more than a few places. As a result, Abbie thought they looked very convincingly like a small gang of heavy street thugs.

Reading the unspoken question on her face, Mr Thompson chuckled. "We weren't lying, you know, when we told you we all come from humble beginnings."

Abbie nodded, astonished by their transformation. This man only became more intriguing – and even more attractive – every time they met.

"Let's go," Mr Thompson said. He led his curious party to the front door, but then stopped. "On second thought, we'd probably better leave by the servants' entrance. Or else the neighbours might be tempted to think we're burglars who've just ransacked the house."

Once outside, they went to the nearest busy street corner, where they waited and hailed a carriage large enough for the five of them.

Bill, Tom and Georgie were squeezed together on one bench, while opposite them Abbie and Mr Thompson sat side by side. She was acutely aware of his physical presence, made even more powerful by the energetic drive that had come into him due to the mission he was on.

The setting reminded her somewhat of their outings in happier times. *If only the circumstances had been different,* she mused sadly.

"What's our plan, Joe?" Tom asked.

"To be perfectly honest," Mr Thompson replied, "I don't know yet. First, I need to get the measure of the man. Figure out how he thinks, and what his weaknesses are."

"But we'll make him release Jane, won't we?" Georgie asked, not bothering to hide his feelings for her.

"Don't you worry, lad," Mr Thompson said. "We won't be leaving that house without her. One way or another."

There was no mistaking the firm determination in his voice, Abbie thought. "You're not going to do anything that will get *you* into trouble, are you?"

Because as much as she wanted to save her sister, she didn't want Mr Thompson to end up behind bars or on the gallows if things got out of hand. With Percy, there was no telling how far that scoundrel would go.

"I'm not planning on going to prison over a worthless individual like Percy Yates," he reassured her. "But we'll put some sense in him... somehow." He balled his gloved fist as he gazed through the window while their carriage wound its way through the slow traffic.

When they arrived at Percy's house, Mr Thompson was the first out of the carriage and onto the doorstep. He waited for the others to join him and then he knocked.

Just like Abbie had suspected, it was Alice who opened the door. The timid woman eyed the visitors with alarm and apprehension.

"Mrs Yates, I presume?" Mr Thompson asked.

Alice merely nodded. Her frightened eyes darted over to Abbie for a second, before returning to the intimidating gentleman and his younger companions.

"We'd like to have a word with your husband," Mr Thompson said.

"He's not in," Alice replied in a feeble murmur.

Before she had a chance to shut the door, Mr Thompson shoved past her, forcing his way in while being careful enough not to hurt her. "We'll verify that for ourselves if you don't mind."

"It's all right, Alice," Abbie said softly as she too entered the house, following the men. "We've come to get Jane. You won't be harmed."

"He's in his study," Alice whispered. Her fear was tangible, and once again, Abbie found herself pitying the poor woman.

Mr Thompson and the other three were already on their way to the study, and Abbie rushed to catch up – with Alice in tow.

"What's the meaning of this?" Percy demanded gruffly when Mr Thompson barged into the room without knocking. He had a fat cigar in one hand and a large glass of brandy stood by his other hand on the desk.

"Alice, you stupid woman," he grumbled at his wife. "Did you let these vagrants in?"

"I tried to stop them, Percy. But–"

"Oh, shut up already, you worthless hag."

Standing right by Alice's side, Abbie could feel her shudder under Percy's spiteful words.

"That's no way for a man to address his wife, sir," Mr Thompson said sternly.

"I'll talk to the wench any bloomin' way I please, *sir*." His last word was dripping with sarcasm and contempt.

"Abbie!" Jane exclaimed in surprise from somewhere behind them. She had come out of the kitchen to see what the commotion was about, and now she stood in the hallway, staring at the scene before her in disbelief.

"Stay back, Jane," Abbie warned. Until she was sure there wasn't any danger, she didn't want to take any chances. Out of the corner of her eye, she spotted Georgie moving closer to Jane, so he could protect her at the first sign of trouble.

"State your business, sirs," Percy growled menacingly as he rose from behind his desk. "Before I decide to send for the police."

"Certainly, Mr Yates," Mr Thompson replied pleasantly. "And then perhaps afterwards, I shall be the one who calls in the police."

"Is that so?" Percy glowered.

"I've heard all about your despicable plans and disgraceful intentions towards both Miss Lee and her sister."

"Have you now?" Percy grinned and slowly puffed on his cigar. "I don't know what exactly you've heard, good sir. But may I remind you that Miss Lee is an actress?"

"I am aware of that fact."

"And are you then also aware that actresses constitute a very special breed of the female species? They are prone to exaggerated fantasies and elaborate schemes to exploit decent men like you and I."

"Decent?" Abbie shot back angrily. "You? There isn't a shred of decency in your entire being!"

Smirking, Percy turned to Mr Thompson. "And did I mention their hysterical tendencies?" He took a few steps closer, trying to assert his control over the situation.

"I'm a respectable businessman, who only wanted to help the Lee family in their time of need. And as you can see, I even took one of these girls into my own home – purely as a charitable gesture."

"Funny ideas you have about charity," Abbie scoffed.

Undeterred and unsmiling, Percy went on. "But it saddens me to discover that my good intentions have been taken advantage of. So perhaps, it would be better if I sent both of the Lee sisters away. Let them go to prison if they won't accept my generosity."

Suddenly, Alice burst out in furious anger at her husband. "You're the one who should be going to prison, you lewd and lecherous monster! You wanted to push me off the stairs."

All heads turned towards her, and she seemed to take courage from this. Because her ferocity was unabated when she continued, "I heard what you said to Abbie. You'd love to bump me off, so you can take one of them as your new wife. Well, maybe I should bump *you* off, you evil brute!"

In a heartbeat, Percy closed the distance between him and his wife, lashing out at her. But Mr Thompson intervened just in time, grabbing the fiend by the arm.

"I don't like it when men hit a woman," he snarled. "Even less so when the lady in question is with child."

Alice's strength left her and she turned to Abbie, with tears in her eyes. "I was young and pretty like you once. Until *he* came along," she said, gesturing at Percy with a short nod of her head. "He wooed me, and then he corrupted me. He even managed to trick me into helping him with some of his dirtier business dealings – using my charms on other men, so he could more easily fleece them."

"Enough of that, woman," Percy said darkly.

"On the contrary," Mr Thompson replied. "Tell us more about these ploys, ma'am. They sound interesting and quite possibly illegal."

Wriggling to escape Mr Thompson's iron grip, Percy shrieked at his wife, "I'll kill you, you miserable–"

Coolheaded as ever, Mr Thompson hit him over the head. "One more word out of you, Mr Yates, and my associates here will gladly beat you to a pulp."

He pushed Percy towards Bill and Tom, who caught the villain and held him by his arms, subduing him as much with their strong hands as with the steely look on their hardened faces.

Shocked, but finally feeling safe, Alice broke down and cried, prompting Abbie to put an arm around the poor creature's shoulder.

"He used to be so loving and caring to me when we first met," Alice wept. "But the moment I fell pregnant and stopped being useful to him, he started treating me like filth. I'm nothing but a rag to him now."

"We came here to save Jane – initially," Mr Thompson spoke softly. "But I can help you too, Mrs Yates. I'm a wealthy man and I own many properties. I could provide you with a modest little house that will suit you and your baby. You'd be able to make a fresh start."

Alice looked at him, not sure if she could believe him.

"All I ask in return is that you would be willing to testify against your husband in a court of law, when and if the need should arise."

Percy opened his mouth to utter further threats and insults, but one look from Bill and Tom quickly made him change his mind.

"You can trust Mr Thompson, Alice," Abbie said. "He has money as well as honour, and I guarantee that he will keep his promise to you."

Looking from Abbie to Mr Thompson, followed by a quick and cold glance at Percy, Alice finally nodded. "Yes, I accept your offer, sir. And I'll gladly do as you want."

"Wonderful," Mr Thompson grinned and looked at Percy next. "Now to you, Mr Yates. I'm going to make you an offer as well... but only once."

"I'm all ears," Percy sneered.

"I'll pay off the full amount of Miss Lee's family debt–"

Abbie wanted to protest, but Mr Thompson calmly raised his hand, turned back to Percy and waited.

"All of it, you said?" Percy asked, mulling the offer over in his head.

"Correct. The full amount, in one single payment."

"What's the catch?"

"I see you're a clever man, Mr Yates. In return, you will leave the city and never bother the Lee sisters again."

Percy rubbed his chin. "And if I refuse?"

"Then I set the dogs on you. I have many friends in the judicial system and I have a feeling that if they did a bit of digging, they would find enough dirt to convict you. Especially with a star witness such as Mrs Yates."

Mr Thompson smiled, confident in his victory.

After a moment of silence, Percy sighed. "I may be a coward, but I'm not a foolish coward. I accept your offer."

"A sensible decision," Mr Thompson replied. Immediately, he produced a long, rectangular booklet from his pocket, went over to the desk and started filling out a money cheque in Percy's name.

"Miss Lee, will you write down the amount, please?"

When Abbie hesitated, he presented the pen to her with a friendly smile. "Think of your sister," he said softly.

"But it really is a substantial amount," she whispered.

He chuckled and whispered in her ear, "And I'm really substantially rich. Write down the full amount please. And round it up, just to make sure."

Steadying her jittery hand, Abbie filled in the amount and handed the pen back. Mr Thompson didn't bat an eyelid when he saw the amount. He simply signed the cheque and gave it to Percy.

"That concludes our business," he said. "Remember your side of the bargain, Mr Yates. I'm not a man to be trifled with."

Percy nodded and then stared down at the cheque in his hands. "When do you want me to leave London?"

"As soon as possible. My associate Bill will stay here this evening to ensure that you start making preparations for your lasting departure. And he'll come round every day to keep track of your progress."

"What about me?" Alice asked tentatively.

"Go pack your things, ma'am. Tom will take you to Mrs Haywood's boarding house. I'm her landlord and she will look after you. In the morning, I will send for you and we'll sort out a more permanent solution. I gave you my word and I intend to keep it."

Abbie gave Alice's shoulder an encouraging squeeze. "It's your chance at a new life," she said. "Make the most of it."

"I will," Alice said, smiling weakly. When Tom led her out of the room, she still looked somewhat dazed and incredulous.

"As for the rest of us," Mr Thompson said, "I want you all back at my house for a little celebration."

He gazed at Abbie with an enigmatic look in his eyes. "And to talk through certain other matters."

Chapter Thirty-Four

During the carriage ride back, Abbie and Jane were so happy they held each other's hand all the way to Mr Thompson's house. They didn't talk much, but they smiled each time they looked at one another, while a grateful bliss warmed their hearts.

Abbie's mind was troubled however, by a myriad of doubts and a whirlwind of questions. Her debt to Percy had been paid off, but it hadn't gone away; she owed the money to Mr Thompson now.

Would this change anything between them? She couldn't see how it would make things better – but there were many ways in which it could make matters worse than they already were. Much worse.

As the carriage hobbled along the cobbled streets, she stole a furtive glance at Mr Thompson, who sat next to Georgie, opposite her and Jane. He remained silent, his melancholic gaze directed outside, while looking at nothing in particular.

What's going through his mind, she wondered? Wishing she could catch a glimpse of his true feelings, she studied the solemn expression on his handsome face.

Was it merely her imagination, or did she detect a faint trace of a smile there as well? Whatever his thoughts were about, she concluded, they had to be of a profound nature.

She sighed and stared down at her hand that lay resting on her leg, intertwined with Jane's fingers.

Their momentous visit to Percy's had shown her a different side to Mr Thompson character: bold, valiant and resourceful. She had begged him to save her sister, and he had agreed. How could she ever repay him for that?

Telling him the whole truth would probably be a good start, a wise inner voice suggested. Because even though she had told him about their family debt and how it had come about through no fault of her own, he still didn't know that she was actually a simple charwoman.

The last of my secrets, she agonised.

The trotting horses slowed down to a walk and then came to a complete stop in front of Mr Thompson's elegant residence. Abbie's heart grew increasingly restless now that the moment of truth drew nearer. At Percy's, Mr Thompson had said he wanted to celebrate. But what would happen afterwards?

With an air of joviality, he ushered everyone into his home. "Come, come," he urged them merrily. "Let's make our way to the drawing room."

To the maid who had opened the front door for them, he said, "Tell the kitchen to prepare two full platters of refreshments for us. No, make that three. And ask Mr Jenkins to bring up a bottle of my finest champagne."

Turning to Abbie, he smiled, "Simple tea and biscuits won't do for such an occasion."

He then led the small party through the hallway and into the spacious drawing room. Just like the rest of his house, this place too was exquisitely decorated. In the middle stood two stately sofas, upholstered in a deep red velvet that gave the room a warm and inviting feeling. Natural light fell through the high windows overlooking the garden and bounced off the cream coloured walls, while bookshelves filled with thick leather-bound volumes and tastefully chosen antiques reached up to the ceiling.

"He has even more money and better taste than I thought," Jane whispered playfully in Abbie's ear.

"A toast," Mr Thompson announced cheerfully once champagne had been poured into fine crystal glasses and his staff had brought in three silver trays stacked with delicious finger food.

The four of them raised their glasses. "To happy endings," Mr Thompson said with a twinkle in his eyes.

"Hear hear," Georgie agreed. He looked at Jane, who suppressed a nervous giggle.

Soon, the room was filled with pleasant, trivial chatter while they enjoyed the champagne and sampled the wonderful spread of food that had been laid out for them.

But when the first bottle of champagne was empty and the food had dwindled, Mr Thompson cleared his throat.

"Georgie, my dear lad," he began. "And Miss Jane, of course," he added in a less formal tone. "If it wouldn't be too much trouble, I would like to ask you to excuse Miss Lee and myself."

His gaze drifted over to Abbie and stayed there. "She and I have some rather pressing matters to discuss."

"Certainly," Georgie replied with a straight face and a polite nod of the head. Turning to Jane, he smiled, "I'm sure the fresh evening air would suit us after today's adventure, Miss. Care to join me in the garden for a stroll?"

Jane smiled back at him, her eyes sparkling in anticipation. "I would love to," she said softly.

By the time the two of them had left the drawing room, Abbie's heart was beating in her throat.

This is it, she thought. Mr Thompson didn't seem mad at her – rather on the contrary, she would have said. But that didn't stop her from worrying about the impending conversation.

"Before you say anything," she began after a deep breath, "I have another confession to make."

He looked at her with the kindest and most patient smile on his face. "Yes?"

I might as well blurt it out, she decided. No use in beating about the bush.

"I'm not a professional actress. I work as a charwoman. The only reason I'm in Mr Parker's play is because I like to act out silly make-believe fairy tales, and the Parkers believed I would do well on stage."

There, she sighed with relief. *I've said it. I've finally said it.* Biting her lip, she stared at Mr Thompson and waited.

"I know," he simply said.

Abbie's jaw nearly dropped. "You... know?! How?"

"Mrs Parker told me."

"She told you?" Abbie wasn't sure how she felt about that. Mrs Parker hadn't struck her as the sort to gossip and betray other people's secrets.

"It's not as bad as you think," he reassured her. "Bess is an old friend of mine, remember? She and I have been through a thing or two together.

And she happens to be an exceedingly wise and caring woman."

Abbie nodded. That sounded more like the Mrs Parker she knew.

"She suspected there was more to your distress than you were telling her," Mr Thompson continued. "And being a keen observer, she had spotted my own tormented state of mind as well. So she took me aside and explained your situation to me."

"I see," Abbie said. Feeling somewhat aimless now that the truth was out, her eyes wandered round the opulent room. *So much beauty and wealth on display.* She didn't belong here.

"Doesn't my lowly status bother you, sir?"

"My dear Miss Lee," he nearly laughed. "Remind me to tell you about my youth some other time, but for now, suffice it to say that I was far less respectable back then. You are a lofty queen by comparison."

"So you keep saying, sir. But–"

"I was the ringleader of my own little pickpocket gang, Miss Lee," he said in all seriousness. "Bill, Tom and Georgie were my underlings."

Abbie was flabbergasted. Never had she expected such a revelation – that the dignified Mr Thompson had been a common thief in his youth.

"I've come a long way, haven't I?" he quipped. "But that's all in the past. What matters now is the present... and the future."

His gaze intensified. But since it also retained his typical tenderness, she didn't look away. Their eyes locked.

"Miss Lee, I owe you an apology."

She blinked, utterly confused. *He* was apologising to *her*?

"I should have trusted you about Percy. I should have known better than to think that you would–" He paused as the hot, reddish mark of his embarrassment rose up from his neck. "Someone as honest and pure as you would never do the sort of thing I so callously accused you of."

His temperament suddenly turned fiery and impassioned. "But I was mad with jealousy when I saw Percy waving at you in the street," he continued. "If I'd been a wiser man, I would have realised what my reaction meant, there and then: I was wildly in love with you, Miss Lee."

He hung his head. "Instead, my foolishness turned on you and I drove you away. Abbie, can you ever forgive me?"

In between her stunned astonishment at his emotional confession, one single thought kept coming back to her over and over again, like a delirious obsession – *He loves me!*

She swallowed. Her throat felt raw and dry, but she needed to get the words out. "I should apologise to you as well. If I had revealed the full truth to you right from the start, then perhaps none of this unpleasantness would have happened between us."

"You had your reasons," he replied lovingly.

"Perhaps. But they were stupid, irrational reasons. I was afraid that if I told you the truth about my work and my father's debt, you wouldn't love me any more."

"I love you for who you are, Abbie," he said, stepping closer and taking her hands in his. "Always have, always will."

She trembled with delight. "And I love you, Joe."

"Marry me, Abbie. Make me the happiest man alive and say you'll be my wife."

"Yes, Joe," she replied in a sensual, husky voice. "I'll marry you. And I'll be the happiest woman and the most devoted wife in the world."

As if drawn closer by an invisible yet unstoppable force, their lips found each other in a sweet embrace. She felt as though she was in an endless dream, unable –and unwilling– to escape the rapture of his touch.

When their kiss ended, they held onto each other, relishing the blissfulness that bound them. With her head resting on his chest, she dreamily stared through the window to the world outside. The sun was beginning to set, causing the skies to blush with a radiant orange halo.

But despite the fading daylight, she could still see the figures of her sister and Georgie, sitting on a bench underneath a large rose bush.

"Oh dear," she sighed.

"What is it, my darling?"

"I think we might have to organise a second wedding in the not too distant future."

When he looked at her, frowning, she smiled and gestured at the window with a nod of her head. And when he too saw the two youngsters outside, talking quietly but so evidently in love with each other, he laughed.

"What can I say, the lad has excellent taste. He can't do any better than marrying a Lee girl."

"Charmer," Abbie whispered before inching closer and letting her lips caress his once more.

The End

Continue reading…

You have just read Book 2 of The Victorian Orphans Trilogy. Other titles in this series include:

Book 1 ~ The Courtesan's Maid
Book 3 ~ An English Governess in Paris

*For more details, updates,
and to claim your free book,
please visit Hope's website:*

www.hopedawson.com

Printed in Great Britain
by Amazon

36473639R00189